The Desiderata Stone

Other titles in The Blind Sleuth Mysteries:

Belgian legal deposit D/2024/Nicolaas Jan Ouwehand, publisher
ISBN 9789464982916

Nick Aaron

The
Desiderata
Stone

A Blind Sleuth Mystery

ANOTHER IMPRINT PUBLISHERS

And out of the ground the LORD God formed every beast of the field, and every fowl of the air; and brought them unto Adam to see what he would call them: and whatsoever Adam called every living creature, that was the name thereof.

Genesis 2:19

Salute every saint in Christ Jesus. The brethren which are with me greet you. All the saints salute you, chiefly they that are of Caesar's household.

Philippians 4:22

Contents

I 1964: Doris Day goes to Rome

"Even today," Daisy explained, "although we are preparing to go to the moon, blind people are still not allowed to touch the sculptures in museums."

"Do you really believe we will go to the moon?"

"Oh ye of little faith, of course we will! Haven't you heard about the last Apollo mission that was launched on the 28th of May?"

"But you are still not allowed to touch the sculptures..."

"Yes, exactly! But, get this: these days I never go to a museum or a gallery without a pair of surgical gloves, you know, those thin rubber ones, so that they can't turn down my request without looking silly."

"Oh, I see: so you *force* them to let you touch the sculptures!"

"Exactly."

Father Boudry chortled amiably. The French Catholic priest—*l'Abbé Boudry*—spoke good English, albeit with an accent, but sometimes he and Daisy's friend Beatrice lapsed into his mother-tongue, and a few times that afternoon Daisy had found herself speaking French without even noticing: she mastered it better than she thought. This made her feel quite sophisticated.

On the modelling stand right in front of her there was a clay head set up on a steel armature. This was the first time she made such a big piece: a life-size portrait of her best friend, Bee, who was sitting on a high stool within reach.

Daisy was working hard, struggling; she palpated her friend's face at arm's length and probed her features with her fingertips. Her sitter shuddered, "This always gives me gooseflesh, Daise…"

"Just don't move… I'm trying to get a clear understandding of the transition between these two edges… here… and here. Am I smudging you with clay?"

"I don't know; I can't see my own face. *Qu'en pensez-vous, mon Père?*"

"*Juste un peu,*" the man answered, "but nothing to be ashamed of, surely."

He got up from his own stool and started walking around the two women. The blind sculptress had impressive dark glasses hiding her eyes, and her sitter, indeed, had comical smudges on her face. He scrutinized them both with great interest as Daisy kept probing Beatrice, and again he chuckled contentedly.

As he paced close to her, Daisy could smell him distinctly. He not only had his signature odour, like everyone else, based on breath, after-shave, and sweat propensity, but there was something different, that she associated with soldiers and police, even with mailmen and milk delivery boys. Uniforms; dry cleaners… Father Boudry was a man of the cloth, literally, you could smell it. And if you listened carefully, you could even hear his cassock swishing along his legs as he walked around.

It was very quiet in the large hall of the abandoned brewery, where a local artists' collective had fitted out their studios. Most of the members had day jobs, but Daisy, who worked part-time as a physiotherapist, was off-duty that afternoon.

"My dears," Father Boudry said, "I am reminded of our great Rodin. He was renowned for making his sitters pose uncomfortably close to him, within reach of his hands too, but whether his models ended up with clay smears on their face... or elsewhere, that I don't know, though with Rodin one might suppose *que si.*"

"Yes, but obviously I *really* need to touch my sitter's features. That is why I have to be quite intimate with people if I want to do their portrait. But maybe this is a good thing, as I'm told that the result of my work is rather brutal and can be very confronting."

"Brutal, yes. I am also reminded of Daumier. You may not know his work, but he made sculptures too; portraits... caricatures, really."

"Well, it is not my intention to caricature people, but rather to render reality as I perceive it... Sighted people rarely stop to think about how we blind-since-birth might picture things in our minds: that is what I'm trying to show."

"A very worthy endeavour, I'm sure."

The priest now stopped in front of the modelling easel and eyed the work in progress and the sitter, alternatively. Daisy had let go of her friend's face and was kneading the clay head again. Beatrice said, "I don't like that look, *mon Père.*"

"What look would that be?"

"You're laughing at my predicament; you think the joke is on me!"

She said this fondly; she'd known the priest all her life; a friend of the family... Anyway, as Father Boudry kept looking from her to the piece, and as he knitted his eyebrows satirically, Beatrice burst out into giggles, then snorted through that rather prominent nose of hers, and tried to stifle her merriment, hiding her mouth behind her hand. Very much aware of the fact that she was no beauty, she turned quite red with embarrassment.

"My dear girl, don't blush on account of *me*, I'm only a priest, and I know you have a beautiful soul."

11

"That's what everybody keeps telling me, so they don't have to mention my ugly mug!"

"What's going on here?" Daisy asked.

"Father Boudry thinks your efforts do not do me justice!"

"Well, I haven't finished yet."

"That's the right spirit, *ma chère Dési*," the French priest said. Now he stared at the artist for a while: she was quite pretty, with a shock of blonde curls on her head, half-long, probably natural. You didn't expect someone like her to have a perm, somehow. The woman reminded him vaguely of one Hollywood star or the other, although he would have been at a loss to say which one. Like most French, however, he adored *'Ollywood*.

People started to arrive: other artists from the collective and their hangers-on. They needed their day jobs to keep the kettle boiling, and became painters, sculptors, etchers or photographers only after office hours. They repaired to different corners of the echoing hall: the painting studio, the photo and etching labs with their attendant dark room and printing press, and finally the sculpture studio with its clay-stained modelling stands. Fellow-artists greeted Daisy and her sitter, and were introduced to the visitor. Then, sometime later, she decided to call it a day. She covered the clay portrait with damp rags and a sheet of plastic, before she and Beatrice went to a washbasin by the wall, the former to wash her hands, the latter her face.

"Shall we go for an early dinner? There's a new Italian place in the neighbourhood; really nice; I'm inviting you both."

Using her cane, Daisy led the way out of the derelict brewery and into the streets of Tufnell Parc. She knew exactly where to find that new restaurant, and while they walked over in the mellow early summer evening, she explained that Italian restaurants had become all the rage in London, lately, because of hugely successful pictures like 'Roman Holiday', 'La Dolce Vita', or more recently 'The Roman Spring of Mrs Stone'.

"Did you attend projections of those films?"

"I certainly did! Didn't we, Bee?"

But when they entered the establishment, with its red and white checked table cloths and empty Chianti bottles set with dripping candles, the priest cheerfully pronounced all of it "completely bogus". However, after talking with the welcoming proprietor in rapid-fire Italian, he had to admit that the man, at least, was genuine. They were the first customers of the evening, and settled down with a bottle of the establishment's "best wine", served by the *padrone* himself. Father Boudry pronounced it "adequate".

"Obviously, as a Frenchman, you must be hard to please," Beatrice remarked.

"Oh well, in France we always say: 'As long as you're in good company.'"

Daisy raised her glass and shot back: "In Britain we say, 'As long as there's alcohol in the plonk!'"

"Ah, my dear *Dési*, I' can't tell you how happy I am to have made your acquaintance at last, and how impressed I am. My darling Beatrice had not exaggerated her praise of you. The fearless way you go out into the world with that white cane of yours, and the assurance with which you navigate the streets!"

"Oh, but I know Tufnell Park like the back of my hand."

"And then the way you throw yourself into your art. It is quite marvellous!"

"Though you doubt whether my efforts do poor Beatrice justice, am I right? Well, I can assure you that I *love* Bee's face, no matter what other people may say. At least she has *readable* features, when I touch them, with clear volumes and edges."

"Ah, but that is not the issue here… You see, as soon as you start 'rendering' someone's *face*, then you are confronting them with their sense of self, their identity, maybe even their very soul! Therefore the process of rendering reality as you *perceive* it suddenly becomes… rather brutal."

"I see, yes; I guess you're right."

"You know, you could learn a lot from the classics of antiquity… My advice would be: go to Rome and study them."

"You mean the sculptures?"

"Yes, the Roman sculptures and the copies of the Greeks… There's this program, organized every summer at the Vatican Museums by an Irish priest, Father Cadogan, a good friend of mine, where blind people get an opportunity to study archaeological artefacts by touch. Would you be interested?"

"Of course, *mon Père!* So they're not only allowed to touch the sculptures, but are even *encouraged* to do so?"

"That's right, and I don't think they're required to wear those rubber gloves you were talking about."

"But surely this is only open for Catholics?"

"Oh, you're not one of us then, are you? Well, it doesn't matter, I guess… this is not a religious event." And after a moment's reflection he added, "They may expect you to attend Mass once in a while, if that is all right."

"Yes, but would it be all right with Father Cadogan, too?"

"We wouldn't tell him… just promise not to partake in the Holy Communion, is all I'm asking."

"Nor in any other sacrament; I get it."

So that summer, just like that, Daisy ended up in Rome for a fortnight's holiday. That busybody Boudry had been true to his word, but now Daisy was wondering if it had been such a good idea after all, to set off on such a daunting

14

venture on the basis of such a flimsy invitation. It had all gone so fast. She'd taken two weeks off from work, and her husband Richard, who was a pilot with BOAC, had arranged a flight over the phone from Sydney, in Australia, where he happened to be at that moment. It was the first time she went abroad without an escort: Bee would have liked to come along, but Father Cadogan had vetoed the idea, as Daisy would be part of a group. Fair enough.

The trip had been all right, she'd taken a taxi to London Airport, and Richard had made sure that a stewardess would be there to help her through customs and bring her to the aircraft. At Fiumicino, the airport of Rome, Father Cadogan had come to pick her up personally. So far so good.

Then she and the other participants had been taken to a meeting room somewhere within the depths of the Vatican Museums. The only thing Daisy knew for the moment, was that the museums were a huge maze of galleries and corridors, and that they had been taken to a part of the complex that was not even open to the public, but was used by visiting scholars and researchers.

Once they were all gathered in this room, Daisy could hear the conversations of half a dozen people around her, speaking Irish English and sounding very youthful. She expected that most of them would be blind, and as she listened more carefully, she was able to ascertain that this must indeed be the case, although there was no telling if they were totally blind or not. None of them spoke to her, as she had just joined them, a late arrival, a newcomer, and the only non-Irish member of the group. *They* had all travelled together from Dublin. And as they couldn't see her, how could they even think of making an effort to include her in their conversations?

So right there an then she suddenly realized that this was going to be much more difficult than she had foreseen.

For the first time since leaving school she became aware of the fact that she was no longer used to being with other blind people. At the 'Anne Sullivan', her old boarding school for blind girls, it had been second nature, automatic, for many years. You knew you couldn't rely on your friends for assistance because they were just as blind as you, and you learned to rely on yourself only. But since then she'd lived exclusively among the sighted and had come to take the convenience of seeing the world through the eyes of others for granted. Wistfully she thought back to that afternoon and evening with Bee and Father Boudry: how relaxed and easy-going all three of them had felt! When the priest had pronounced the Italian restaurant "completely bogus", he had immediately proceeded to describe the décor to Daisy in order to substantiate his harsh judgement. The plastic vines hanging from the mock beams of the ceiling, complete with ripe grapes 'made in Hong Kong'; and the gaudy fresco of Mount Vesuvius on the wall, with non-descript ruin-pillars ("Pompeii-style") on the foreground... Daisy had raised her arm and fingered the plastic grapes; for the gaudy Vesuvius she had to take Boudry's word. But she'd acquired a very clear picture of her surroundings. Now she had no idea where she was, and her young Irish companions would not be able to supply a better sense of the place for her.

Then Father Cadogan made his presence known, but even before he started his welcome speech, he told the room that as some of them were deaf, there was a "friendly lady" standing right next to him, Sister Maria Elizabeth, who was a very competent sign-language interpreter, and that she was signing every word he was saying, "as I speak".

"I'm only telling you this because the true blind among you are not aware of Sister Liz's presence, nor, perhaps, of the presence of your deaf fellow-participants... Liz, do you want to say a few words?"

16

"Yes, Father. Hello everybody. Obviously you are going to wonder if it is possible at all for the blind and the deaf to communicate directly... we'll see about that later. But for the moment it seems that all your exchanges will have to pass through me, so feel free to use my services as you need them, but please be aware I can't help everyone at once. Please don't overwhelm me."

These words created a slight stir, a flutter among the blind youths around Daisy. "Of course!" she thought: she'd already noticed that there were more than half a dozen people in the room, maybe twice that much. You could sense their presence by their odours, the shuffling of feet and scraping of chairs. But she'd just assumed they were 'the silent majority', people too shy to say much on a first meeting, just like herself. Now it turned out that they might have been chattering as freely among themselves as the blind youths... but in sign language! After all, they too had travelled together and got to know each other beforehand. And at least they could *see* who was there.

This was strange and disturbing: blind and deaf people together in a group. As father Cadogan continued his little welcome speech, Daisy reflected: why exactly were deaf people so disturbing? Probably it had to do with the fact that you couldn't communicate with them at all, as Sister Liz had already pointed out. So why bring them together? And then there was the fact that you just had to wonder—you couldn't help yourself—which was worse: being blind or being deaf? Perhaps that was only a matter of degree, but Daisy always felt that being totally blind must be a lot worse than being totally deaf. After all, *they* could still see their loved ones and read their faces, enjoy normal books, admire art, and the far vistas of foreign landscapes... Oh, to *see* Rome for just one minute!

In the end Father Cadogan asked all those present to

introduce themselves one by one, and Daisy went into mind-mapping mode, concentrating fiercely. She put the name and voice of each blind participant in a mental pigeonhole in her head, together with any particulars he or she mentioned. All of them were still at school or at a Uni and were very proud of it. When her turn came she decided to be deliberately vague.

"Hi, my name is Daisy Hayes and I'm from London. I'm no longer at school, but I work part-time as a physiotherapist, and part-time as a sculptress."

How about that for size? But when the deaf introduced themselves in the same way, you already had a problem: it was Sister Liz who translated what they said. She sounded very friendly and competent, but how would Daisy ever be able to keep all those deaf people apart?

Then came the real shocker. Father Cadogan announced that they were going to be paired up, because they would all be staying two by two at different convents near the Vatican. "Now, part of the set-up of our stay in Rome is that the blind and the deaf get to know each other better, so I will assign a partner for each of you: ladies with ladies and gentlemen together, but one deaf and one blind on each team."

This announcement caused quite a stir, Daisy could hear, at least with the blind. And you could imagine the deaf commenting excitedly in sign language as well. But what could they do? They had to go along with it.

Daisy was assigned a girl named Morag. ("Hi, I'm Morag," Sister Liz had interpreted, "I'm Scottish, but also a Catholic. I'm reading History of Art at the University of Dublin. So now you can imagine why I'm here.") Then, at length, the two of them were escorted to their residence by a Roman youth, a volunteer from a local parish who didn't speak English at all, but was quite proficient in Latin; Daisy remembered some Latin from school, not much, but it did help a bit. They followed this Giovanni into the streets outside the Vatican, up the Janiculum hill, while Daisy tried to map their route in her mind. In fact, they'd been told, it would be the deaf partner's responsibility to guide the blind to their digs, but you could never be too careful. Starting the next day, the two were supposed to shuttle on their own between the Vatican and the 'Congregation of the Sisters of St Plautilla', the convent where they would share a room.

And the next day, sitting on a hard chair in another lecture room, or maybe it was the same one as the day before, Daisy decided that she would have to speak to Father Cadogan privately about her misgivings.

They were listening to a presentation by some priest whose English sounded atrocious. He was explaining that throughout antiquity, people had assumed that Homer had been blind. "Now, some writers thought up completely fanciful biographies of Homer, it was all the rage, but these had no historical validity whatsoever, except for one thing: the fake 'lives of Homer' reveal a lot about the daily life of blind people in ancient Rome and in the Hellenistic world, where these fanciful biographies were written, between a few centuries BC and a few centuries AD... So, thanks to the Homer myth, we know quite a lot about the daily life of the blind at the time!"

The man's English was quite good, actually, albeit a bit long-winded; it was his Italian accent that was atrocious. And Daisy felt too tense and nervous to take an interest in what he was saying, although she realised it must be com-pelling enough.

While the scholarly priest droned on, Daisy reflected carefully about what she should tell Father Cadogan. For starters, she was the only adult in the group: there were a dozen teenagers and young adults in the room, and she could have been the mother of most of them. Secondly, she hadn't realised there would be lectures and guided tours; she'd expected that she would be free to roam the museum galleries, probing the antique sculptures at her leisure. And thirdly, she wondered if she shouldn't own up right away to the fact that she was not a Catholic. Now that she was actually inside the Vatican, she felt like an intruder. Pope John XXIII had died a year back and Paul VI had just taken over; the Second Vatican Council was still in full swing, she'd heard; all that was happening right here, at this very moment.

The Italian priest was telling them, "It will surely not come as a surprise to you that sign languages for the deaf already existed in antiquity... Saint Augustine, who was writing around 400 AD, was fascinated by how deaf people and their carers communicated by means of gestures; how they could answer questions, or even give explanations of their own without being asked. Not only could they refer to visible objects, but also to quite abstract notions. After all, the Church Father wrote, mimes in the theatre can tell quite elaborate stories by gestures alone, without using spoken words... Elsewhere he wrote about a family where the healthy parents had invented a sign language in order to communicate with their deaf children. So you see, sign languages already existed, but people were not aware of the fact that *the deaf themselves created them!* Because probably it were not the carers who had invented those gestures for their charges, and it must have been the deaf children themselves who had taught their hearing parents to communicate with them, not the other way round. After all, as Joseph Schuyler Long writes somewhere, 'So long as there are two deaf people upon the face of the earth and they get together, so long will signs be in use.'"

Ah, yes, interesting. That was another thing Daisy wanted to tell Father Cadogan, the thing that bothered her most but that she would be almost too ashamed to mention: her aversion for her deaf partner. Morag was a very sweet person and all that, but deep down, for no good reason at all, it made Daisy's skin crawl to be thrown together with her like this. She'd hardly slept a wink that night.

The scholarly priest with the Italian accent had come to the end of his 'introduction' about the daily life of the blind and deaf in antiquity. A short and polite applause helped him on his way to the exit, coming mainly from the blind, supposedly, although maybe the deaf *knew* about applause as well, and applied that knowledge. This introduction had been the last item on the day's agenda, so it was time to go back to their lodgings.

Daisy expected that her deaf partner would be making a beeline for her now; here she was; she recognized her by her odour. But as her partner could not hear her if she spoke to her, and as she herself didn't know the first thing about sign language, she had no choice but to turn her face towards the girl and to mouth the name "Morag" histrionically with her lips. Voicelessly, Daisy pinched an emphatic M between her pressed lips, then formed a nice round O before displaying the tip of her tongue against her palate for the r-sound, and she finally widened "-ag" into a little smile. The deaf girl responded by tapping Daisy's forehead twice with the tip of her forefinger, meaning "yes". Well, this was the first sign Daisy had learned from her new friend, the other being a light bump with the closed fist on her forehead, meaning "No". Both of these improvised signals were derived from the standard Irish Sign Language, or ISL, that was being used by the deaf participants. Morag also 'spoke' British Sign Language (BSL), which in fact was her 'mother-tongue'; she was bilingual, and very proud of it.

21

Anyway, Daisy now raised her hand, palm forward, in what she hoped was a universal sign meaning "Wait!" Then she called out, "Father Cadogan? Could I have a word with you?"

"Yes of course! Over here!"

Daisy now motioned Morag to follow her, also with a pair of signs she hoped would be self-evident, a 'pulling along' movement of the hand and forefinger and an emphatic nod of the head 'that way'. They navigated between the chairs and tables to the front of the room.

"How did you like old Contini's lecture?" the Irish priest asked.

"Interesting, but that's one of the things I wanted to discuss with you. Can we talk in private?"

"As the others are leaving in a hurry, we'll be alone in a moment, yes."

"All right. Well, to start with, I'm a bit... disappointed that we don't get to explore the collections more... on our own, you know?"

"Fair point. But I'll ask you to be patient, Daisy dear; in due course you will have more freedom, I promise, and by that time you will also be more familiar with the lay-out of the place and the location of all the stuff."

Then, as she could hear that they were quite alone now, except for Morag of course, Daisy explained how uncomfortable she felt to be the only adult participant; "I could be the mother of most of these kids!"

"Only if you'd had a teenage pregnancy," Cadogan chuckled, "and nobody is accusing you of that!"

"How old do you think I am?"

"Erm... thirty to thirty-five, at most? You're not supposed to discuss her age with a lady."

"Well as a priest you should be able to handle that... I'm forty-one, going on forty-two, so no need for a teenage pregnancy, either."

"Sweet Jesus! If only I'd *known* I'd have turned you down... just kidding, of course."

"And I'm not even a Catholic."

"That I'm aware of; my friend Boudry confessed; but my secret hope is that you might become one of us... one day. No, believe me, Daisy, you're the right person at the right place as far as I'm concerned. Boudry was right to sing your praises; he told me about your sparkling personality and your inquisitive mind, and he was not lying about that."

"But then why am I feeling so inadequate, so out of place all the time?"

"Maybe it takes some getting used to, to be in a group with other blind... and deaf people."

"Yes, well, speaking of that, why on earth did we have to team up like this, each blind person with a deaf partner?"

"So that's what is making you uneasy? Well, you're doing just fine, my dear Daisy. I observed your little inter-action with Morag just now, and how you led the way to the front of the room with your cane... a case of the sheep leading the sheepdog! And right now young Morag is sitting next to me, waiting patiently for the end of our conversation, and she's just looking at you all the time... looking at you *adoringly!*"

"Really?"

"Absolutely, and this demonstrates how right I was to team you up with her. Only, she must be wondering what has brought that cross frown onto your beautiful brow."

"Are you going to tell her?"

"I'll give her a quick rundown in a moment, yes."

"So you can *sign* too?"

"Yes, but I'm not an interpreter like Liz, in case you're wondering."

"That I am. Where *is* Sister Liz anyway?"

23

"Just powdering her nose. What is this, the Spanish Inquisition? I still perceive some slight hostility here."

"Sorry about that, but I'm still not clear in my mind: is this a pet project of yours, this mixing of the deaf and the blind?"

"You could say that, yes."

"But *why?* Can you just explain why?"

"Well, in my work with impaired young people, back home, I've often noticed that the deaf and the blind feel a deep aversion for one another. It's a bit like cats and dogs. And I find that a great pity, especially as blind people always seem to think that they are worse off than the deaf, and the deaf believe they are worse off than the blind! It is only by getting to know each other that you'll find out this is not true. I want you to realize how good you have it. I believe this can reconcile you no end with yourself and with your condition... In my experience it can be very therapeutic."

"But there's a little flaw in your reasoning: which one, deaf or blind, should find out that they're better off than the other?"

"Well, *both* of course!"

A moment later Daisy and Morag were following endless, echoing corridors on their way to the exit. Morag knew how to get there and was leading her partner by the hand, but Daisy still kept tapping her cane on the hard floors, so she could *hear* the numerous statues and paintings they were passing. Besides, it was always good fun to make such a racket in a hushed museum. They went out into the gardens, suddenly feeling the heat of the summer afternoon, and Daisy could hear the changed acoustics of being out in the open. They took the shortest route to the south gate of the Vatican fortification, and once outside, followed the wall, going down to a thoroughfare by the Tiber, very busy with cars. It was the rush hour. They crossed over, Morag obeying the indications of the impressive, uniformed policeman who directed the traffic with waving arms at this hour of the day. Morag would have liked to describe his white gloves with wide, starched muffs attached. Daisy could only smell exhaust fumes and hear a lot of honking, like everywhere in Rome. It always gave you the feeling that everyone was on the brink of a nervous breakdown.

On the other side of the road they climbed a flight of stairs and followed a small street up the Janiculum hill. The blind woman and the deaf girl had to walk in silence all the while; there was not much they could communicate to one another. That was a pity, Daisy thought, as the Scottish student must be incredibly smart, studying art history at the Uni in spite of her disability. You had to admire that. She tried to simply enjoy the other's company; it was nice to be holding hands; Morag showed much care and consideration for her older companion all the time. And Daisy had to think of what Father Cadogan had said: that she had looked at her adoringly... With hindsight, Daisy felt a bit ashamed of her truculence with the priest, and of the implied hostility towards poor Morag. After all, she was really sweet.

Suddenly a man, walking downhill on the other side of the street called out, *"Ciao bella! Ciao Doris Day!"* Daisy giggled and waved him on; it was the first time anyone called her that: Doris Day... "Do I really look like her?" she wondered, "Maybe only because I'm blonde, or because of the dark glasses." She'd never seen the Hollywood star, obviously, but knew that much about how she looked. She'd 'attended' a couple of her movies, too, and found them nice enough, albeit a bit jejune. At least old Doris, who was her age exactly, also believed in human goodness. And at least she could sing.

But already Morag had stopped in her tracks and pulled

Daisy aside. Then, holding her shoulder with one arm, she started tapping her partner's forehead with her forefinger, five or six times in rapid succession, like a funny little woodpecker. This was the third 'word' in sign language that had spontaneously been introduced between them: it meant "What? What's going on?" and was always accompanied by a great deal of excitement and urgency from the deaf girl. Daisy tucked her cane away under her arm, opened her handbag, and retrieved a little notebook. With the attached pencil she scribbled a few words in caps: THE MAN CALLED ME DORIS DAY!

Daisy smiled, and Morag patted her shoulder, bouncing up and down on the balls of her feet, then raised herself on the tip of her toes and nibbled at the taller woman's earlobe. Another sign of great merriment, Daisy knew. The girl was such a fun-loving creature, but somehow she could never giggle or laugh audibly; instead, nibbling at your earlobe was her way of letting you know how funny she found a situation. This was another signal that had emerged between the two of them, spontaneously expressed and understood at once on both sides. Daisy thought back to the lecturer's remark, that two deaf people thrown together would create their own sign language; it could even work with a blind-deaf pair.

The catcalls from local men appeared to be part and parcel of life in Rome, but what made the two women laugh was that as a matter of course they had been aimed only at poor Daisy. Morag was small and mousy and slight; even scrawny, and just a kid: they would never call *her* Doris Day! But apparently she knew how the actress looked, had perhaps also watched a few of her movies, and she found the likeness between the Hollywood star and her companion very entertaining.

As for the trick of writing something down in a notebook, that was a *cheat*, as Sister Maria Elizabeth had already pointed out to them, and it only went so far, as Daisy could not read anything that Morag might want to write in reply. Sister Liz had also remarked it was a good thing for the "project" that not all the blind participants could write in Latin script like that. Daisy had answered she could even use a typewriter. "I could write Morag a *long* letter if I wanted!"

They arrived at the convent and were welcomed by many friendly voices chattering enthusiastically in rapid-fire Italian. The Congregation of the Sisters of St Plautilla was clearly *not* a silent order. In fact all the sisters were nurses, or carers, and worked at the children's hospital across the street. And the convent where they lived was another one of those big buildings with many rooms and long echoing corridors, where the stone floors smelled of the mop. Daisy expected to be passing her whole vacations in those, rather than outside. But that was quite all right, as it was rather hot, the Roman summer not exactly what one was used to, coming from London. She now wore a light summer dress at all times, and even sandals, which was quite exceptional for her, who at home was known by all as "Miss Sensible Shoes". Inside the Vatican Museums or in this convent, at least, the temperature was bearable.

And in here, once again, the assistance of her deaf partner was invaluable, as they made their way to the upper floor, dropped their things in their room, and went over to the communal bathroom to refresh themselves, before going down again for dinner. Daisy didn't understand much Italian, could only react with *"sì"*, *"no"*, and *"grazie"* from time to time, which again encouraged the sisters to keep chattering away. Morag, on the other hand, had one advantage: like all Italians, the nuns just couldn't keep their hands still when they were speaking, and she could *see* their very expressive gestures as they talked... The nuns realized this:

they thought the friendly blind woman was rather vague, but the little deaf one had a sharp mind, *she* understood. So they would gesture and mime any messages they needed to convey, and Morag caught their meaning quite well and guided her blind partner accordingly... Time to go to the refectory now; we're supposed to sit here today; the ground-floor lavs? Wait... Aha, yes, follow me. At their first 'debriefing', Morag had told Sister Liz, "The Italian nuns just *know* my language... somehow... almost."

Later that night they retired to their room. It was just a cell, really, where a sister would normally have lived on her own, and with two beds it was rather cramped. But for Daisy this didn't matter, as she couldn't even see it, and Morag seemed to appreciate their little nest well enough. In the evening they liked to settle on their beds and do some reading. Daisy had taken a Braille book along on her holiday, *Les Antiquités de Rome*, by Joachim du Bellay, a collection of French sonnets she'd found in Paris just after the war, almost twenty years back. The slight volume of verse made for a bulky book in Braille; the French poems made for a challenging read that whiled away the evening hours.

Nouveau venu, qui cherches Rome en Rome
Et rien de Rome en Rome n'aperçois.

Morag, at least, could read normal books; she had a couple of mystery novels in pocket editions to keep her amused. She also had a book about Renaissance art that she'd borrowed from the museum library.

But on that particular night they had something else to amuse them besides. In the morning the whole group had taken a guided tour of the *Forum Romanum* together. Their guide spoke adequate English and had been asked to describe what he showed them for the benefit of the blind; Sister Liz had interpreted for the deaf. Then, as the guide kept mentioning columns of one 'order' or the other, Daisy

28

had asked him to *describe* those orders to them, although she already knew about them in theory. Then, after they'd returned to the Vatican in their small chartered bus, Sister Liz had taken Daisy along to the museum's 'educational service', and to make a long story short, they had given her a set of miniature columns on loan. Three plastic models of the three classical orders, which Daisy now retrieved from her handbag. She started to finger and caress the little pillars delightedly.

The three orders of classical architecture. The Doric one had a simple, sausage-like ring at the top; the Ionic column had two opposed curly scrolls, forming a square-sectioned top; and the Corinthian one had frilly leaves and four smaller curls in a kind of inverted pyramid. Interesting. The Doric pillar was sturdy and had few grooves, the other two were more slender and the grooves were finer. The plastic models just gave you the *feel* of the ancient pillars, of their beauty and permanence. "Oh, I adore miniatures," Daisy told herself, thinking back to her childhood and to the Dinky Toys models her father used to give her.

Morag came over to sit by her side; Daisy felt her weight depress the mattress. She turned her head to her companion and smiled, holding up the three plastic pillars to share her delight with her new friend. Morag took them away and placed another object in her hand: she had also received an interesting item on loan from the educational service. It was a replica of a pair of Roman wax tablets: writing tablets. Two wooden planks tied together by a pair of string hinges; on the inside, the framed lower planes were covered with a layer of beeswax; there was also a stylus with a dull point to scratch words into the wax, and a spatula at the other end to erase them.

Daisy fingered the object, frowning; she knew what it was, but... then she realised that Morag had written some-

29

thing. Clever girl: the scratches were as deep as possible, and the letters were so big that you could follow the grooves of each letter with your forefinger to make out its shape; and in doing so you could make out the words:

C A N
Y O U
R E A D
T H I S

Of course! Daisy giggled, and nodded emphatically: yes, I can! She groped for Morag's face and kissed her on the cheek. The deaf girl nibbled her earlobe with relish, and then she took away the writing tablets and set to work again. A moment later she gave them back to Daisy, who deciphered the next message:

H E L L O
D O R I S
D A Y

II AD 64: A hot summer night

Sextus Pomponius Sacer was proud of his slave. That is to say, the poor girl was deaf and dumb, and probably a bit retarded too, and she was not really pretty. So he was not particularly proud of her as a person, but he was proud of *possessing* her. In the tenement block where he lived with his little family, that was quite exceptional. In fact, none of their neighbours had a slave. No one could afford it. When you bought one, even a dirt-cheap bargain like Felicitas, you needed to register the transaction at the *tabularium*, on the Forum, and pay a fee for that; and once a year you had to pay a tax for the privilege of owning a slave. Then, for all your trouble, you had another mouth to feed in your household.

Reclining on his bed, leaning Roman-style on one elbow, Sextus sighed and looked despondently into the gloom that a single oil lamp, nearby on a stool, struggled to dispel. It was hot and stuffy and he was sweating. His home was just one room under the roof beams of the five-story building. There were no windows, but there was a gap between the top of the low wall and the overhanging eaves; all the noises from the street below came through and were reflected by the slanting roof tiles overhead. In Rome the nights were noisy, as carts were forbidden to enter the city by day; the deliveries were brought in from dusk to dawn, the wheels rattling and the drivers cursing. The summer sun had beaten down on the roof all day long and the garret remained incredibly hot. In the winter the place was draughty and freezing cold, but that was only a distant memory now. Still, the home is a man's castle.

Sextus had to look hard for reasons to be proud, but fortunately he was quite good at that. To start with, apart from the fact that he owned a slave, he was also a Roman citizen, albeit a dirt-poor one. That meant a lot to him and had many advantages: you were entitled to a free ration of grain, distributed once a month courtesy of the emperor himself. You had the right to go to the baths free of charge and had free seats at the circus or the amphitheatre for various shows and games, gladiator fights and chariot races. You were entitled to go to any public library without paying an entrance fee; not that Sextus made much use of *that* privilege. And what else? Ah yes: you could even take your little family to the zoo in the gardens of Lucullus for nothing... Anyway, when his good wife Claudia complained about their numbing poverty and hinted that he was no more than an idler and a parasite, he would tell her, "Never forget that your husband is a *real* plebeian, a free citizen of Rome. Always remember that I have the vote!"

And that was the second thing he was proud of. Sextus loved politics and spent a lot of time supporting his patron, senator Antonius Soranus Canio, one of the 600 members of the Senate, a minor but ambitious politician, and wealthy enough to patronize dozens of poor clients like him. In fact he'd spent all day hanging out with his patron, as a member of his numerous retinue. In the morning he'd passed a couple of hours waiting in the lobby of Canio's big *domus*, or townhouse, on the Esquiline hill, being fed some bread and olives and served some wine. Then, as the boss went out and about town, visiting friends, the baths, or attending to business on the Forum, he'd accompanied him with all the others, jostling for a position close to great man, loudly approving every word he said and laughing at every joke he made. On that day Sextus had even managed to place a witticism of his own, which had been well received by all; he'd done himself an excellent turn, therefore. But how exhausting it was to be a hanger-on at the very bottom of the ladder; it was hard work; people had no idea! Still, Sextus had no complaints: Canio, for instance, had paid the fees when he'd bought Feli. After all, when one of your protégés became a slave-owner, it reflected well on the patron. And Canio was the owner of the tenement block where Sextus lived. His home might be modest, but at least he didn't have to pay any rent.

Looking into the gloomy room from his bedstead, Sextus contemplated his household. First his eyes wandered over to the shelf in the corner, where a little terracotta Venus statue presided, given to the couple by his in-laws, on their wedding day, to protect their home. Then he looked over at his wife, Claudia, who was sitting close by on the chest where they kept their clothes and blankets; she was spinning some wool. She twisted a fine thread between her slender fingers, keeping the wooden spindle twirling steadily, her elegant nape bent forward in utter concentration. He had no idea how his wife did it, creating such a fine yarn from some fluffy raw material loosely tied on a stick; it looked effortless; at least it was an honourable occupation for the wife of a Roman citizen. Or it used to be in the good old days... Anyway, his dear Claudia was always hoping to get a fair price for her fine thread, but somehow the money never seemed to materialize.

And then there was his young daughter, Desiderata, sitting on the floor, playing an apparently fierce game of brigands—*latrunculi*—with the slave. In fact the two girls, who were the same age, where great friends, inseparable companions. They'd carved a grid of eight squares by eight into the wooden floorboards and used two sets of stones:

smooth round pebbles from the Tiber and rough, angular clumps from a building site. They were in the process of taking prisoners without mercy. It was typical: he, Sextus, had taught his dear daughter the game, and now she spent hours every night playing with her great friend, the slave, instead of her own father! Not that he would have demeaned himself into crouching on the ground with her and using mere rocks... but still: it rankled a bit.

However, this was the third thing Sextus could rightly be proud of: his household, his family, and the fact that he was a *paterfamilias*. In the good old days he would have had the right of life and death over his kin. He could have killed his daughter at birth because she was not sound in body and limb, and he could have sold her on the slave market whenever he wanted... well, he could not have done both, obviously, but anyway... Of course the old laws had been mellowed somewhat by successive emperors, starting with the divine Augustus; nowadays the *mores* of the Romans were more civilized, and perhaps that was better. As *paterfamilias* he still had the right to decide who could marry his daughter; it was at his absolute discretion; not that anyone had come forward yet, even though she was already fourteen years old. Or was it fifteen? Sextus had lost count a bit, he was slightly ashamed to admit; how did other fathers keep up, especially if they had several kids? Anyway, in the old days girls were all married off at twelve, and good riddance. Ah, the *patria potestas!* Sometimes he said jokingly to his wife, "The law is hard on you ladies, I have to admit, but it can't be helped: that is the way of the Romans!"

"Yes, but don't forget the *lex Claudiae*."

And he would chortle expectantly, "The *lex Claudiae?* What would that be? Please remind me!"

"It's the law that applies under this roof, the one that is based on all the promises you made when you were wooing me, remember?"

And they would both smile fondly. It was true, Sextus knew, he'd made many idle boasts about their brilliant future, and Claudia had been a great catch!

Sextus looked over at his daughter again, sitting on the floor in front of the carved-out board. The deaf girl had just made her move, and now Desi patted the pieces with her flat hand, not looking down at the game, but her head slightly turned to one side. She was rather pretty: like her mother she had nice round cheeks, full lips and a pert little nose. Her thick black curls were bundled up with ribbons above her slender nape. She had a beautiful brow too. But where her eyes should have been, you only saw these shocking *holes*: empty slits sunk in deep sockets, caving in on the shrivelled remnants of withered eyeballs. She'd been born like that, poor thing, totally blind, a cruel joke from the gods!

They'd named her 'Desiderata', which in Latin could have two meanings: 'she who was longed for', or 'she who was regretted'. A very apt name, Sextus always said, as at her birth he and his wife had done both. And because of such remarks, the girl disliked her name and insisted on being called Desi.

She made her move on the board, and immediately started to 'chatter' silently with her deaf friend. She used her hands to make all sorts of complicated signals, half mime, half military semaphore, and Feli looked on intently and 'listened'. Then, when the deaf girl wanted to say something back, she'd prod Desi in a special way, and the blind girl would immediately raise her hands, her spread fingers like a cage. Feli would perform her signs and mimics between the blind girl's fingertips, and sometimes she would let a broader gesture play itself out against the other one's chest in such a way that her friend could feel its sweep. At other times Feli would seize Desi's fingers or wrists and use her friend's hands like two puppets performing in between them, alternatively thumping one girl's chest, then the other girl's, in a self-evident choreography of 'me' and 'you'. At this stage they would look like two little girls playing at hand games, totally absorbed, but without ever clapping, which seemed strange. And they could carry on like that for hours, chattering incessantly... in complete silence. What a freak show! What a wonderful joke from the gods: a *blind* daughter and a *deaf and dumb* slave... the joke was entirely on *him*, Sextus sometimes thought.

How hot and stuffy it was in the room! He decided it was time to make use of the perks of owning a slave—just for once. He tried to catch Feli's eye and mimed what he wanted from her, but he couldn't help bellowing at the top of his voice as well.

"Come over here, will you? I'm hot! I want *you* to *fan* me!"

And with his hand he pointed at Feli, motioned her to come over, and imitated the flapping of a fan. They had an old fan made of mangy ostrich feathers; and Feli was emphatically not looking in the direction of her master, knowing all too well what he wanted.

"It's no use bawling like that," Desi remarked, "Feli *really* can't hear you."

"Well, *you* tell her what I want from her."

Desi relayed her father's message and then held up her hands to receive an answer, and before you knew it they were having a whole conversation again.

At length Desi reported, "We've just concluded that my slave is not available right now, darling PF, as she's attending to her *mistress*. If it can be any consolation to you: she's beating the stuff out of me on the latrunculi board. I am *not* enjoying myself!"

Gracious *love!* The girl kept calling him PF, making fun

of the last shred of dignity he still clung to with more desperation than he cared to admit... the cruelty of youth!

"She's not *your* slave, she's mine! As paterfamilias I am the owner of everything in this room."

"Yes, yes, dear PF, if you say so."

"Well, I do! So send her over here."

"No. Even if she's *your* slave, her job is to care for your poor, helpless blind daughter, remember?"

"Such a stupid slave; such an impertinent daughter!" Sextus grumbled.

"Shall I sponge you down, *carus?*" Claudia offered placatingly, "And then fan you for a while?"

She wound the smooth length of yarn around the axle of the spindle and put the wool aside. She took an earthenware pitcher from a corner, and pouring water on a sponge she started to rub down her husband's naked body. He lay back and sighed, then smiled ruefully at his wife.

"How do you manage to always stay so cool, *cara mea?*"

Meanwhile the two girls were finishing their game, a heated battle that played itself out in increasingly rapid moves.

Desi didn't believe for one moment that Feli was *stupid*. She reflected crossly that after all, her friend had probably *invented her own language*. How many people could say that? Surely Feli hadn't learned to speak from her own mother—whoever that may have been—like most toddlers. Not even with hand-signs. And Claudia admitted she'd never managed to teach her *anything* when she'd arrived in their household, when Desi had been a mere baby. (Thus, Feli must be a few years older than Desi.) No, as a little girl she had invented her own language, and then she had taught that to Desi, although she was blind, which made it even more difficult. But Desi could not *remember* learning their private sign language at all: it must have happened when she was too young to remember anything... So there, anyway: Feli was not stupid. Besides, right now she was beating her, again, at a very complicated game that required strategic thinking and a lot of cunning. And Desi thought she herself had plenty of both, but Feli had even more... so there.

There was another disturbing fact that now pressed on her mind: sometimes Desi and Feli had lively discussions about what it meant to be a slave or not. About what it meant and didn't mean.

"It means nothing," Desi would say, "I love you like a twin sister."

"Yes, I know," Feli would reply, "but that's easy for you to say. You're not the one that is treated like a piece of furniture."

"I *never* treat you like a piece of furniture!"

"Maybe not you, but your father does. Or he tries to, anyway."

"I don't let him! I'll never allow it, you know that."

Feli often sighed, and signed: "I wish I also had a pretty little jewel like yours!" And she would fish out the tiny silver medallion hanging from a thin cord deep inside Desi's tunic. It was shaped like two moon crescents, one inside the other, which was unusual. Now, every freeborn Roman child received a pendant like this as a baby, which they always wore around their neck. The boys were given a *bulla* when they'd survived their first nine days, a tiny pouch filled with lucky charms; the girls a *lunula*, a moon crescent. And Feli did not have one, it was not for slaves.

Meanwhile Claudia had sponged and fanned her husband so nicely that the PF had fallen asleep. In the street below they heard the call of the second night-vigils' patrol. "Citizens!" one of the *vigilēs* cried, "it is the sixth hour! Don't forget to extinguish your lamps and your fires before you go to bed! Lock your doors and your windows if you can, and enjoy a good night's sleep!"

"Psst," Claudia whispered, "shall we go to bed like the man says?"

Desi transmitted her message to Feli, and silently the girls cleared the pieces lying around the game board and crept over to a corner of the room to retrieve the straw mattress that stood there, rolled up into a large bundle. They picked it up and carried it together, Feli leading the way, and Desi's mother quietly opened the door, holding the oil lamp high. On the landing in front of the door, there were already a number of mattresses laid out on the floor, with young children asleep on them. This was the usual setup: the attic garrets were so small, that Sextus and Claudia, and some of their neighbours, had to accommodate their offspring on the landing at night, especially if they wanted to enjoy some intimacy themselves.

Claudia stepped outside and hung the oil lamp on a hook next to the door, then she silently closed the door behind her. As soon as the two girls had settled down on their mattress, just in front of their own threshold, she crouched next to them, and stroked Desi's forehead. Speaking very softly, *Mater* told her daughter that she should let her father order Feli around a bit more, from time to time. "She's very lucky to be the slave of a decent little family like ours."

"Hmm."

Desi was already shifting her body so that she could translate her mother's words for her companion.

"Stop that!" Claudia hissed, "what I'm saying now is just between you and me, all right? No, really, believe me, a crippled girl like that, with very little commercial value, she could have been grievously abused in any other household. They could have given her to a young child as a plaything, to be handled and ordered around at will, teased constantly, or even *tortured...* and the child's cruelty only applauded and

39

encouraged by the parents, you know what I mean? And they call such a human pet a *delicata!* Most Romans want their kids to learn to be *hard* on their slaves."

"What do you want me to say, my sweet Mater? I *hate* it when the PF orders Feli around like that. She's like a *twin sister* to me. Even more: she's my eyes and I'm her ears. At home you don't notice it much, because that's when *I'm* serving *her*, mostly, but as soon as we go out on the streets, it's Feli who's helping *me*, and I can tell you, she really looks out for me like a she-wolf!"

"All right, but be nice to your father, yes? He's a decent man. Believe it or not, they don't often come any better than him… You're old enough to understand that now."

"Well, I never want to get married anyway; I don't want to be any man's possession."

"Hmm. That won't solve anything, sweetness: if you don't marry, you'll just stay in the custody of your father for the rest of your life."

"Yes, but *him* I can handle!"

They both giggled. Feli looked at them inquiringly, visibly burning to be let in on the joke. She always loved a joke. And Claudia, feeling a bit guilty for monopolizing her daughter, asked, again very softly, if they would like her to tell a bedtime story.

"Oh yes, please!" Desi whispered, "It's been a long time!"

And although they'd both spoken under their breath, some of the other children on the landing, who were listening in from their makeshift cots, overheard them and perked up at once. *Matrona* Claudia was famous for her stories. They woke the other kids and before you knew it, they were all sitting around her in front of her door. She sighed, and then smiled.

"Which story shall I tell? You decide, Desi."

"*Androclus and the Lion*, of course!"

Of all of Aesop's tales, this one was her favourite, her mother knew.

"All right then, so here goes:

"Once upon a time, many years ago, a slave named Androclus escaped from his master and fled into the wilderness, and fearing he would be caught by his pursuers, he hid in a deep, dark cave.

"And just as he was catching his breath he heard a lion near him roaring terribly. The poor slave jumped up and cried, "Androclus, you're dead meat!" He'd fled into a lion's den! And when he thought the lion was going to devour him, the beast raised its paw, and in the dim light Androclus could make out that the beast had a big thorn stuck into the flesh between its mighty claws, which was causing him great pain.

"Picking up his courage, Androclus took hold of the lion's huge paw and drew out the thorn from between the sharp claws. The lion roared in agony when the thorn came lose, but soon after found such relief from it that he softly put his paw on Androclus' shoulder, and licking his face, showed that he was truly grateful for being relieved from the constant, throbbing pain.

"One day, a few years later, a detachment of soldiers came marching through the wilderness and chanced on Androclus as he was fetching water and gathering wild berries for his next meal. They took him prisoner and brought him back to Rome, and he was condemned to death because he had fled from his master.

"Now, as you know it is our custom to throw murderers and other criminals to the lions in the arena, and on the appointed day, Androclus was taken to the arena to be fed to the wild beasts.

"On that day, the emperor himself was present in the

41

royal box and he gave the signal for the beasts to come out and devour the condemned prisoners. But when the first and biggest lion came out of its cage and got near Androclus, what do you think it did? Instead of jumping upon him and shredding him to pieces, it rubbed up against him, and stroked his arm with its huge paw.

"It was of course the very same lion that Androclus had met and helped in the wilderness a few years before.

"The emperor told the arena guards to bring this lucky prisoner to him, and asked him to explain what had just happened. Androclus then told the emperor that the lion was only showing its gratitude, because he'd once relieved it of a thorn that was bothering it. Then the emperor pardoned the escaped slave in recognition of this testimony to the power of friendship, and he let him go free together with the lion.

"Afterwards the people of Rome used to see Androclus walking the streets with the lion attached to a simple dog-leash, making the rounds of the taverns throughout the city. He was given money to buy meat for his big pet, he was offered drinks, and the lion was wreathed with flowers by the young girls, and many of those who met them exclaimed, 'This lion is a man's friend, and this man is a lion's healer!'"

All the while, as Claudia was telling her story, Desi, sitting straight on the mattress, kept translating it for Feli, signalling wildly with both hands. The deaf girl looked on intently, patted Desi's knee approvingly, and seemed to enjoy the tale immensely. This still annoyed Claudia a bit: why couldn't her own daughter just listen, without getting in a flap over sharing this with her *slave?* Translating it into their sign language cost Desi a lot of effort, frowning and gesti-culating, and soon she was sweating profusely, while the deaf girl, reclining comfortably, kept cool and wriggled her toes with pleasure.

42

When she'd finished telling the story, Claudia shooed off the other kids, who returned to their own beds, and she wished everyone good night. Desi thanked her for the tale, hugging her passionately with both her arms around her mother's neck, telling her how wonderful she was.

"You're the best Mater in all of Rome! What would we *do* without you?"

Claudia let go of her daughter and made her lie on the mattress, she bent low and kissed her, and as she looked down on her empty eye-sockets, she thought, "Oh Desiderata, how brave and cheerful you always are; how much I love you!"

Then she noticed Feli looking at her expectantly, lying right next to Desi, her head very close to her daughter's. Feli was looking at her with those big inquiring eyes; those huge eyes; both reflecting the flame of the oil lamp, looking up *adoringly...* What could Claudia do? She bent down and kissed the slave girl too.

III 1964: The Italian typewriter

Daisy and Morag were visiting the Colosseum, just the two of them. It was part of the project. They had skipped it when they'd all visited the Forum together; now the teams were to explore it two by two. Father Cadogan and Sister Liz had given Daisy and Morag detailed instructions the day before: they were to take a taxi directly from the convent; Daisy would pay the fare, as she could easily afford it. Sure, no problem. She'd also paid for their entrance tickets.

But they'd both had some reservations from the start. For one thing, visiting a famous monument in a foreign city had by necessity to be a vicarious experience for a blind person; there was nothing wrong with that. On top of the Eiffel tower in Paris, or on Sugarloaf Mountain in Rio, Daisy had enjoyed the views immensely, as her companions had *described* them to her. Morag, on the other hand, would have preferred to be with someone who knew sign language and could *communicate* with her and share the experience. For both of them this muted, silent outing was a bit awkward at first.

Then again, Daisy had to admire Morag: she was a resourceful girl, full of good will, and she'd instinctively found the right approach. She'd taken her by the hand and they'd *walked* to every corner of the huge ruins complex. Up and down worn-out staircases, through echoing tunnels and along the walkways at different levels. Your *feet* conveyed the dimensions of the monument to you. Sometimes Morag made them stop at a spot where you could gauge the thickness of a wall: Daisy had to open her arms wide, and even so barely managed to touch the outer surfaces left and right. And she was made to pat the top of another wall and feel the difference between the smooth outer layer of masonry and the rough filling of angular clumps and concrete on the inside. She recognized a smell like that of the cathedrals or medieval castles she'd visited at home, and her white cane produced a satisfactory range of echoing sounds. The sounds of the Colosseum were unique, as in contrast to a church or a castle, you were mostly in the open air. The sounds of the traffic, outside the thick walls, were muted.

By the entrances there were stone slabs with inscriptions; Morag made her probe the carved letters, which were perfectly legible under her fingers, even more so than those on a wax tablet. But her Latin was not good enough to make out the meaning of the words. And then there were *a lot* of cats roaming these ruins; the two of them delighted in stroking their soft fur, and Daisy couldn't help cooing when they purred or meowed sweetly. Then Morag would look on and puzzle.

So, yes, just by making use of the senses you had, you could indeed get to know the famous monument, even as a blind person. After all, on top of the Eiffel tower Daisy had also been able to *feel* that she was high up in a fresher atmosphere, and to *hear* that the sounds from the city down below were very far away. And even without the possibility of talking, Morag's companionship was real and engaging and warm. They held hands or put their arms around one another's waist; Daisy giggled and even laughed, a lot, she couldn't help it, and Morag nibbled her earlobes in return; they huddled and hugged for no good reason at all.

Daisy was starting to understand the meaning, the purpose of their experience. She hadn't uttered a *word* since

45

they'd left the convent that morning and she'd said *"arrive-derci"* to the nuns. In fact, as she didn't speak much Italian, really, she hadn't had a true conversation since the last briefing at the Vatican Museums on the previous afternoon. So Father Cadogan had sent them off on a mission to find out how it is to be the *other* person. Daisy was discovering how it must feel to be deaf, unable to communicate, and to visit the greatest monument of Rome as if you were a goldfish, swimming around in a glass bowl full of water, looking out at the world around you from a different place, a place of utter silence and aloneness. And Morag must have been experiencing something of how it is to be blind, to risk bumping into a wall or tripping down a staircase at every step... and not to be able to *see* the Colosseum!

The tourists around them, by contrast, were chatting among themselves all the time, taking pictures with their cameras, which Daisy could hear clicking repeatedly. The visitors came from all over the world and exclaimed in many foreign languages, *"Impressionnant... Wunderschön!"* Verbal communication was so much part of their enjoyment!

And taking pictures, too. That at least was something Morag could have enjoyed as well, but apparently the penni-less student didn't have a camera. Then Daisy remembered that she wanted to take away a souvenir of her own: a little model of the Colosseum! Just like she had a miniature Eiffel tower and even a tiny Sugarloaf Mountain at home. "We must find a souvenir stand," she decided. So she stopped Morag and turned her around so that they faced one an-other, and the deaf girl did her little woodpecker thing, "What's up?" Daisy started to mime what she wanted. They'd left the notebook and the wax tablets at home, because they didn't want to cheat anymore. First Daisy showed Morag her purse, taking it briefly out of her handbag, then she gestured widely, with both hands, at the Colosseum all around them, and made a motion of shrinking all that into the palm of her hand. With her forefinger she traced a circle above her flat hand, "See the miniature Colosseum?" and finally made the universal gesture of "paying", "buying", rubbing her fore-finger against her thumb… Morag tapped her forehead twice, "Yes, I understand," and off they went, to the exit of the ruins complex.

Soon they were standing by the stall of a souvenir ven-dor, and Morag had guided Daisy's hands to the models on display. When she'd selected one, Daisy gestured to her com-panion, "Do you want one too? It's on me!"

Yes, Morag was delighted to accept the offer. It was amazing how well they could communicate, as long as it concerned only such practical matters. Meanwhile it had be-come very hot; the Colosseum was not the ideal place to be, as the Roman summer sun started to bake the stones. Daisy proposed that they go to a local restaurant for lunch, and they went up the Esquiline, across the avenue in front of the Colosseum, to a small place with some tables on the pavement, on the shadow-side of the street. The spot was rather noisy from the traffic, which of course didn't disturb the deaf girl in the least, and also smelled of car fumes. But the strange thing, again, was that once they were settled and having a nice meal, after they'd solved all the practical pro-blems brilliantly, they just sat there and ate, and could no longer communicate. Small talk or a friendly chat were still out of reach for them.

The whole thing came up again later that day, at the "debriefing" that had been scheduled by Father Cadogan. Just like Daisy and Morag, the other teams had been exploring the huge amphitheatre on their own, and they reconvened in their usual lecture room at the Vatican Museums to share their experiences. Sister Liz interpreted and the Father moderated. It was actually interesting to hear what the other pairs had been up to, and how they'd experienced their visit. It sometimes sounded as if they'd explored different monuments. Daisy let Morag do most of the talking for the two of them, and listened intently to the Sister's rendering of what she was saying in sign language. It was fascinating to *hear* what she was thinking, this way.

Then, when Father Cadogan asked them for examples of "spontaneous" or "improvised" communication within the teams, Daisy contributed the example of the crazy little woodpecker Morag had come up with to ask what was going on. "I find it intriguing how I immediately understood what she meant."

Morag, sitting right next to her, tickled her earlobe with her finger, then said, by way of Sister Liz, "I find it hilarious, partner, that you call that sign 'the crazy little woodpecker!'"

A moment later in the proceedings, Daisy volunteered her observation that as long as they were only dealing with practical matters, it was quite easy to communicate, but that a friendly chat was impossible to achieve.

"True," Morag agreed, "very annoying, that."

"Interesting," Father Cadogan said, "do any other teams want to comment?"

And comment they did. They all agreed with Daisy's remark; the consensus emerged that communication between them only went so far. Miming was not the same as signing, and even if the blind would learn sign language, how would the deaf answer them? "Maybe they should learn to write in Braille," a young man volunteered hopefully.

"It's not like we're going to need sign language on a daily basis," a blind girl answered, "or that our deaf friends will ever need Braille."

"Yes, but what do you think of the *principle* of the thing?" Father Cadogan asked.

"Too much trouble," most of them answered.

Daisy reflected smugly that if the good Father had expected they would come up with a workable solution to this intractable problem, just like that, he was wide off the mark. But in the end she did volunteer an unexpected contribution of her own again.

"For those who're interested, I happen to know of only one example of *perfect* communication between the deaf and the blind, but it concerns *one* person who happens to be deaf *and* blind: Helen Keller!"

"Ah yes," they said. Everybody had heard about Helen Keller.

"Again, that's an excellent contribution from our oldest and wisest participant," Father Cadogan remarked wryly, "So what you're saying is that there exists a solution: communication between the deaf and the blind is possible after all."

"Yes. And it turns out that it's the blind who would have to learn sign language."

"But how can you learn signs if you can't *see* them?" someone wanted to know.

"Well, the interesting thing is that even before Anne Sullivan was hired to teach her, little Helen created a sign language of her own. As a little girl she used to spend her days playing wild games with the daughter of the family cook, Martha Washington, who was a bit older than her. And while playing with her young black friend, she spontaneously thought up about sixty different 'words', all of them relying only on the sense of touch. For instance, pinching a small piece of skin on the back of the hand meant 'small'; expanding one's fingertips in the other person's open palm meant 'big'. Later, when Anne Sullivan taught her sign language, Helen Keller had to raise her hands, her open fingers forming a cage, and the teacher would perform her

49

signs between her pupil's fingertips and communicate with her that way."

The rest of the afternoon was spent among the collections. The Vatican Museums were a real maze, so the deaf had to escort their blind charges to the location of their choice before they could go their own way. Later the blind were escorted back to the meeting room by the employees. Sometimes they were even provided with stepladders, when the sculptures they wanted to study were too high. But eventually Daisy and Morag separated and were free to roam the museum galleries on their own, to study the collections at their leisure. That is to say that Daisy was interested in some plaster copies of antique statues, and Morag in the paintings, and that was why they didn't stay together. They would meet again at closing time.

The uniformed museum attendants, although they were impeccably polite, were also a bit wary of the blind visitors, those groping youngsters that had been imposed on them by "that crazy priest from Ireland". But for the older woman among them, the one that "looked like Doris Day", they made an exception. She moved slowly from one plaster cast to another, using her white cane carefully, so that she never bumped into anything, and she made a point of always wearing surgical gloves, there was no need to be afraid of sticky fingers with her. And then she visibly enjoyed herself so much, spending hours probing the faces of Roman consuls and emperors. "Ah, the classical portraits of our ancestors," they would tell themselves, "the pretty lady has good taste!"

Daisy lost herself completely in the sculptures. She lost track of the time and was hardly aware of the other visitors. Sometimes she did become aware of one of the attendants shuffling in and staying in the room for a while, apparently keeping an eye on her; the Italians working here all smelled strongly of cigarette smoke. She would reflect that if she were so bold as to explore their features with her fingertips as well, she would be able to compare the Romans of antiquity with those of today. But there was already enough to explore among the exhibits without pestering the employees too.

One advantage of the plaster copies was that their pedestals were modest and that the sculptures, therefore, were within easy reach. No need for a stepladder. The educational service had prepared a list in Braille of all the exhibits in these rooms, so at some stage Daisy knew that she was probing the portrait of a young Nero. It was astonishing: the infamous emperor as an innocent boy, smooth-faced, with big, drooping eyes, an endearing little nose and an impish chin… Was this impression genuine? Had this portrait really been made when Nero was still young, or had it been ordered after the fact by the adult ruler to refurbish his image?

"Do you know who he looks like?" a young man's voice asked, right next to her, making Daisy jump out of her skin.

"Erm… No?"

Why could people never understand that you shouldn't sneak up on an obviously blind person like that?

"He looks just like Paul McCartney… you know?"

"Who's that?"

"You don't know about Paul, as in 'John-Paul-Georges-and-Ringo'? The Beatles! The Fab Four!"

"What are you *talking* about?"

"They're a group; a band; pop singers! Haven't you heard about Beatlemania?"

"Well… are they on the radio?"

"Of course they are!"

"On the BBC?"

"Yes, of course, the BBC too! If you listen to the Light Program; Saturday Club; Pop go the Beatles?"

51

"All right… So what were we saying?"

"That young Nero looks exactly like Paul McCartney… it's uncanny!"

"I see; I'll take your word for it. I'll check this out at the first opportunity. 'The Beatles', you said?"

But the young man had already moved on. How had he even known that she spoke English? Was it that obvious that she was British?

Finally the bell rang, and the attendants started roaming the rooms, announcing in Italian that it was time to leave, and they corralled all the visitors towards the exits. Daisy was reunited with Morag and they set off for the convent up the Janiculum hill. Again they just enjoyed one another's company, holding hands, but were incapable of conversing about what they'd been up to in the afternoon. Morag was clearly in a playful mood, as she kept rushing them, running along the pavements, pulling her older companion's arm.

Then, after dinner, they settled down on their beds as they always did, and tried to read. But Daisy kept putting down her Braille edition of French sonnets, and even her tiny model of the Colosseum couldn't engage her for long. This plastic thingy was a bit of a disappointment, sad to say. She kept thinking back to the discussion after lunch. Fancy finding something relevant to say, based on dear Helen Keller's life story; she had become so old hat nowadays! She was an elderly lady now, in her eighties, and she had retired from public life. But still, wasn't it something, that a deaf and blind woman had set such an example to the rest of the world?

And then there was this disturbing portrait of a young Nero, and his likeness to Paul McCartney, whoever that may be.

Suddenly Morag, who must have noticed these musings, landed on the mattress next to her and tapped her forehead with her finger, "What's up?"

How can I tell you, Daisy thought, where do I even start to explain what I'm feeling? Her notebook was in the drawer of the nightstand, right next to her, but instead of writing something down, she decided she would like to use a typewriter. Surely the nuns had one in the office of the convent secretariat? So she raised her hand: "Look here, watch this," and then she mimed typing on a machine with ten wriggling fingers and pushing the return chariot back from time to time at the end of the line.

"Yes, I understand" her companion signalled by tapping on her forehead, "follow me," she conveyed by pulling Daisy off the bed. Together they slipped into the silent corridor outside their room. Then Morag led the way down the stairs and into a musty-smelling office on the ground floor. There she settled her roommate into an upholstered chair in front of a desk and pushed the typewriter towards her. Daisy immediately started probing it with her fingers, and while Morag inserted a sheet of paper and turned the drum further with a ratcheting sound, Daisy settled her fingertips in the correct position. And finally, after a short pause to gather her thoughts, she started typing. Morag quickly went over to close the door, and coming back, looked on in fascination. It was quite impressive: even on a clunky old Olivetti, the blind masseuse had enough strength in her fingers to keep up a rapid-fire rat-tat of 'blind typing'.

When she'd finished her letter, Daisy pulled it from the drum with a flourish and handed it over to her deaf friend. Morag held it up, started reading, and was taken aback: "Dear ?orag". Then she looked over at the typewriter, and understood at once: it had an *Italian* keyboard, QZERTY, so not only were the letters W and Z switched around, but where the 'm' should have been, there was a comma, and the

53

capital M, when typed, came out as an interrogation mark. Looking at the jumbled message, the deaf girl was shaken by silent giggles of merriment, but she didn't want to give away the game. With a little bit of good will you could read the text anyway, so she just carried on, regardless:

Dear ?orag;

There are a fez things I zanted to tell you after our visit to the Colosseu, (thank you for being such a zonderful guide) but I didn't zant to say the, in front of the others at our daily debriefing; because this is just betzeen you and ,e:

I still find you a very ,ysterious creature; as I have no visual contact zith you; and no verbal co,,unication is possible either: But I love you very ,uch; for you are alzays kind and friendly to ,e; and incredibly patient: I zant you to knoz hoz ,uch I love you:

Father Cadogan zas right zhen he predicted that I zould change ,y opinion of deaf people: I no longer think you have it any easier than ,e; rather the opposite: I ,ust ad,it I alzays believed being deaf zas only a light i,pair,ent; not that I ever gave it any serious thought; obviously:

By tea,ing us up; I guess the good Father is forcing us to realiwe hoz it is to be the other person: This ,orning at the Colosseu, I have finally experienced your lack of co,,unication possibilities; your sense of isolation ,aybe; and you ,ust have felt ,y helplessness; ,y sense of stu,bling in the dark so,eti,es:::

Anyzay; it is nice to be going through this experience zith you; ,y dear ?orag; I couldn't have zished for a better tea,,ate:

Love; Daisy

IV   AD 64: Two beggar girls of Rome

Desiderata could not hide her feelings. As soon as she became aware of Feli's presence, she showed her delight, smiling from ear to ear. Sometimes Desi woke up first, from the prattling of the children around them on the landing, and because Rome was a noisy place that you couldn't ignore once it got going in the morning. And sometimes, less frequently, it was Felicitas who woke up even earlier from the light of dawn pouring in under the eaves of the roof and through the small window at the front of the staircase. In both cases the girl that woke up first would immediately shake the other one's shoulder. And in both cases Desi's welcoming smile was the first thing Feli saw at the start of the day.

However, there was no time to dwell on all that; they had to get up. They were hungry; being poor was hard work; they needed to get cracking. They rolled up their mattress and brought it back inside their tiny apartment.

"PF! Mater! Are you awake?"

"We are now," Sextus would grumble.

The girls went down to empty the chamber-pot and draw fresh water from the nearest public fountain. This was the only moment of the day when they served their parents or masters willingly, and both of those were grateful for it, especially as they lived on the fifth floor. Then they would all breakfast on the bread and olives left over from the previous day. Soon they would leave their garret and go on their different errands. Poor Romans like them lived on the streets, mostly, and only went home to sleep at night.

Sextus led the way and closed up the place, securing the wooden latch with a wedge as best as he could. Their front door didn't have a lock with a key: that was a luxury they could only dream of. Instead they hung a wax tablet on the hook next to it, with a message promising unspeakable plagues from the gods for any trespasser. The last time Sextus had read out his latest malediction to his daughter, she'd roared with laughter and translated it for the slave, who'd sniggered silently. Hardly the desired effect.

Anyway. First he'd go to his usual barber for a shave. He went straight to a cosy open shop under an arcade at the end of his street. Even poor, a proper Roman wanted to be clean-shaven, and wouldn't dream of taking care of this himself—sharpening and wielding a shaving knife was better left to a professional. And he'd want to have his face whitened a bit with chalk powder, and his lips rouged just a smidgen so he'd look healthier; his eyelashes blackened just enough to make him look smarter and seductive. His barber, fortunately, didn't expect to get paid until his customer came into funds again.

Speaking of which. Sextus was expecting a windfall. Rumour had it that the emperor had just issued a new coin to honour his dead little daughter Claudia Augusta and his wife Poppaea Sabina. This would be a silver *denarius* at least: you didn't issue copper or bronze to honour your loved ones. Now the nice part was: when Nero issued a new coin, he would give a few to each citizen who came in to pick up his free ration of grain, and as luck would have it, on that day Sextus was due to do precisely that. And that was why he was even wearing his white plebeian's toga, a gift from his patron Canio.

And by the way. When he mentioned his high hopes to

his barber—you had to give the man something to look forward to—the other customers waiting for their turn started to exchange all the latest gossip about little Claudia's death.

"They say it's the *Christians* who cast a spell to make Nero's daughter die... You know, that Judean sect they talk about... they sacrifice human babies on their altars and drink their blood, as everyone will tell you."

"Yes, but why would they have wanted poor little Claudia to die?"

"Because they believe in nothing! They are ghost-worshippers; they hate Rome... despicable people, all of them!"

Sextus was sceptical about this story and said so. But he had to admit there was something fishy about the poor little mite's death. You'd expect that the emperor's baby had received the best care in the world, and that when she got poorly, the best doctors and magi of Rome would have done their utmost to save her. Yet she hadn't lived longer than four months.

"But that's what happens all the time when you have kids," someone remarked, "it can happen to any of us, so why wouldn't it happen to the imperial couple as well?"

"Careful what you say, Mucius... the emperor is not like you and me."

"I know, Sextus, I'm not saying he is! Just that his grief is the same as ours, that's all."

"True. And he deserves our full sympathy."

After his shave and 'touch-up', poor Sextus had to go out to the Campus Martius, outside the city walls, to a special warehouse, the *Porticus Minucia Frumentaria*, to pick up his monthly ration. Passing through the *Porta Ratumena*, he made his way to the sprawling complex, where he had to report to one of the 45 offices situated under the arcades. There he waited for his turn, and then he had to fill in a wax tablet with his name, 'address'—a brief description of where he lived—, the date of this appointment and the number of the office he'd been assigned to: XXXIII.

"You already know all that, man," he grumbled to the familiar clerk.

"It's for the record, Sextus, you know the rules. But cheer up, the rumour you've no doubt heard about a money handout is correct!"

And with a flourish the man handed over two clay tokens to the smiling 'beneficiary'. One was the *tessera frumentaria* that entitled him to a grain ration, the other a *tessera nummaria* for the gift in cash. Sextus went inside the building. He had to wait in line in front of a table guarded by two uniformed members of the urban cohorts, where another clerk gave out the money in exchange for the tokens. When his turn came, Sextus collected nine *denarii*, for a household of three. In wonderment he looked down at the freshly minted silver coins in the palm of his hand, and said to the attendant, "Isn't this the *prettiest* thing in the world?"

"Next!"

Hurriedly he cleared off and went over to the corner of the hall where they were distributing the grain. He gave an attendant his token and an empty, folded sac he'd been carrying with him all along, and that was filled with wheat by a public slave. Then he had to lug the full sac back to office number XXXIII, where the clerk made him press the seal of his signet ring—the one he'd inherited from his father—into the wax of the tablet he'd filled in earlier, and gave him the token he would have to show the next time he came, a month from now. Finally Sextus was off with his haul.

The sac was heavy, containing enough grain for two loaves of bread a day. He had to bring it to his baker, who every day would take a portion of your wheat, and for a modest fee would grind it and bake your bread for you. Each bakery had a millstone operated by a donkey tethered to a wooden beam and turning round and round in the courtyard, day after day. It seemed kind of symbolic. As he carried the heavy sac on his shoulder, stopping every hundred paces to take a breath, sweating profusely in his thick, woollen toga, Sextus reflected that being a subsidized citizen was damn hard work! And where was your accursed *slave* when you needed her help to shoulder your burdens?

Feli was having a great time with her mistress Desiderata. They both had something very specific on their minds: urine. That morning, when they'd taken down the chamber-pot so willingly, they hadn't emptied all of it in the great urn by the entrance of the building. They'd gone into the backcourt of their *insula*, their apartment block, and there they'd emptied a part of "the family pee" in a smaller pot of their own. The big urn on the street, out in front by the entrance, was owned by the local launderers, who took away the smelly production of all the tenants as soon as it was full. They needed big quantities of stale urine, reeking of ammonia, as a detergent to scour their customer's clothes.

After breakfast, and after the PF and Claudia had gone off on their errands, Desi and Feli sneaked back into the backcourt. They retrieved the pot with urine from its hiding place behind a pile of junk, then slipped down into the cellar, that was only used as a storeroom by a local potter. There they took off their regular tunics and changed into old rags, remnants from their childhood that were full of holes and way too small. Then they went over to a wall that had a big patch of saltpetre on it. In the dim light coming in from a small basement window you could just make out the fluffy white powder. Feli scraped some off and dissolved it in the urine with a little stick. Finally the two girls started rubbing the smelly mixture in their hair, on their faces, shoulders, arms and legs. Desi signed to Feli, "If you're going to rub it all over yourself, you want it to come from your own folks."

"Certainly!"

The saltpetre had been Feli's idea: if you wanted your skin to look like a peeling wall, why not use the white stuff that 'grows' out of such a wall? It worked like a charm; as the mixture dried, they both looked like genuine lepers: their skin had taken on a kind of flaking aspect. They looked repulsive! From the hiding place in the backcourt they now retrieved a pilgrim's walking stick and a beggar's bowl, and Desi picked up a cheap little bell made of stoneware. They were ready to go.

For a short moment Feli kept a lookout around the corner of the backdoor, with Desi right behind her, until they were able to leave the building unseen. They didn't want people to know about their secret lives, but the entrance archway was quiet: most tenants were off to work or out to the shops. So they hurried into the street and went straight to the 'Argiletum', the main thoroughfare in their neighbour-hood, where they could melt into anonymity, no longer Desi, the blind one with the sharp tongue, and Feli, the deaf and dumb one, but just two ordinary little beggars of Rome.

The Argiletum was incredibly crowded and cluttered, like always. The main streets from the Quirinal, the Viminal and the Esquiline hills came together here, in the lower part of town, and this narrow street led straight to the Forum. So it was bustling with crowds of pedestrians moving in both directions, some of them hauling heavy loads and bumping into other people. The rich were being carried in litters by sturdy slaves, preceded by guards who shooed away the passers-by in front of them. Groups of women were clustered by the shops and makeshift food stalls, examining the wares and chatting, and urchins at play ran everywhere and got in everybody's way.

If you looked up along the sickly facades with their bawdy graffiti, you could see the street at its prettiest. Balconies and windowsills decorated with pots of flowering plants; clotheslines with towels, handkerchiefs and underwear fluttering brightly in the sun, and beyond the red rooftiles of the eaves, a narrow strip of deep-blue summer sky. But it was better not to look up for too long, or you would be overrun by the relentless tide of the moving mobs.

It was heavy going on the flagstone pavement. There were high kerbs, stepping stones across the roadway at each corner, and deep ruts that had been carved out by the wheels of countless wagons and carts. The street was dusty and smelly too, littered with garbage and hazy with smoke. The food stalls were belching acrid smoke straight into the open. There were all kinds of businesses housed in arcaded shops on the ground floors of all the apartment blocks lining the street: a riot of odours came from the bakeries and smithies, the laundries smelling of urine, and the even more pungent public latrines. Then there was the noise, the clamour: haggling, cursing; even normal conversations were held in the loud and pushy tones typical of the Romans.

And suddenly, adding to the confusion, two mangy-looking creatures appeared on the scene. Beggar girls straight out of the sewer, that you wouldn't want to touch with a ten-foot pole. One was clearly blind, helpless, with horrible slits where her eyes should have been, the other was scrawny and shifty, her squinting eyes darting left and right. Both in rags, unkempt, with stringy hair, their skin scaly-looking. The blind one had a little bell jingling in her hand and probed her path with a stick, the other one held on to her shoulder but seemed to be led as much as she was leading her companion. Bizarre pair. People hurriedly moved out of the way as they passed. You wouldn't want to come into physical contact with these repulsive creatures; they

61

looked like they might spread all sorts of awful diseases by mere touch. As they progressed down the street, a path opened in front of them through the crowd and bustle; probably the guards clearing the way for the wealthy and mighty couldn't have done a better job. At some point, being in a playful mood, the skinnier one made them rush forward, running in the middle of the roadway, pulling her blind companion's arm. People dashed aside, scattered in a panic... for Desi and Feli the most difficult part was to keep a straight face, a tragic mask even, instead of bursting into helpless giggles.

But it was not all play. Rome was a dangerous place, especially for two unchaperoned girls of marriageable age. The fact that they were wearing young girls' tunics that left their arms and legs bare didn't make it any better, on the contrary. As Feli remarked, "Marriageable? In my case that would be: ravishable!" Her sign for this was rather crude; her language could be very graphic sometimes.

"Ravishable? Not as long as *I* have anything to say about it," Desi replied, "and Mater, of course."

The truth of the matter was that Sextus could in theory do as he pleased with his slave, but at the same time this protected her from unwelcome attentions elsewhere: no one would want to interfere with another man's property.

Still, as they walked down the street both girls were extremely vigilant; danger lurked everywhere; this was no joke. Feli kept scanning the street left and right, on the lookout for any threats; Desi kept her ears open. You had thieves and louts and gangs, the girls were the ideal target, completely defenceless, but on that day at least they also looked repulsive, which was an advantage. And then you had to keep an eye out for the police, the patrols of the urban cohorts, who might not look kindly on alleged lepers roaming freely through the streets of Rome. At least these cops were easily spotted by their bright red tunics and the crests on top of their helmets.

The girls had become very proficient at disappearing from the scene when needed. If Feli identified any threat coming their way, and she had a sharp eye and an uncanny ability to anticipate trouble, she would rap her knuckles on top of Desi's head and Desi would prepare to run. The rap on the head was a very subtle signal, because it could easily convey a wide range of alarm levels. In its softest form, it meant they would suddenly veer off, at a brisk walk but without running, into a narrow side alleyway, hardly visible to a casual passer-by, or into a building's archway, leading to a backcourt. A sharper rap and a tugging would have the two girls galloping at full clip in the opposite direction they'd been following. In a sticky situation, Desi became totally attuned to her guide's directions and together they were able to react to danger with perfect coordination. And when she *heard* something alarming happening, the crash of some accident, of something falling, and the cries of the by-standers, she would rap her knuckles on Feli's head and immediately point in the direction where the noise had come from, so her friend could see if there was any danger for them.

But on that day they reached the Forum without pro-blems and crossed it as fast as they could. Desi stopped ringing her bell, Feli steered them clear of the cohort patrols that were always present there, and so they quickly melted away between the buildings on the other side. They were going to a place where they hoped to make some money.

In the meantime Claudia was on a mission of her own. It was market day all over Rome, like on every ninth day— the *nundinum*—and she had gone to a street market on the Viminal hill, where they sold raw wool in bulk. Not just any old wool, but fleece from Northern Italy, the best, famous for its silky sheen and soft feel. Of course it didn't come cheap, but Claudia had a lot of money in her purse. She had organized a cartel of housewives in her neighbourhood and had collected the contributions of around twenty matronae like herself, who had learned to card, spin and weave from their mothers when they were little girls. The husbands found it a quaint women's activity and had no idea how much money you could make out of it. Of course the 'ladies' had to compete with every domestic slave in Rome who was ordered to spend every idle moment carding or spinning. But Claudia had figured out that the wives of free citizens who actually *liked* the work could produce a much superior thread. What could you expect from overburdened slaves who were forced to work the cheapest wool while they craved a well-deserved break? So the plan was to work with the best raw materials available, and buy it in bulk so that you could get it at the best price, then distribute it among the participants of 'the housewives' cohort', who would produce the finest yarn from it. As she sauntered from one stall to the next, fingering and comparing the goods, Claudia was already dreaming of setting up weaving looms. For the moment the cartel had to sell their yarn to professional weavers, and they got a fairly good price, but if they could produce their own cloth they could make even more profit. On the other hand, most of the members lived in cramped quarters, like she did, but you could set up a traditional vertical loom against any wall, and it didn't need be expensive... still, it would be a big step... as things were now, each woman's entire equipment and materials—raw wool, a pair of carding bats and a spinning spindle, plus the spools of finished thread—fitted into a single, average-sized basket... Finally Claudia selected a promising bale of fleece and proceeded to haggle with the stallholder. "No, no, you misunderstand, sir,

I want to buy the *whole bale*, if you can send someone over to deliver it at my place... how much?"

If you went straight to the Tiber, taking the *Vicus Jugarius* from the Forum, and you turned to the right through the *Porta Carmentalis* in the Servian wall, then passed in front of the Marcellus theatre, you could soon cross a stone bridge on your left, to the island in the middle of the river. And there you had the famous temple of Asclepius, the Greek god of medicine and healing. Very potent and popular, this god, and his temple a crowded marketplace of ailments. Desi set up shop on the broad steps leading up to the colonnaded, Greek-style front portico; Feli went on the look-out at the top of the same stairs, leaning nonchalantly against a column with one shoulder.

The business plan was quite simple and straightforward. Hundreds of ailing people came here to be healed, and they knew that if you gave an offering to someone who was worse off than yourself, it would put the divinity in a better disposition to help *you*. And Desi, with her hollow eyesockets, her scaly-looking skin and stringy hair, was clearly worse off than anyone else, including the other beggars, who put it on a bit, all of them. She didn't smell too good either. On the streets, coming over, people had felt so much disgust at the sight of her, that she could almost *hear* their aversion humming in the air around her; now suddenly she was at the top of the game, the queen of the dung-heap!

She was sitting on the temple stairs, jingling her bell pitifully, with a little bowl in front of her. And in that bowl there were already a handful of small coins. That was the finishing touch for setting up shop. Mater gave her money in the morning, "Buy something to eat for lunch, sweetness, for you and Feli, and come home when you get hungry again." She always seemed to have some cash to spare, and made sure the PF was not around when she gave it to her. And the thing was, if you already had a number of coins in your bowl, people were easily induced to give you some more, as they assumed that others had already done the same. Meanwhile Feli kept an eye on things, not even hiding, to make sure no one tried to steal their earnings.

People came to the Tiber Island's temple not only from Rome itself, but from far and wide: its reputation had reached all the corners of the Empire, on a par with the original temple at Epidaurus, in Greece. The sick and the wounded, no matter what was ailing them, came to this place to be healed by the god, by the waters of the miraculous spring inside the dark, cave-like temple, by the priests and the snakes and the dogs. The priests, as far as Desi could make out, must have had oodles of experience and were effectively among the best physicians of the day. The serpents and the dogs also lived in on the premises, and once the patients had explained their symptoms, the priests burned incense, chanted incantations, and would make the sacred animals flick their tongues at the ailing spots or lap up the pain from the sufferers. And they would also give you drugs. Very often, it worked.

But what interested Desi most, was that the square in front of the temple was also a marketplace of religions. People came here from all over the Roman world and were followers of a wide variety of gods and faiths. Most of them came to worship Asclepius *beside* their normal gods, because it couldn't hurt to beg a specialist deity for help, but some hung around to make publicity for the healing powers of the *competition*. "Asclepius is old hat, the temple of Apollo on the Palatine is the place to be for what's ailing you.—No! you should appeal to Isis and Serapis, I myself was miraculously cured." Apart from the usual crowd of Greek and Roman gods, say all those living on the Olympus, you also had the likes of Cybele the Great Mother, Atargatis the Syrian goddess, or Mithras from Persia. Feli had told Desi that there was a tall obelisk from Egypt, covered with hieroglyphs, in the middle of the square, to add to the exotic atmosphere of this colourful marketplace. And to add to the confusion, some Judean enthusiasts from the Trastevere neighbourhood across the river came over to preach that there was only *one* true god: theirs! Desi found all this very entertaining.

And then some of the followers of these widely different religions wanted to recruit the blind beggar to prove their case: "My poor girl, you should try this or try that, go to such and such temple; your eyesight might be restored; wouldn't that be wonderful?" But Desi put them back in their place implacably. She was a true Roman and defended the traditions of her people.

"*I* am not *ill*: I was *born* like this. Why would the gods want to heal me? It would only mean that they've changed their minds, and the gods never do that."

Recently Sextus, judging his daughter old enough for such serious matters, had told her, "If you could ask one of the gods, 'Why was I born blind?' he or she would just shrug and answer, 'Why not?' That's how indifferent the gods are to the fate of mere mortals. Believe me, the important thing is to worship them properly and keep your nose clean so that you don't incur their wrath. But if you're smart, don't expect any sympathy from our gods!"

"That's the Roman way," she would tell the people who were pestering her with miracle cures. Some of them were put out, some impressed, even shaken. "Did your father teach you this? He must be a wise man!"

"Well of course: he is a true plebeian!"

Desi thought, "If only the PF could hear me singing his praises like this!"

When the obelisk's shadow indicated that it was noon, Feli would decide it was time for a lunch break. Her stomach had been telling her the same for quite a while, but was not as reliable. So she would join Desi, count the money, tell her how much they had, and they would buy sausages and pastry from the food peddlers in front of the temple and stuff their faces. Then, still belching, they would 'chat' for a while. The people around them marvelled at those two, standing there facing one another, and playing endless rounds of 'hand clapping'; they weren't little girls anymore; they see-med way too old for such games. But Feli wanted to know what Desi had been discussing with her 'customers'. Feli always wanted to know everything, and Desi accepted this: after all, there was no one else in the world who could tell her. So she reported the discussions about all those reli-gions, and how she'd defended the Roman attitude, the idea of the indifference of the gods.

"Yes," Feli commented, "the gods are hard on you people like you people are hard on your slaves."

"Yes... but not me."

"No... not you."

A few hours later, as she'd taken up her vigil at the top of the stairs again, Feli spotted a group of youths crossing the bridge on the Trastevere side of the island. She'd noticed them before, on other days. They were a local gang of toughs; thieves of the purse-snatching kind. They would hang a-round on the temple square, by the stone parapet, feigning a great interest for the view across the Tiber. But they were keeping an eye on the beggars, waiting for an opportunity. At other times Feli had seen them following a beggar going home at the end of the day, at a distance, like a pack of wolves. Until now they'd never shown an interest in Desi, a mere girl, as blind as a bat. But on that afternoon one of them, the youngest and smallest, crossed over to the temple steps and passed very close by Desi's spot, glancing into her bowl. They were scouting; time to call it a day and leave the scene as discreetly as possible. Feli stepped down and rapped her friend's head with her knuckles, very lightly, meaning, "Something's up; let's go".

Desi put away their earnings inside her belt, and the two girls crossed the bridge on the Forum side of the island. Then Feli led them down the incline to the riverbank and followed the Tiber. She knew a spot upstream from the main sewer, where the water was clean, more or less, although the river was very low. Without further ado they stepped into the muddy stream to wash the scales and the pee off their skin a bit.

The two girls liked the Tiber and the riverbanks a lot. Even when they were quite small they'd spent endless days playing here, roaming up and down the meandering stream, even as far as the countryside, outside the city. They were real river rats and felt at home here.

As they bathed, Feli thought of Claudia's stories about gazelles in the wilderness that go for a drink at a waterhole: they were now at their most vulnerable and she had to be particularly alert. She was thinking about the youths from the Trastevere neighbourhood. While the two of them were bathing like this, up to their middle in the water, they were a very tempting prey; she would soon find out if they were being hunted or not. And sure enough, the group of toughs appeared at a small distance on the riverbank, coming straight for them. As soon as they saw that Feli had spotted them, they started running, with the relish of predators who know their quarry can't escape.

But they were wrong. Already Feli had rapped her knuckles on top of Desi's head, hard this time, meaning "run as fast as you can". Immediately they splashed out of the water and flew off at top speed, holding onto one another lightly, their movements perfectly coordinated.

At a strategic location just thirty yards from where they'd been bathing, there was an entrance to one of the seven sewers of Rome, or rather its finishing point, where it poured its sewage out into the river. The girls even had to run *towards* their pursuers in order to reach it, but reach it before them they did, and there they just jumped into the rivulet of slurry and rushed into the sewer tunnel at full speed. The young toughs stopped in their tracks, disgusted; they went "Ugh!", and decided to wait outside until the beggar girls would come out again. They sat down around the tunnel opening; they were quite certain those two had collected a lot of money at the temple; they were willing to wait for that booty.

But Desi and Feli had no intention of turning back. As soon as she heard the hollow, echoing sounds of the vaulted masonry around them, Desi took the lead and they kept running. Even without her walking stick—still lying on the riverbank—she was quite proficient at finding her way with her outstretched arms. Soon Feli could no longer see a thing, but her blind friend just kept rushing her along in the pitch darkness. This was not the first time they did this. When they were certain that the boys weren't after them anymore, they slowed down, panting, and gagging on the incredible stench of human excrement. As they walked on they could feel the stuff squishing under the soles of their feet and between their toes. Sometimes they were wading through it up to their ankles.

Every public latrine in Rome was being flushed permanently into the sewers by a trickle of fresh water from one of the numerous aqueducts that supplied the whole city. But normally the ancient underground tunnels should also have been evacuating rainwater and local brooks, and draining the marshlands on which a part of Rome was built. However, in that hot summer of 817 AUC a terrible drought had been going on for a while, and the sewer sludge was particularly concentrated and pungent.

They soldiered on regardless. Desi tried to gauge the distance they were covering; the idea was to reach a point beyond the Forum and emerge somewhere in the vicinity of the Argiletum or the Subura neighbourhood, near where they lived. From time to time Feli tapped Desi's shoulder to indicate she wanted to say something, and her friend held up her hands. She would announce, "There is a little bit of light above us." A drain hole or an access well, but it was too soon to get out, and they kept advancing.

Finally, after what seemed like an endless slog, when Feli had signalled another source of light, Desi groped at the walls around them, and could make out a narrow staircase cut away in the wall on one side of the tunnel. It had to be an access shaft; from time to time gangs of public slaves would be sent down into the sewers to dredge and unclog them; this was one of the places where they entered.

Desi tapped Feli to make her hold up her hands, so she could tell her something. She assumed it was too dark for Feli to see her signs, so they needed to use Feli's signs instead. This was no problem: Desi just mirrored the signs she normally *received*, and Feli read the signs she normally *transmitted*. "This is a good place to get out. You go first. Go for the light." Feli pulled her along and they started climbing up into the shaft.

They had to lift and raise a heavy wooden grate, which they only just managed to do, combining their efforts, before they emerged in a deserted side street of the Subura neighbourhood. Then Feli led them to the nearest public fountain, where they could wash. As was usual, this one had a rectangular basin carved out of a huge chunk of stone, like a big bathtub, so the girls just climbed in and wallowed. The other people who wanted to use the fountain were not happy.

And finally they got back home.

From the archway they could hear Mater's familiar voice, cackling with her friends at the back, in the shade of the tenement building. The two girls slipped into the potter's cellar, where they'd left their good tunics, and changed back into them. Then they went into the backcourt, where half a dozen women were carding or spinning, sitting out in the open on wooden stools.

"When you speak of ghosts they always turn up," Claudia exclaimed at her daughter's appearance, "we were just wondering what you two were up to."

"*Salvē, dulcis Mater,*" Desi replied as she hugged her mother. Then Feli led her from one woman to another, and she hugged them one by one. "*Salvē, matrona* Domitia... Tullia... Rufina.*" The women didn't say a word until she'd greeted them; they wanted the blind girl to guess who they were; and Desi, who'd known them as long as she could remember, easily identified them by their familiar odour.

"Incredible, Desiderata, you haven't lost your touch!"

They kissed, caressed and petted her in their matronly way, like the little girl she had been not so long ago.

"Do you wash properly, my pet? You smell a bit... peculiar."

"I know. Maybe I stepped on a dog heap somewhere."

"How big you are now! When is your father going to find a husband for you?"

"Well, forget it, *matrona* Aemilia, who would want a horrible blind girl like me?"

"Oh, but all the rest of you looks good; you've become a beautiful creature!"

And so they went on and on. Desi did all she could to ingratiate herself with these women and laughed heartily at their banter and jokes; she wanted Mater to be proud of her, even if she was only a pitiable cripple.

When Sextus came home, he greeted the company in the backyard very formally, and Claudia took her leave from them. The other matronae reacted demurely: they knew what was proper. Only young Desi, as usual, introduced a light note by flinging herself at her father like a lively little girl, clinging to his neck, "*Carus* PF, you're back!"

She could smell that he'd just been to the baths, the scented oil on his skin wafting up her nose. She liked to feel her father's body against hers: so strong, so hard. As soft and pliable as her mother was, as tough and unyielding her father. It gave her an inkling of why women could long for men, and probably vice versa.

With stiff dignity Sextus led the way up to his shabby little garret, with his wife, daughter and slave in tow. Feli for once played her part convincingly, lugging Claudia's stool and work basket up the steep wooden stairs. As soon as he'd unlocked the door and looked around in the dim light from under the eaves, Sextus noticed the big bale of wool standing in a corner. "What's that?" he demanded.

"Oh, you know, *carus*" Claudia replied levelly, "the women pooled their small change for some wool... it costs almost nothing, but you have to know your stuff... so they asked *me* to buy it for them."

"It's hot in here," Desi said to change the subject.

"And how was *your* day, Sextus?" Claudia asked, "Tell us all!"

"Well, the good news is: I collected nine denarii from our beloved emperor."

"Bully for him!" Desi cried, "What do you want me to buy for dinner?"

"The special feast menu, please, waitress, and a pitcher-full of wine for me and my love."

73

"Don't forget some vegetable soup," Claudia added, "we could all use something healthy and digestible."

So Desi and Feli set out with a pitcher and a pan, a basket and the large water jug. The flats in the tenement did not have anything like a kitchen or a hearth; people never cooked, but bought their food from the countless shops and stalls in the street. Water had to be tapped at the nearest fountain. Down the five stories they went again, exulting at the idea of buying something special to eat for all of them: they were famished!

First stop at the bakery, where they ordered two *panes focacii*, large flatbreads with an extra topping of goat cheese, onions, and anchovies; they had to wait while their order was simmering in the hot oven. They also bought some honey buns for the next morning. Then on to their usual *thermo-polium*, the tavern where they had their pan filled up at the counter with the thickest, most expensive soup from a big built-in urn with a small hearth beneath it; this was also the place where you could have your pitcher filled to the brim with wine. And they bought some extra olives to replenish the stock at home.

The PF had placed lavish orders, but had not given them nearly enough money to pay for it all. This was not a problem, as the traders knew the blind girl well and were only too willing to charge their purchases to her father's account. Sextus had an impeccable record for always settling his debts... in the end. But on this occasion that was not even necessary, as Desi simply made up the shortfall with her own earnings from the temple square.

And after passing by the fountain to draw some fresh water, they slogged up to the fifth floor again with all their supplies. They could all have gone down to the thermopo-lium and eaten there, in the noisy tavern, huddling around one of the small tables, shoulder to shoulder with their neighbours. But that was precisely what Sextus didn't want. He claimed that he liked nothing better than sharing a meal with his family and slave in the peace and quiet of his own home. Even if that happened to be as hot as the baker's oven.

And Desi liked to listen to her father's stories. He always had interesting things to tell when he came home at the end of the day. As a hanger-on of Senator Antonius Soranus Canio, he went places and met a lot of people. He often picked up the latest news on the Forum. Besides, the never-ending narrative of how Sextus tried to keep up appearances was very entertaining too: how he pretended to be a man of importance, time and again suppressing the fact that he was a dirt-poor nobody.

"This morning, at my barber's, the 'Christians' were the talk of the day, all of a sudden."

"Really?" Claudia said absent-mindedly.

"What's that: the Christians?" Desi wanted to know, wolfing down a big chunk of panis focacius.

"It's a new religion, apparently. I'd never heard of it either, before now. Then they start telling you that *everybody* knows about the Christians, making you feel stupid, because you don't… yet. I hate it when they do that!"

"Yeah. I know the feeling. So what about those Christians?"

"They were saying that they'd cast a spell to make Nero's daughter die. You know: the Emperor's and Poppaea's little baby, Claudia Augusta."

"The poor little mite!" Mater cried.

"Why on earth would they want her to die?"

"That's exactly what I said too! They told me the Christians are ghost-worshippers, that they sacrifice human babies on their altars and drink their blood. They hate Rome. They believe in nothing!"

"What kind of religion is that!"

Desi didn't believe a word about all the horrors, but she was intrigued: to believe in *nothing*, wouldn't that be something, in a way?

"You know, PF, apart from all the rest, I can understand the appeal: life would be so much easier without being constantly pestered by the gods."

"Careful what you say, girl... it is every Roman's duty to honour our gods and the emperor. But anyway, just like you I was kind of intrigued. So as I was lugging my sac of grain over the Forum, I buttonholed the first Judean peddler I could find—they'd told me the Christians are a Judean sect—and right in front of the Basilica Aemilia I asked him what he knew about these people. This dignified old gentleman in his strange costume explained that the Judeans are waiting for what they call a *Messiah*, an envoy from their god who will come one day to be their king and rule the world so wisely that all men will live in peace and joy forever... It was the first time I'd heard of it... I wonder if our emperor knows about this... But anyway, the funny part is, it turns out the Christians believe that this Messiah has very recently come, and gone, and that *no one has even noticed*... How about that?"

Desi and her mother sniggered, genuinely baffled.

"Talk about believing in nothing!" Desi cried, and then she had to explain to Feli what the joke was about. That was not so easy.

She and Feli were sitting on the chest and on a stool, facing one another so they could easily communicate. Sextus and his wife were reclining on the bed, leaning on one elbow, the pan of soup on another stool in front of them, as if their double bed were part of a *triclinium*. As if this were the dining room of a fancy *domus*. While they were eating their flatbread with their hands, they would dip it in the soup, taking turns; Claudia insisted that the four of them have their share. "We need to eat something healthy as well," she declared. Meanwhile she and her husband were also drinking wine mixed with water from earthen beakers; the girls had only water.

Sextus now told them that he'd found Canio and his retinue on the Forum too, later in the afternoon. They had just come back from the gladiator fights in the new arena on the Campus Martius, the beautiful wooden amphitheatre erected by Nero. Desi knew why her father sounded so wistful: when you went to the arena with Canio you could always count on front-row seats!

"It's ironic," Sextus said, "I was also at the Campus, picking up my ration, but that was earlier, at the public warehouse. Anyway, Canio and the men were on their way to the baths, and I joined them. All the while they were grumbling about the fights they'd just attended; too tame; not enough blood on the sand. They assured me I had missed nothing."

"Oh, that again," Desi commented, "I'm glad our emperor has put an end to all the bloodshed. We live in different times now."

People like Canio, the PF, and all the other grown-up men she knew kept deploring the new rules that forbade public executions in the arena. Nowadays a runaway slave like Androclus would no longer be fed to the lions, and the gladiator who lost a fight could no longer be put to death by the winner to please the crowd. Nero had even built the first sports stadium of Rome, where games could be held for amateur athletes, like in Greece, but the Romans found athletics boring. It was a good thing, Desi thought, that you had to be careful about criticizing the Divine Emperor, otherwise the bloodthirsty populace could have caused a lot of trouble!

Everybody called Nero "the young emperor", because he was still in his twenties, but as he had come to power at the age of seventeen, Desi herself could not remember a time when he'd not been there. It had always been "young Nero" this and "young Nero" that. So surely he could not be all that young anymore. What old men also objected to was that the young emperor appeared to be greatly influenced by Seneca, his tutor, and something of a father figure to him. Seneca was a Stoic philosopher who dreamed of a society governed by the highest moral principles. Nero was said to listen carefully to him and to follow his advice, so the old guard called him "the philosopher king", dismissively. Desi thought, "What's wrong with a philosopher king?"

And Rome was full of buildings that bore the young emperor's name, in particular the very lavish Nero baths, and the brand-new *Macellum Magnum*, the indoor market on the Caelian hill—everybody loved to go wish-shopping there!—and then you also had the Neronian aqueduct across the same hill. There was a new Nero Bridge over the Tiber, north of the Campus Martius, that led to the extensive Nero Gardens on the Vatican Fields, and also near the Vatican hill the Circus of Caligula had recently been refurbished.

For as long as the blind girl could remember, Rome had been prosperous and peaceful, the only wars you ever heard about being glorious conquests taking place on far-flung Eastern outposts. Only recently Sextus had reported that the emperor intended to ceremoniously close the "doors of war" at the temple of Janus on the Forum: the empire would then officially be at peace again. And the reforms of Roman law started under Julius Caesar and Augustus had been completed: nowadays even the slaves had rights! Therefore, as far as Desi could make out, it was a very good thing indeed to have a "young emperor". She said so to her father, and concluded, "Next time you see that Judean peddler, you should ask him if our own beloved Emperor could possibly be the Messiah he was telling you about."

"My dear girl," Sextus answered ruefully, "even if that

were the case, I don't think the Judeans would ever admit it!"

"Anyway, you can tell your precious senator Canio that the days of mauled convicts and chopped-off heads are over; no more blood on the sand; all that will never come back in Rome."

"Don't be so sure, girl. You're still very green and naïve; I've lived long enough to know that these things come and go."

Sextus frowned while his blind daughter relayed their conversation to his deaf and dumb slave again in that strange sign language they had. It still irritated him no end, but what could he do about it?

Suddenly the neighbour's cat irrupted into the room. Desi heard a crazy bouncing sound as if a leather ball had been thrown in their midst.

"Gattus!" she exclaimed.

The gaps between the walls and the roof of the building allowed the tenement cats free rein to hunt mice wherever they wanted. In fact Desi now realized she'd also heard the scratchy patter of one of those darting over the wooden floor.

"What's the cat doing?" she asked Feli in sign language.

"He's caught a mouse... wait, the mouse escaped... no, he's cornered it again... the cat is *playing* with his dinner!"

"That makes me so angry! Let's try to distract him."

Desi started whistling like a bird, something she was very good at, but that didn't make any sense to poor Feli. After twittering and warbling for a while, she asked her, "Did it work?"

"Only for a short moment. The cat is still holding the mouse prisoner."

"Can't *you* do something?"

Feli let go of Desi's hands and crawled on all four to the corner where Gattus was torturing his prey, his tail sweeping

79

the floor with relish. A moment later the deaf girl was back and told her friend, "I managed to free the mouse and punish the cat. I blew into his nose, real hard, you should have seen him jump!"

"Well done!"

As much as cats were useful for controlling the mice that plagued them all, Desi could not tolerate this mania they had of toying with their victims.

Without registering the irony of the incident with respect to the cruel arena shows they'd just discussed, Sextus said, "It's a good thing our ration of wheat is stored at the baker's, out of reach for these grubby little pests... Speaking of which: when I'd collected the cash gift from the emperor this morning, I decided the first thing I'd do was to settle my accounts with my suppliers and my barber. And as I had to deliver the sac of grain at the bakery anyway, I asked Antonius the baker how much I owed him..."

"Uh-oh," Claudia said.

"Exactly, *carissima*. He assured me that I owed him nothing, because you'd already settled the bill a while ago."

"Yes, I used part of the money for the wool. If I can buy it real cheap, I get to keep the difference."

"Well, that's great, but you could at least have told me before I went and made a fool of myself. Then picture my even greater surprise when later on I went over to our thermopolium, and this time I was told that my *daughter* always pays our orders cash in hand!"

Desi signed to Feli, "The PF has discovered our little secret!"

"Well? What do you have to say about this, young lady?"

"At least your *barber* must have been glad that you paid him."

V   1964: The Desiderata stone

As she came out of the museum room, Daisy probed the side of the doorway with her cane and knew she had to make a sharp turn to the right to proceed down the corridor. Just as she did so she bumped head-on into another person moving in the opposite direction.

"Accidenti!" the man cried, dropping the books and papers he was holding in his hands.

"Drat!" Daisy cried, jumping out of her skin.

"English, eh?" the man said with a heavy Italian accent, "can't you look where you're going?"

"Well no, I'm blind!"

Daisy raised the handle of her white cane to underline her words.

"Even so: you were not paying attention!"

"I beg your pardon?"

"It is true, no?"

Already the man had picked up his documents and publications from the floor and stepped past Daisy. She could hear his footfalls receding down the corridor behind her. She righted her dark glasses and turned to him.

"Excuse me!?" she called out harshly, intending to hector him about his bad manners.

The man's footfalls stopped.

But just at that moment Daisy realized in a flash that he'd been right: not only had she not been paying attention, but also he was right not to treat her any differently from anyone else because she was blind. So she repeated in a much softer voice, "Excuse me, you were right, I was not paying attention."

She took a few steps in his direction and bumped into the man again, softly this time. Apparently he'd just turned around too and walked back towards her. He was a priest of some kind, as she could feel a many-buttoned cassock stretching over his belly.

"I apologize also. It just struck me how crazy this is, me dedicating my whole life to disability studies, and now I'm missing this opportunity to get to know a real-life blind woman!"

"You're Father Contini, our lecturer! I recognize your voice now."

"And you're one of our Irish interns."

"British, actually. Shall I tell you why I was not paying attention? I just made a momentous discovery, a moment ago, in that gallery back there."

"A discovery, really? Do you realize that scholars have been studying these collections for almost a thousand years? So I doubt very much that you could have discovered anything new."

"Well it's new for me, and I'm very excited, and besides, you have to ask yourself: how many *blind* people have studied these collections in a thousand years?"

"Not many, I'll grant you that. So what is it; what can only the blind find out in that gallery?"

"Well, I was probing the funeral inscriptions in there, and it came to me in a flash that in ancient Rome, *the blind didn't need anything like Braille.* They could easily learn the normal alphabet from the carved inscriptions all around them, and read those. They could even learn to write, using the wax tablets that were widespread at the time. If you wrote large enough, you could feel with your fingertips the script that you or someone else had scratched into the wax."

"Interesting. So what exactly is your discovery?"

"That in antiquity, the blind could read and write without a problem. Don't tell me you already knew that?"

"No, I had never thought of it, I admit. But it stands to reason, yes; it's not a discovery as such; it's just a practical inference and it's purely speculative."

"You are hard to please, Father Contini!"

"Well I'm sorry, but from a strictly scholarly point of view this is not really... relevant."

Daisy shrugged: never mind the strictly scholarly point of view! She was thinking of why she'd been in such a hurry in the first place, and decided that the man standing right in front of her could come in handy anyway. She tapped his belly lightly with the back of her hand, which was still holding the cane. "Listen: do you have a moment? I need your help."

"I was on my way to lunch. That is why I was in such a hurry: I'm famished!"

"And I was on my way to the educational service, to see if I could find someone to help me translate an inscription: it will only take a minute."

"All right, young lady," the priest said, "let's have a look at your inscription, and then you'll have lunch with me."

He felt some relief that this lively blind woman was not challenging his authority, and he looked forward to her company: sharing a meal with a pretty woman, whether blind or not, was never to be sneezed at. Daisy turned around, and sweeping with her cane she went back into the room, leading the way.

This was another collection of plaster casts, but here they had brought together copies of interesting inscriptions from antique monuments and funerary stones. The blind woman stopped in front of one of them, with the priest by her side, and after putting on her surgical gloves again, she started probing the inscription with rapid movements of her fingertips, and read aloud the words and letters of each line.

N·QVINCTIVS·Ɔ·L·COMICVS
SIBI·ET·QVINCTIAE·PRIMILLAE
COLLIBERTAE·ET·CONIVGI·SVAE
VIXI·CVM·EA·ANNOS·XXX

The man in the cassock was impressed in spite of himself; his thick dark eyebrows bounced up and down; this was unprecedented, you had to give the blind woman her due.

"Now," Daisy explained, "I have some Latin from school, like everybody else, and what struck me was the last line: 'Vixi cum ea annos triginta—I lived with her for thirty years'. Is that correct?"

"Absolutely. Very good."

"How romantic!"

"I agree: tidings of a good marriage from almost two thousand years ago. What could be more moving?"

"But I have difficulties with the rest."

"Let me start at the beginning then, yes? Numerius or Naevius Quinctius is the author of the inscription. His *praenomen* starts with N, and we also learn that he was a comic poet, 'comicus'. But then the mysterious code 'Ɔ L', or Ɔ libertus' tells us that he was a slave, freed by two women: that is the meaning of the inverted Cs. They were probably the sisters of the slave-owner, and they 'manumitted' the comedy writer or actor when they inherited him, together with the rest of their brother's estate."

"Again, very romantic."

"It gets even better. The inscription is dedicated to himself, 'sibi', and to Primilla Quinctia, his wife, 'conjugi', who was freed together with him. And then the man declares, 'I lived with her for thirty years'. Then she died and he buried her, and commissioned this stone for the grave where he expected to be joining her soon... Is everything clear now?"

"Yes, thank you, kind sir. So:

"I, Numerius Quinctius, freed by two women, comic poet;

"for himself and for Primilla Quinctia,

"who was freed together with him, and who was his wife;

"I lived with her for 30 years... That is incredibly moving!"

Father Contini chuckled, "My dear lady, they know what they're doing at the Vatican Museums."

A few moments later they were sitting together at a small table in the museum canteen. This was where the attendants, the staff, the researchers and the interns had lunch. It reminded Daisy of the refectory of her old boarding school, but instead of the din of giggling blind girls, you were overwhelmed by the harsher hubbub of countless loud conversations in Italian all around you. Still, the smell of this place was almost the same—the whiff of watered-down vinegar from the kitchens—and the food was almost as bland. Well, a lot better than in England, but bland compared to the restaurants in town.

The gruff priest turned out to be surprisingly obliging and helpful in assisting his blind table companion; they'd had to choose a menu and collect what they needed at a counter; father Contini had insisted on shuttling back and forth to their table, first with Daisy, then twice with their trays. And now at last they were tucking in.

Daisy was delighted to be with a sighted companion this time. On previous occasions she'd shared her meal with some other blind participants of "the project", but the fact that they were so young had made her uncomfortable. Well, that and the fact that they were very Irish, and blind too. Now at least she had the feeling she could see through the old priest's eyes, vicariously: she could ask him where her bread bun had gone, or tell him to describe the view through the window. Wonderful. As for Morag, she thought with a pang of guilt, she was probably sitting at another table somewhere, having a great time with other deaf girls, conversing animatedly in sign language, completely oblivious to the hubbub around her.

"I must confess that I was impressed in spite of myself by your little demonstration, back there, my dear lady. I'm starting to realize how clever you must be."

"Call me Daisy, Father... But you still think it is not relevant from a scholarly point of view?"

"That's right: your skill, as extraordinary as it is, proves nothing."

They both had to lean over the small table and huddle over their spaghetti in order to hear one another. And even so they had to speak loud and clear. Besides, Daisy was struggling hard with her very messy spaghetti Bolognese.

"What I would like to ask you, erm... Daisy: is it normal nowadays, for a blind person, to be so familiar with the Latin alphabet?"

"No, as a matter of fact it is not... As a girl I went to a very special school, where they insisted we should learn 'Braille and self-reliance'. That was before the war. They wanted us to be able to write an address on an envelope, say, or to use a typewriter. They wanted us to lead 'a productive life in the real world', as they called it. So later I studied to become a physiotherapist, and now, at work, I still use these skills on a daily basis."

"I see! Interesting. But it proves my point exactly: not everyone who is blind could read an inscription the way you just did."

"True, but I was just trying to imagine an intelligent blind girl in ancient Rome, middle-class and well-educated like me. Now, even if there existed no such thing as Braille, wouldn't such a girl just naturally find out about all these inscriptions around her in the city, and on the tombs along the roads outside the city?"

"Ah yes, each road outside the gates was literally *lined* with graves, as it was forbidden to bury people within the city walls."

"Exactly! And my doppelgänger in ancient Rome would have been as fascinated by them as I was in that collection room just now. So she would have pestered her mother, or her father's secretary, or the slave that taught her siblings, to please teach her the alphabet, and she would have carried on for as long as it took, until she could *read the stones.*"

"You make it sound so easy!"

"I'm trying to make it sound *inevitable!* So what do you think?"

"I'm starting to understand your point of view, but what *I* would want to see is some written evidence from the past, any inscription or document from antiquity that tells me directly, or even by implication, that a blind individual was ever known to read inscriptions with his or her fingertips."

"*Scusi, Monsignor*, I couldn't help overhearing."

A man sitting at another small table right next to them said these words, half in Italian, half in English.

"Vanetta! You were eavesdropping!" Father Contini cried, and to Daisy he said, "It's all right, Vanetta is an old friend, and a great scholar."

"Possibly I know of a record by implication about such a blind person in antiquity, who could read and write."

"Really, Vanetta? Well I'm curious: out with it!"

"It is in the *Compendium*, by Bishop Rorick of Trier. Do you know it, Monsignor?"

"Of course! A well-known historical source for disability studies, although I must confess I never read it *in extenso*. You know how it is: you see quotations by others all the time and you end up thinking you know the work, but you don't, really."

For Daisy's benefit Contini added, "The *Compendium Mirabilium Sanationum* is a list of holy relics people could go and visit as pilgrims, to heal specific ailments. This was in the Merovingian age, in the 6th century, when such practices were current."

"Yes, Monsignor, and at some point Rorick mentions that on his first pilgrimage to Rome, he saw a miraculous stone from antiquity, with an inscription. He calls it the 'Desiderata stone'. He reports that it was a very powerful relic for healing blindness as well as deafness. Now the interesting part is: he also claims that this Desiderata person, who was supposed to be blind, *had carved the inscription herself*. Of course many scholars have argued that he makes that claim only because he wants the stone to be a true relic, not a mere inscription..."

"Desiderata!" Daisy exclaimed, interrupting the man at the next table.

"Do you know her, Madam? I mean, have you heard of her before?"

"No, but I was just fantasizing about a doppelgänger in ancient Rome, right? Well, if Desiderata really existed and was blind like me, her family and friends would have called her 'Desi' for short. And *my* name is also Daisy!"

The two men chortled fondly: what a girlish thing to say... and how completely irrelevant!

"There are *three* questions arising in my mind, my dear Vanetta," Contini now said very earnestly, "the first one being: is Desiderata a Christian saint? Is she on the list?"

"No, Monsignor, I don't think so. She must have been a

normal Roman woman. But valid point nonetheless."

"Secondly: do we find her name in the Corpus?"

"I have no idea; I would have to check."

"Oh, don't bother, I'll do that myself, it will amuse me."

"What's the 'Corpus'?" Daisy wanted to know.

"The *Corpus Inscriptionum Latinarum*. All the Latin inscriptions—and graffiti—that have ever been found anywhere have been collected in a kind of encyclopaedia by German scholars. If Desiderata is not mentioned in the index of that work, it would imply that the stone, or plaque, mentioned by Bishop Rorick, has never been found."

"Oh no, it can't be, that would be such a pity!"

"And the third question, Monsignor?"

"Do we know the name of the church where Rorick saw the stone?"

"I suppose so, yes: that's the whole point of the Compendium, isn't it? Go to this church in that town or convent and pray in front of such and such a relic to heal this or that ailment… However, I can't remember the name of the church, only that it didn't ring a bell, particularly, which is strange, because I know my Roman churches."

"Very well. I'll have to find the relevant heading in the Compendium, and check that detail too. Again, I'll do it myself, I find this thing intriguing."

In the meantime they'd finished eating, like all the other people around them; the noise level in the museum canteen had gone down and it sounded like everybody was about to go back to work.

"So what's the plan, Father Contini?" Daisy asked, "I may be very ignorant, and I'm not sure I understand everything you two gentlemen have been discussing, but you intend to go looking into this thing, right?"

"Yes, my dear Daisy. I propose we meet again tomorrow, same time same place, and have lunch together. Then I should be able to tell you more about Desiderata, and explain all the ins and outs. I have a feeling that you are very passionate about her already."

Daisy sighed, smiling. "But of course! Wouldn't it be wonderful to discover a stone that tells us her story? Just like Quinctius the comic poet and his wife Primilla?"

Daisy found Morag at the debriefing right after lunch, or rather, Morag found *her*, and they sat down next to one another in the little lecture room and waited for the start of the discussion without even attempting to communicate. They'd all spent the morning scattered among the collections, in small groups or on their own. You'd have thought there would not be any new developments to "debrief" by now.

But as soon as Father Cadogan and Sister Elizabeth opened the proceedings, it became clear that there was a small crisis at hand, and that the mood was rather sour. Through the voice of Sister Liz a couple of deaf girls started complaining about being partnered with blind girls all the time. Daisy suppressed a smile: now that she had finally accepted the strange rules of engagement of the "project", it turned out that other participants found it just as hard to stomach as she had at first.

"Why can't we stay together and just use our own language?" one of the deaf girls pleaded, "At home, when we go to the Uni and all that, we have to do *everything* in English *all the time*. Now that we're on holidays we'd like to relax."

"You know why we're doing this," Cadogan replied calmly, "we've discussed this repeatedly. I know it's a sacrifice, but I truly believe it's a beneficial experience for all of you."

"I agree with you, Father," Morag said by way of Sister Liz, "I don't mind being partnered with Daisy at all, on the contrary. And it's not even like we have to use English all the time, it's more like using 'mime', just the same as with the Italian nuns."

Daisy was pretty sure Morag was very chummy with the two girls who were complaining. In the canteen she was always sharing a table with some deaf girls; you could smell her and her friends' distinctive odours when you passed them with your tray. And Daisy assumed that they were always silently chatting in sign language, having a good time. So it wasn't as if her deaf partner didn't have the same reasons to complain as the others.

"Very good, Morag," Father Cadogan exclaimed, "I like the way you call it 'mime'! So in fact English as such is not really an issue here."

"Wait a minute," Daisy now said, "what's all this about 'English'? Do I sense a certain *hostility* towards my mother-tongue? Is this some Irish thing?"

The priest and Sister Liz both tittered; Morag leaned over and pulled Daisy's earlobe, which meant that the other deaf participants must have been sniggering silently too. But it struck Daisy that she didn't hear any reaction from the blind in the room, so it wasn't some *Irish* thing after all; it must be a *deaf* thing.

"What?" she demanded, "Did I say something funny?"

"Sorry, my dear Daisy, you couldn't possibly know. Neither could the other blind in our group. So let me explain. The issue here, is that our deaf friends would rather use *sign language* than English, and the point is: *it's not the same thing at all*. Morag, you know BSL as well as ISL, can you tell our blind friends more about this?"

"Yes, Father, I'll try. So, as it happens, the British and the Irish have completely different sing languages. ISL, just like the American version, is based on the French system. But BSL, on the other hand, is not: it's… different. Anyway, the thing is: ISL, ASL and especially BSL are not only com-

91

pletely different languages, but they've got nothing to do with English either... For us, English is a *foreign* language!"

"All right, I had no idea... But in that case, what was Anne Sullivan using when Helen Keller went to college at Radcliffe, for instance, when she interpreted the teachers' lectures for Helen?"

"She was probably doing just that," Father Cadogan replied, "interpreting from spoken English into sign-supported English. As it happens, I believe Helen Keller never learned ASL, poor thing. Didn't she learn to lipread and to use voiced speech?"

"Yes, that is quite incredible: Helen Keller can lipread with her fingertips! And she learned to speak too. It took her more than twenty years to learn to speak in such a way that others could understand her. I mean, don't forget she is deaf *and* blind: she *really* has a handicap!"

"Of course!" Father Cadogan said placatingly, "that's not the issue here."

"The issue," one of the deaf girls said through Sister Liz's voice, "is that it took the poor creature twenty years to learn to voice English speech properly. That only goes to show how *unnatural* it is for the deaf. I am certainly not going to break my backside doing the same!"

"But still," one of the blind boys said, "if you're talking about communication between the deaf and the blind, lipreading and voicing is a viable solution, definitely."

"Hah! You only say that because that way *you* don't need to make the effort. It's not fair!"

Daisy recognized the blind boy's voice; he'd been in her lunch group a couple of times; he was very Irish, meaning rather sarcastic and opinionated. And after he'd bickered for a while with the very Irish deaf girl, Father Cadogan put an end to the debate.

"To get back to the complaints we started with: if you

two girls want to team up, I have nothing against it, as long as your blind partners don't mind being thrown together as well."

The two blind girls assured him that it would not be a problem. They both could find their way to their digs un-assisted by now, or rather, using their canes only, so it was just a matter of choosing the most convenient location of the two.

"Well that's great, girls, thank you ever so much. Any other teams who'd like to split up, no? Daisy and Morag, you two are good, yes? In that case we're dissolving just two of our six partnerships, after almost a week... not bad... I've seen much worse on this project; we've hardly ever had a better set of participants than you people."

During the priest's little pep talk, Daisy smiled waggish-ly and started wriggling her fingers on her lap as if she were typing, then gave a sweep to an invisible return chariot with her right hand. Morag leaned over and fondled her earlobe.

Dear ?orag;

So ,uch to say::: I zas thinking about our biwarre debriefing all afternoon: And suddenly it hit ,e: Inside your head and in your drea,s you ,ust be thinking in sign language; BSL or ISL: Incredible::: People often tell ,e they can't i,agine hoz ,y ,ind zorks because I', blind since birth: Even our teachers at school said that: Zell; noz I have the sa,e feeling about YOU; darling ?orag: I can hardly i,agine hoz that ,ind of yours zorks: So you still re,ain a very ,ysterious creature: And ,uch cherished; of course:

Another thing: Today it also hit ,e that in antiquity the blind could read inscriptions by touch: No need for Braille::: I should have knozn that already; after our little experi,ent zith the zax tablets: Anyzay; I deciphered a fascinating stone zith a little help fro, Contini; our lecturer: You ,ust have seen ,e having lunch zith hi, and another scholar: It zas very interesting: Ze discussed a blind zo,an; Desiderata; fro, the 6th century or earlier; zho ,ight have left an inscription so,ezhere in a local church:

Ro,e is a place zhere the stones can speak; and I've found out they can have a ,ind of their ozn: I', hoping to get a ,essage fro, a distant past; because the Desiderata stone ,ust still be here so,ezhere: Stones can't just disappear:

I'll soon knoz ,ore; and I'll keep you posted:

Love; Daisy

VI   AD 64: Two masseuses at the baths

Cominia Gariliana was a freedwoman working at the new baths, outside the city wall, on the Campus Martius, and she loved her job. She'd come a long way, starting as a slave at a local third-class *balneum* in the Subura, where she even had to scrub the shithouse. Thinking back to that time still made her shudder. No, nowadays she didn't dirty her hands anymore: she was in charge! At least in charge of all the household matters at Nero's baths. Organizing everything; making sure there were always enough towels and that they smelled good; ditto for the bathing oils, which had to smell even better; that kind of thing. All the cleaning was done by slaves or by lowly freedwomen that she bought or recruited herself to work for her: let *them* do what *she* used to do.

And then: Nero's baths! Top notch… the emperor had really made a splash! ("Pardon the pun," Cominia thought wryly.) For the first time public baths had been put up on the scale of an imperial palace, rather than a patrician villa. Huge echoing halls, with swimming pools rather than mere bathtubs, following one another along a central line. Left and right you had changing rooms, *palestrae* for all kinds of sports, steam baths, and private meeting rooms. Everywhere you could enjoy the sight of friezes and frescoes on the walls, dedicated to Venus; all kinds of erotic scenes; nude couples or threesomes doing every trick imaginable, but very tasteful. Oh yes, and at the entrance you had this incredible fountain basin made from a huge, polished slab of porphyry—purple granite—from Egypt. Very classy!

Anyway. On that day, Cominia was busy in her store-room, stacking clean towels on the shelves in her cupboards. She made sure to place enough lavender and rosemary pouches between the stacks to dispel the slight whiff of human pee the linen had when it came back from the launderers. Suddenly a man entered her domain, without knocking or saying a word. Cominia looked up in alarm, then relaxed: it was one of those wealthy regulars who rented a private meeting room and always behaved as if they owned the place. Tall and broad-shouldered, with a shock of greying curls above a handsome-looking face, he stared at her with the cold eyes of a cobra ogling its prey. She knew the type: patricians, equestrians or senators; they always behaved as if they owned half of Rome, witch in a way they did. Filthy rich and mighty powerful.

"Do you know who I am, woman?"

"Yes, Sir," Cominia answered with a slight bow of the head, "I am honoured to greet you, Praefect Rufrius Crispinus. What can I do for you, Sir?"

"You know that I entertain an informal little circle of friends in my private meeting room… I need a couple of slave girls to do some massage for us. Can you provide that? I'll make it worth your while."

"Sure. But if you want them to tend to your pleasures, why not just go to a brothel and pick up a couple of girls you really like? I don't know what you and your friends would fancy, and I guess a high turnover is always better for this kind of thing."

"You misunderstand, woman. We *really* want only massage. But I want to *buy* a couple of competent slave masseuses from you, so I can kill them at my convenience, should one of my friends inadvertently reveal any state secrets, you know? Just as a precaution, so to speak."

"I understand, Sir. But you do realize that killing a slave like that is illegal nowadays? Our emperor has recently made the laws a lot stricter that way."

The man waved this off with a frown and a dismissive gesture of his hand. "Well, in that case I'll just sell them on to someone in the provinces, you know, remove them far away from Rome: the effect would be the same."

"Erm... I see, yes. But I have an even better offer, if you'll allow me, Sir. I can hire two *crippled young girls* I happen to know, both experienced masseuses, but one of them is totally blind, the other one deaf and mute. They can do an excellent job serving you gentlemen, but they are so *retarded*, that even if the blind one should overhear any sensitive information, she wouldn't have a *clue* of what you're talking about... She hardly understands what's going on around her... Pitiful little lambs, both of them."

"Sounds good. You can bring them in. The sooner the better."

Desi was fascinated by the stones, Feli knew. So that morning she led her up the Esquiline Hill, all the way to the *Porta Esquilina*, the gate in the old city wall, and then they ventured out on the *Via Tiburtina*, the main road to the town of Tibur. Right behind the gate the road was lined with graves, and where there are graves there are tombstones, and where there are tombstones there are inscriptions. They walked briskly along the road for a while, until Feli spotted exactly what she was looking for: a fresh grave. And a brand-new gravestone with a beautiful inscription.

The fresh grave was situated more than a hundred yards off the road, so they had to swerve through a thicket of older tombstones. Then at last Desi could start probing the inscription with rapid movements of her fingertips, spel-

ling the letters one by one in her mind, reconstituting the
words of each line.

N·QVINCTIVS·ƆƆ·L·COMICVS
SIBI·ET·QVINCTIAE·PRIMILLAE
COLLIBERTAE·ET·CONIVGI·SVAE
VIXI·CVM·EA·ANNOS·XXX

When she was satisfied that she understood everything,
she turned to Feli and started telling her what the stone said.

"It's a man who writes comedies: you should like that.
He used to be a slave, but he and his wife were set free by
two women. Now the man's wife died and he says that he
lived with her for thirty years. That's twice as long as you or
me have been on this earth!"

Feli was mighty impressed. She knew the stones with
the carved 'letters' could speak to Desi. Not only in the grave-
yards along the roads, but on every temple and monument
in town as well. Only, in that case, most inscriptions where
out of reach for her blind friend's fingers, and sometimes Feli
would painstakingly copy one of them on the PF's wax
tablets, if they could 'borrow' them, and Desi could 'read'
from that, if Feli wrote large enough.

In this way they'd found out that there were quite a lot
of houses with the inscription "Felicitas lives here" above the
door. These were brothels, as Desi could hear plainly from
all the panting and moaning coming from inside. She explained that the word Felicitas, above the door, was not only
the name of her friend, but that it also meant "joy" or "bliss".

"Yes, 'bliss', that's me!"

"And it says 'bliss lives here' because it's a place where
men can pay for sex."

"I know: there's a big penis carved in stone left and right

of the inscription."

You also had many interesting graffiti written in charcoal on the walls in the back alleys of the Subura. Feli would take Desi's forefinger and guide it along the letters, getting it all smudged with charcoal. But then Desi could tell her what the message said: "Caius is a big turd," and Feli laughed out loud, barking a bit like a dog, which she rarely did, but there was nothing she enjoyed more than a good joke involving poo or pee.

In fact it had been Feli who had started the whole thing, many years back, when Desi had been eight or nine years old. One day she'd asked what all those 'squiggles' carved in stone were for. "They don't seem to be of any use, so why do they bother to carve them everywhere?"

Desi had investigated, as soon as Feli had been able to lead her to an accessible inscription. And from that moment on, the blind girl had been fascinated and obsessed. She'd asked her mother what this was, and when she'd been told about reading and writing, she'd started to pester Mater and demanded to learn "the language of the stones".

"You'd have to learn the alphabet first," Claudia pleaded, "I don't know how to teach you."

"Yes, but if *you* know the language of the stones, how did you learn it?"

"I went to school for that."

"School," Desi told Feli, "don't we have one of those a few streets off?" Yes, that was the place under the arches of a portico where you heard kids reciting their lessons all day long, under the severe tutelage of an old Greek slave they called a 'teacher'. It didn't sound very exciting, or even interesting, on the contrary, but if that was what it took, Desi was willing to try.

The Greek slave, Tassos, had been quite astonished. He knew the girls, of course, they were well-known in the neighbourhood, and he had already come to the conclusion that the blind one, at least, must be rather clever. But fancy her coming to him and demanding to learn to read! Apparently she'd figured out how to recognize carved inscriptions by touch. He explained that you had to pay for the teaching; that his master, the owner of the portico, collected the fee; that it was not free.

"I will pay you when I grow up, Tassos. Teach me!"

The old slave had sighed, and smiled inside his Greek beard. "Oh well, why not. But don't tell anyone."

And when his regular pupils went home, he'd taught the blind girl. It was Tassos who'd thought up the trick of writing the twenty-three letters of the alphabet on a couple of wax tablets. Desi had then learned to recite them in the correct order.

A B C D E F G H I K L M N O P Q R S T V X Y Z

And she'd learned that each letter in fact represented a sound, or two, and that all the sounds in a word were represented by the corresponding letters. Great invention! "Yes, a *Greek* invention," Tassos claimed.

But then it had soon become clear that this system didn't work for poor Feli. Of course she had to sit in on every lesson Tassos gave to her blind friend, and Desi fully expected her to participate in this new, exciting venture. So in the beginning she'd translated every word the teacher said for her deaf companion. But very soon she encountered an unsurmountable difficulty. The two had a sign for every word: like "early" was a certain flip of the hand, palm down, but only in a certain context; "late" was the same flip, palm up. In another context both signs could have several other meanings. And when Desi had shown Feli the written Latin words on her tablet: MATVRE, SERO, and explained their meaning, the deaf girl had argued, "Yes, but in what kind of story? You can't just use a word on its own!" And that was when it dawned on Desi that *Feli didn't know Latin at all.*

Not a word.

She could hardly believe it.

"What did you expect?" Tassos asked, "words are sounds, really, and that is why the deaf cannot speak." He was intrigued by the strange sign language the two ten-year-old girls seemed to have invented for themselves, but he would never for the life of him have imagined that this could be anything more than mere playacting. He was firmly convinced that Feli was retarded, poor thing.

Desi carried on as long as it took, pestering her teacher, and then her parents at home, relentlessly, until *she* could read the stones on her own. Then she seemed to lose interest, but that was only to placate her deaf companion. In fact, Feli was sadly aware of the fact that reading was still one of Desi's greatest passions.

That morning, by Primilla Quinctia's grave, the blind girl brought up the subject once again.

"Why don't you want to learn Latin, Feli? You could learn to read and write; I could teach you! You're making such a big mountain out of this; I'm not saying it would be easy, but we could take one small step at a time and get there in the end."

"You're the one who is making a big mountain out of nothing. If I learn Latin, I can chat only with stones!"

"No! I'll give you wax tablets and then you could write messages for other people to read."

"I want to chat only with you."

"But what if a flowerpot falls down from a windowsill on my head? I could be dead in a flash, at any moment, and then you'll have no one else to chat with."

Feli found this thought so disturbing that she changed the subject at once. "It's strange that I don't know Latin, by

101

the way, because I learned our language from *you* when we were little. Why didn't you teach me *then*, when you had the chance?"

"No, Feli, no! *You* taught *me* to use our signs!"

"Really? I can't remember a thing about that; can you?"

"No, I was too young."

"But I always thought that *you* taught *me* because you are a few years *older* than me."

"No! I always thought that *you* were the oldest!"

"Well maybe we're the same age after all."

Desi sighed. This conversation was going nowhere. Then suddenly a man was approaching among the gravestones. "*Avē*," he said, "This is not a place for young girls to loiter. This is my wife's grave."

From his voice Desi could make out that he was an old man. "*Salvē*, freedman Quinctius. May I offer my sincere condolences for the death of your beloved Primilla? You lived with her for thirty years, that's twice as long as I or my friend have been on this earth!"

"And *who* is offering her condolences?"

"I am Desiderata Pomponia, a free citizen's daughter, and this is my slave Felicitas. She's deaf."

The old man eyed the girl's worn tunica, which was no better than her slave's, and he smiled. He knew the type: dirt-poor plebeians who clung desperately to the last shreds of dignity they had, to being free citizens and owning just that one mangy little slave.

"You are obviously blind, my young fellow-citizen, and I like the idea of a deaf slave guiding her blind mistress!"

"Yes, wouldn't that be a nice subject for a comedy in verse?"

"Possibly. What would the story be?"

"Well, surely the faithful deaf slave would be manumitted in the end, and there would be joy, *felicitas* all

102

around."

"You like a happy ending, eh? But it doesn't always work like that. Besides, I no longer write comedy, not since my master died. He used to sell my work as his own, but the theatre people just didn't believe me when I told them that *I* could write more material for them. My career has ended with my master's life."

"That is really sad for you, but at least you had your wife."

"Yes, and the master's two sisters have been very kind to us."

"I was fascinated by your story when I read your stone. I would like to do the same thing with mine and Feli's story. Is it expensive?"

"Very. And it's very strange for a young girl like you to be thinking of her own tombstone... but tell me something: how did you manage to read the stone, if you're blind and your slave can't speak?"

Desi put her fingertips on the stone slab and explained she could read by touch alone. "Feli can't read; I was just pestering her about teaching her, but she doesn't want me to... All right, Quinctius, we'll leave you alone now."

The two girls went back to the road, manoeuvring among the graves, and by the roadside Desi started telling Feli what she and the man had just discussed. Feli said, "Maybe it would be cheaper if we only buy a marble slab, and then *you* can carve our story yourself."

"Excellent idea!"

Numerius Quinctius watched the two girls from a distance, and he marvelled. "Oh Primilla, if only you could have seen this!"

When they got home at the end of the morning, they found Claudia spinning in the company of a few neighbours at their usual spot in the backcourt of the insula.

"Ah, there you are, Desi, right on time. Cominia Gariliana was here a while ago. She has a job for you and Feli. Do you remember Cominia, from our balneum?"

"Of course, dear Mater. She used to scold us so when we bombed the bathtub!"

"Well, she needs two young masseuses for some rich men, to rub them with oil and scrape them clean with a *strigil*. You two can do that, can't you?"

"Of course!"

"I want you to go over to the new baths on the Campus Martius: Nero's baths. Ask around if Feli can't find them. You're supposed to start this afternoon, and Cominia needs to show you the ropes, so off you go, and I mean *right now!*"

Desi smiled from ear to ear, delighted, flew into her mother's arms and clung to her neck. "I'm on my way, sweet Mater! I'm so glad! I hope this is going to work out."

Claudia gave her a few coins to buy something to eat on her way over and grumbled mock-angrily, "Your days of loitering in the streets are over, young lady."

Desi understood all too well how grateful she should be for this job opportunity. It was the result of long and tense negotiations between her parents. As she and Feli set out for the new baths, she thought back to the dramatic scenes that had followed her father's discovery of her covert career as a beggar. He had been furious. He'd lost all of his Roman cool and reserve. How could a daughter of his even *contemplate* taking money from strangers; had she no *dignity?*

"I give them what they pay for," Desi had argued, "I'm blind, I'm worse off than all of them, and that's why their gift buys them some sympathy from Asclepius."

"You miserable girl, no true Roman *buys* or *sells* favours from the gods!" the PF had screamed.

Mater had been in a very difficult position. The PF was

104

still not fully aware of the fact that she too made some money from her carding and spinning, and she wanted to keep it that way. But she'd argued that it would be a good thing if their daughter could find a suitable and honourable way to make a living. "Let's not delude ourselves, Sextus: how are you ever going to find a husband for our poor Desi? And we're not always going to be around to care for her." She'd also pointed out that if Feli earned something extra on the side too, there would be nothing wrong with that for her masters. So in the end the PF had relented. Let the girls find some work, "but only as long as Desi is not married."

At the baths they had an uneasy reunion with their old acquaintance Cominia. Desi remembered her from her childhood as a bad-tempered women who was always criticizing her when they went to the local balneum, where she was the caretaker. She also remembered that she'd often been scolded by her mother when she'd been disrespectful to old Cominia: Mater would not stand for that.

"So there you are, young Desiderata, none too soon… quite a lady now, eh? Good… good. I remember you as a very lively little girl, always causing trouble with your deaf side-kick here."

She asked if they had any experience using a strigil. Desi said of course, she and Feli liked to do some wrestling at the balneum, and then cover their bodies with dust and scrape off the sweat and dirt. "We don't have real strigils, but we use a couple of suitably curved sticks. And we do each other's backside."

"Good… good. This afternoon you can start doing the same for your new paymaster and his cronies. However, I want you to understand one thing, young Desi: I remember your sharp tongue… but from now on, never *ever* say a word to any of these gentlemen without being asked to speak. Not a *word*, you understand? And even then, answer with

105

restraint. I told them you're a bit retarded, so act the part. Got that?"

"Yes, yes, Cominia," Desi said, starting to feel a great deal less enthusiastic about the job already, "they think I'm retarded... keep it that way."

"Exactly! Now listen, Desi, I'm *devoted* to your mother. Matrona Claudia is the nicest woman in the world. Even when I was just a slave she was always nice to me. So don't let me down; I don't want to disappoint her."

Hmm, that was easier said than done. They followed a routine that had been agreed on with Cominia. Desi and Feli stood by at the entrance of the meeting room, waiting, and when the men came in from the palestrae and took place on the massage benches, the deaf masseuse would lead the blind one to her first customer and take care of the next one herself. Then, as soon as they'd finished oiling and scraping the first pair of customers, Feli would bring Desi to another one, wherever he'd laid himself down. Or she'd take her back to their post by the door, waiting for further orders. When the men had taken a dive in one of the pools, they came back expecting their masseuses to dry and rub them down with a towel.

Cominia had recommended they should use their sign language as little as possible, so Desi had to let Feli take the lead. She had the feeling that Feli enjoyed bossing her around very much, as a matter of fact. Sometimes, when a man ordered Feli to rub him "here", or "there", she understood that without hearing, but when she was told, "I want a longer massage from you, girl," Desi would signal discreetly, and her friend caught her drift with half a sign.

In the beginning some of their customers did some amusing little experiments on Feli to verify that she was really deaf, trying and failing to make her jump by yelling

"Boo!" just behind her, for instance. And they commented derisively on Desi's hollow eyes as if she were not even present. Both were used to this kind of thing; this was Rome after all; and the men soon tired of it.

So they were constantly on the alert, on the lookout, trying to anticipate all the whims and wishes of these men who hardly acknowledged their existence. And there was the rub. Desi was made to feel subservient, and she hated that. She also found her new job very boring, although she didn't mind handling those male bodies at all. It was even nice to be using a real, spoon-like, brass strigil, sharp and smooth and elegantly curved. But it was the endless *waiting* in between the massage assignments that was aggravating. How much more fun she'd had as a beggar at the temple of Asclepius!

And she didn't like this praefect Rufrius Crispinus and his friends one bit. He reminded her of her father's patron, senator Canio, only *she* was not his client, more like his slave. But he and his cronies had the same kind of conversations as Canio and his followers. They *complained* all the time. It was clear from the outset that these wealthy and important men did not approve of "the young emperor" at all: everything had been much better in the good old days.

"To start with," a man who sounded younger than the others grumbled, "Nero is not even of Julian stock, but an Ahenobarbus."

"That's right, Lucanus, and until now he has been too much under the influence of Seneca, and of Burrus when he was still alive. What can you expect when an emperor is being henpecked by a *philosopher?*"

"At any rate he has no personality of his own, no maturity. He has become the puppet of his own puppets."

"Good point, Lucanus, a puppeteer entangled by the very strings he is pulling!"

"Huh?" Desi thought, "what on earth are they *talking* about?"

Then an older man with a forceful voice held forth about the military situation: "We lost Armenia, but instead of sending out more legions, the young fellow is trying to reach a peace settlement with the Parthians."

"You're right, Paetus, it is Rome's destiny to keep expanding, to conquer the world. That is the long-term objective we have to keep in mind. An emperor worth his salt should be planning the next stages of our expansion."

"Indeed, Rufrius. Conquest has always been our best opportunity at a military career. What else can a chap do to gather glory and acquire a fortune?"

"Alas, nowadays there's no honour, no spoils to be had."

Desi pricked up her ears: all this sounded almost like seditious talk. You were not supposed to criticize the Divine Emperor, certainly not in such dismissive language... but apparently these men thought they were so special that this didn't apply for them. They spoke of Nero as if they were his *equals*, not his subjects. Strange.

"Do you remember the last time a batch of slaves came in with the returning legions?"

"Ah yes, the Parthian and Armenian prisoners: very good stock!"

"Although I didn't need any fresh slaves at the time, I treated myself to a young girl: a real Armenian beauty."

And then they were off on the subject of the slave girls they picked out to be their mistresses. "At the moment, my friends, I have a redhead whose parents, straight from Gaul, already belonged to my father. You never saw whiter flesh: it almost glows in the dark!"

"Is she willing?"

"Oh yes, Antonius, I make it worth her while, to the extent that even her own mother tells her to be nice to me."

"I don't care if they're willing or not, in fact I rather enjoy having to be a bit rough."

"Oh, Subrius, you're such an animal, they should put you and your sort in the amphitheatre, *instead* of the lions."

"Sure, Flavius, I wouldn't mind showing the crowds how I *devour* a tasty girlie."

That brought on the next subject: these men also deplored that the emperor had put an end to the executions in the arena. Suddenly they were wistfully exchanging reminiscences of the *damnationes ad bestias* from bygone days. "Wasn't it lovely to see those noble beasts at work?"

"Oh yes, and mind you, it's not so easy to get a big cat to attack a human being. The *bestiarii* had to train them, give them a taste for human flesh, make them aggressive and keep them hungry."

"I know, that is an art in its own right, it seems to me. I used to enjoy the thing most in its simplest form: just let the condemned run around in the arena and admire how easily a big predator could dispatch them. You never saw men run faster with less benefit!"

"I always thought that was over *too* quickly. Too merciful a death for those criminals. My favourite used to be when they wrapped the condemned in tight nets, or put them in sacks, and the beasts couldn't get at them the way they wanted. They pawed and clawed, and the victims screamed ten times more, *ergo* it was twice the fun for the spectators."

"What I liked best was when they tied them up on high crosses or forks, and the beasts had to jump or climb to get at their prey. That was spectacular as well as slow: the big cats would rip off one leg first, then the other, and before they managed to gore the torso and kill the guy, he had all the time in the world to see death coming!"

Desi started feeling queasy. "Wasn't this supposed to be *vulgar* entertainment, only intended to amuse the *lowest* classes?"

She frowned: what was wrong with these men? She felt like slapping the one she was towelling off right then, he who liked to see human beings stuffed in nets like big sausages and fed to the lions slowly. But she checked herself, forced herself to wipe the frown from her face while she kept wiping his broad shoulders. She now fully understood why Cominia had ordered her to play stupid, to act retarded: it was best for her own safety. Thank Jupiter Feli could not hear this awful banter. But what a story she would have to tell her later!

And suddenly it hit her what was wrong with these men. They were not only wealthy and powerful, feeling entitled to own the world, no, they were so *healthy* too. Well-fed. Well-trained in the pools and the palestrae. She could feel the muscles and the fat of their pampered bodies under her fingers. And in that respect they were poles apart from the visitors of the temple of Asclepius. There had also been important men coming there, but like everyone else at the temple, those were feeling ill. The people there were all confronted with their limits, their frailty, their mortality in one way or another. And that made all the difference.

After a few hours that had passed so slowly that they seemed an eternity, Rufrius and his cronies suddenly left the baths. They had other things to do. No one said a word to the two masseuses in attendance; they just walked out of their private meeting room, still bantering loudly. Feli took Desi over to Cominia's storeroom. "Yes, I just heard them leaving," the freedwoman said, "the praefect didn't stop by to complain about you two, which means that you did a fine job. Good girls; you didn't let me down."

"And when do we get paid?"

"Not now, that much is clear. You'll have to be patient, Desi. We have to wait until I can decently remind the man

110

that he owes us some pay; then I'll give you your share."

"So you've been hired by Rufrius Crispinus himself?" Sextus exclaimed, "I'm impressed."

In fact the PF sounded positively thrilled, Desi thought.

"He hasn't paid us yet, you know."

"Of course not! But eventually he'll send over a junior secretary to settle his accounts with old Cominia. You'll just have to be patient."

"My 'customers' at the temple, at least, payed me first, and *then* expected a chat..."

"Don't remind me of that shameful episode!"

Once again they were together under their red-hot roof, having dinner in their garret, all because Sextus thought it beneath his dignity to eat in the street or in a tacky tavern. He and his wife were reclining on their bed, the girls sitting on the chest and a stool being used as a table. They were sweating profusely in the sweltering heat. But at least the conversation was lively.

"Tell me exactly what happened, Desi. Did you hear what Rufrius and his friends were saying?"

Desi indulged her father, reporting at length the appalling conversations she'd heard, and conveying the strange mood, the complaining, the criticism, even the contempt these men seemed to have for the emperor.

"My dear girl," Sextus sighed, "I can imagine it is a bit of a shock, but you shouldn't take all this at face value. These men know the emperor intimately; they've always belonged to the inner circle of the court; so in a way they *are* Nero's equals. They've known him since he was a child. They're bound to have all sorts of gripes against him, but that doesn't mean they don't respect him in the end."

Desi started to translate her father's remarks for Feli, sitting next to her on the chest, and Sextus frowned. "Girl! Is this *really* necessary?"

"Yes it is, dear PF. I must be able to rely on Feli to look out for me. Therefore she needs to know exactly what is going on. Believe me, our position is not easy; Cominia even seems to think that we're in danger if we don't watch our step."

"Really? Well that freedwoman has got some nerve! No, as I was saying, these gentlemen are of the highest rank and nobility, but if you want to talk about being in a difficult position, praefect Crispinus is a good case in point."

Sextus proceeded to explain, and Desi kept signing his words with her hands for Feli's benefit. Claudia had finished eating and had left the bed; she took up her spinning again after rinsing and drying her fingers. Apparently she was undisturbed by the heat.

Rufrius Crispinus was a self-made man, Sextus told them, who came from Egypt and had started in life as a fish merchant. "You can imagine what they say about him behind his back!" He'd made a swift and stellar career under the reign of Claudius, ending up as Praefect of the Praetorian Guard. Unfortunately, young Nero's mother Agrippina had given that post to her own protégé Burrus, as soon as her son had become emperor. Rufrius was also Poppaea Sabina's first husband, before she'd divorced him and married Otho, a son of Claudius, and then Nero.

"It's a complicated story, but you can imagine the situation: Rufrius probably still frequents the imperial court on a daily basis, but he was once married to the empress. This must be incredibly awkward for all concerned."

"I understand, yes. And he has every reason to hate the emperor."

"No, no, life at court is something we can hardly imagine: no end of intrigues and settling of scores, promotions and demotions galore. But it doesn't mean a thing, for them it's all in a day's work."

"Hmm. And how about this Lucanus? He sounds very young. Do you know him?"

"Marcus Annaeus Lucanus, yes, I can't believe you've met him this very afternoon, just like that! He's a poet. Very talented and prolific… and you know our emperor is a poet too. The two were very close for a while, but unfortunately Nero doesn't have much time for writing verse, what with the responsibilities of his position. Rumour has it that he and Lucanus had a falling out, and that the emperor's literary rival is no longer welcome at court and not allowed to publish his poetry anymore."

"But that's all in a day's work for him as well. And how about Paetus, the military man?"

"General Lucius Caesennius Paetus! Was he there too? My-my, what important people you've met today, my dear Desi."

"Darling PF, if you're so star-struck by all these big shots, why don't you take over my job? Then *you* can give them massages to your heart's content!"

"Careful what you say, girl, you're being disrespectful again."

"Well, sorry about that, but did I understand correctly that this general has lost the Armenian campaign against the Parthians, and that Nero refused to send more legions and is suing for peace instead?"

"Yes, that's more or less the story you hear on the Forum at the moment."

"Well, the general is very angry because Nero didn't let him keep the loot. So that's yet another man who has every reason to hate the emperor's guts."

"No, no, no…"

But before Sextus could carry on with more arguments and reassurances, Claudia suddenly piped up.

"There's one thing I find strange."

113

"Only *one?*" Desi deadpanned, "lucky you!"

"Well, sweetness, apart from all the appalling vulgarities you just reported of course..."

"Oh, come on, *carissima*," Sextus pleaded, "you know how it is: take any group of men, anywhere, and you're bound to hear some shockingly rough banter."

"Is that supposed to be reassuring? Anyway, as I said, what I find strange is that these men are still in town in the first place. The heat wave has been going on for a couple of weeks now. On the streets and in the shops I hear the people grumble that the rich have it easy: they've all left Rome and are spending the summer by the sea. So how come these wealthy men stay behind? Surely they all have summer residences of their own on the coast?"

Desi smiled from ear to ear. "Oh, but sweet Mater, that is an *excellent* observation! You're absolutely right: it doesn't make any sense at all!"

VII   1964: The Plautilla connection

"Have you ever heard of St Gregory: Bishop Gregory of Tours?"

"Ah, yes, that rings a bell. There was an entry in the encyclopaedia I used to read as a schoolgirl. A chronicler, right? He wrote the history of his times in the darkest Middle Ages."

"Very good! Excellent encyclopaedia... He is famous for his 'Ten Books of Histories', better known as the 'History of the Franks', a chronicle of the Merovingian kingdoms of his time. There also exists a 'Chronicle of Fredegar', but you wouldn't have heard of it... Now I want you to picture the period: the 6th century. The Western Roman Empire had just collapsed, the last emperor, Romulus Augustulus, had been deposed in 476 by a Goth warlord called Odovacar. People now lived under a feudal system that was maybe not worse than the one it replaced, but still we speak of the *Dark Ages*... For me as a Catholic priest, however, there is a silver lining: the Church took over the torch of civilisation, so to speak, and our faith shone over the western world... And that is where Bishop Rorick of Trier comes in."

"Have you checked what he writes about the Desiderata stone?"

"Yes. Patience, my dear, I'm coming to that."

Again, Daisy and Father Contini were sitting together at a table in the museum canteen, eating the *ossobuco* that was on the menu that day. Of Vanetta there was no trace, but

Daisy was now wondering if he'd actually been invited.

"So, as I was saying, our faith shone over a devout populace, and one of the most striking expressions of that faith was the worship of the relics of the saints, and the pilgrimages to the places where these relics were displayed. I want you to picture a world where not much fun could be had, except for one thing: tourism! Because that is actually what we're talking about. People were fascinated by miracles, by divine interventions and especially by the relics involved. People from all walks of life, of all social classes, were travelling—mostly by foot—all over the place to the shrines they'd heard of, or read about: Santiago de Compostela, Tours, Paris, Trier, even Jerusalem... and Rome of course. You could argue that tourism was the number-one *international* business of the 6th century. And Bishop Rorick was the author of one of the best known tourist guides of the day... So he walked all the way from Trier, in what is now Germany, over the Alps, to Rome, and he told his readers about the many miraculous relics he found there, in the many churches."

"I've never visited Trier," Daisy remarked, "but I happen to know that it's the birthplace of Karl Marx."

"Exactly! I went there once, and I visited the man's childhood home. It only demonstrated to me that Karl Marx was a *bourgeois* through and through... Anyway, Rome, when Rorick visited it, was a place of ruin and faded glory. But it was also the seat of St Peter, just like now; the place where the pope reigned supreme; the centre of the Catholic world, already then. He clearly had a great time and visited many relics; he recommended the place very warmly to his readership."

"Yes, yes, but what did he say about *Desiderata?*"

"Oh, yes, silly me, I pontificate, I can't help myself. Once a lecturer, always a lecturer... Anyway, to start with the good news: we have the name of the church, or chapel, or shrine. But unfortunately Vanetta was right: it does not exist anymore. Of course there are nine hundred churches in Rome, but it is easy enough to check a name on a listing of those."

"Nine hundred churches! But the one we're looking for could have been *renamed* since the 6th century."

"Valid point. However, that will not be so easy to figure out."

"And what was the name of the church?"

"Here we're in luck: it is an uncommon name. St Plautilla."

"Really!? And I'm staying at the Congregation of the Sisters of St Plautilla!"

"I'm aware of it, but more about that later. The interesting thing is what this name can tell us. Or rather what the records of the saints can tell us. This is why my first question yesterday was: is Desiderata a saint? Because if she had been, it would have opened up a whole cornucopia of more or less reliable sources telling us her particulars. And although Desiderata is not a saint—I checked—, Plautilla is, and a very interesting one at that. Her hagiography tells us that she was a noble Roman *matrona*, and a widow. She is said to have witnessed the martyrdoms of St Peter and St Paul. When Paul the Apostle was about to be beheaded, she lent him her headscarf, to use as a blindfold. The story goes that St Paul appeared to her after his death to give her back the scarf."

"That is St Paul for you! Always very thorough."

"Quite right," the priest chortled, "the story is completely in character! But anyway, St Plautilla was an early Christian of the very first generation, she is said to have been martyred in the year 67. Now, if the Desiderata stone, as a relic, is associated with St Plautilla, this could mean that our blind woman also lived in the first century, that she was a

117

contemporary of the saint."

"So we could move back in time from the sixth to the first century!"

"Exactly! That is certainly what it looks like. Very exciting! But to get back to the convent where you're staying, I checked the records, and unfortunately it transpires that the Congregation of the Sisters of St Plautilla was founded in 1869 by a wealthy Contessa, who had every reason to identify herself with a noblewoman from ancient Rome. At least she knew her minor saints. But you must understand that on the scale of the Holy Church's long history—the kind of timeframe we are dealing with here—1869 is only yesterday."

"Of course, I understand. The sisters are not likely to know anything more about the case."

"No. However, I took the liberty of making an appointment with your mother superior, to see if she can tell us anything interesting. I will take you and your deaf partner over to the convent at the end of the afternoon, at closing time; we will hear what she has to say."

"Great. That leaves one question from yesterday unanswered: did you find any mention of Desiderata in the Corpus?"

"No, obviously not. If that had been the case, we would also know the *location* of the stone. But no such luck. The Corpus was started in Berlin in 1853, so we must assume that the stone has been missing at least since that date."

"But Father, stones can't just disappear! I mean, long after the Goths and the Vandals were done smashing things up around here, this inscription was still readable, when Rorick saw it in the 6th century. And even broken stones can be put together again, like pieces of a puzzle, as I have discovered yesterday and this morning in the museum collections."

"Yes, yes, all that is true, but unfortunately, between the

6th century and 1853, any number of things could have happened, that we will never find out. But it doesn't matter. The important thing is that Rorick confirms your finding, like Vanetta suggested. The exact words he uses about Desiderata are crystal clear. He chooses the verb 'scabĕre', to scratch, like when you are itching. The complete sentence goes: *Caeca sancta lapidem sua manu scabit*, 'The blind saint—or faithful—scratched the stone with her own hand'. Not 'sculpsit', she carved, or 'inscripsit', like you'd expect. No: 'scabit', she scratched. This inscription must have looked a lot more like graffiti than like a properly carved tombstone. And note the words 'sua manu': by her *own hand!*"

"And what about the scholars Vanetta mentioned, who argued that Rorick wrote all this only because he *wanted* the stone to be a true relic?"

"Rubbish! It's exactly as with St Augustine, who couldn't imagine that it were the deaf themselves, not their carers or parents, who created sign languages. These scholars can't for the life of them imagine a blind person scratching a message on a stone, so they conclude that Rorick must have made it up. I for one believe every word of this entry; only Desiderata's sainthood is doubtful, but 'sancta' could just mean 'believer', or 'faithful'."

"All right, but how could Rorick *know*, really? That Desiderata was blind and all that?"

"The message on the stone must have *told* him! Remember Quinctius? He tells us that he was a freedman, and a comic writer, right? Well, in precisely the same way Desiderata must have told the world at large that she was blind. As Rorick calls it 'the Desiderata stone', we may assume that Desiderata is the first word of the inscription, just like N Quinctius on the stone we studied yesterday. Rorick does not bother to transcribe the message, because he is only interested in its healing powers as a relic. However, we can infer from his entry in the Compendium that not only was Desiderata blind, but that she also mentions another— deaf—person in her message to the world. That is all we know for sure from this source, but it is enough."

"You said yesterday that the Compendium is an important source for disability studies. How's that?"

"Well, like all the Christian authors of his era, Rorick was obsessed with miracles. And each time he describes a miraculous healing he claims to have witnessed personally, he unwittingly gives us interesting details about the daily life of the disabled in his time."

"And did he witness many blind being healed?"

"Some, yes, but not in Rome. What fascinated him about the Desiderata stone, apparently, was that relics for healing the blind and deaf, specifically, were extremely rare. As for the healings of the blind he describes elsewhere in the book, I confess I don't know what to make of them."

"Well, it's very honest of you to admit it. I suppose that when blindness is caused by a mental problem, by what Freud calls 'hysteria' for instance, then a miracle can happen. But let me show you something..."

Daisy paused. She was sitting right across the Italian priest at the small table, just like the day before. She now took off her dark glasses and leaned forward, letting her companion have a good look at the empty buttonholes of her shrivelled eyes.

"Ugh! That looks horrible!" the priest exclaimed, "does it hurt?"

"Sometimes."

"You're such a beautiful woman, my dear Daisy; the contrast couldn't be more shocking!"

Daisy put her glasses back on her nose and smiled. The simple black discs mounted in wire frames were completely out of fashion, everyone had butterfly frames nowadays, but they had the advantage of spelling out 'blindness' loud and clear.

"Now you understand, my dear Contini, why I don't believe in miracles. If I suddenly grew a pair of functioning eyeballs, after I was born like *this*, it would mean that God had changed his mind completely, and in my experience God never does that."

"I see… but maybe the true miracle is that God gave you such a fighting and defiant spirit in the first place."

"Yes, maybe. That kind of miracle I could accept with gratitude… and humility."

"But to get back to the sheep we were tending: for now we have obtained exactly what I wished for yesterday. Written evidence from the past that tells us by implication about a blind individual in antiquity who could read and write. Your hypothesis is now confirmed in history! Isn't that wonderful? I'm thinking of writing a little piece about this for a learned journal. I will mention your name as the finder, of course, it goes without saying."

"Well, I'm not really interested in scholarly glory, but thanks all the same. And let's not forget it was also Vanetta's idea."

In the meantime the canteen had emptied and gone quiet; lunchtime was clearly over. Daisy raised the lid of her tactile watch and checked the time. "Two-thirty already! The daily debriefing must almost be over, Cadogan will be furious!"

"Don't worry, my dear, I'll talk to him. I'll tell him it's entirely my fault, which is true. Just you go and enjoy the stones and the plaster casts."

She did as she was told, going back to the busts of ancient Romans. Now she was interested in the ladies, the matronae with the elaborate hairdos. But then, about an

121

hour later, she had to face the music anyway. A man entered the room and muttered, "Ah, there you are."

"Father Cadogan?"

"You bet... Just one word... I wanted to tell you that you were sourly missed at our little debriefing today."

"Yes, I know, Contini and I lost track of the time... did he talk to you?"

"Yes, and I told him that you two were *not* absolved for all that. These meetings are important, Daisy, it's the only moment of the day when you people can communicate through Sister Liz. Morag was very disappointed."

"I'm so sorry! But I'll make it up to her. I'll write her a long letter tonight and apologize, and tell her everything a-bout the exciting discoveries we've made, Contini and I."

"A letter? So you're still cheating on us?"

"That's right; I use the convent's typewriter."

"I suppose that's pretty impressive in a way, but it's not what I want to achieve, here."

"Well, what *do* you expect: that we develop *telepathic* powers?"

"Oh, Daisy," the priest tittered, suddenly mollified, "there's so much more at stake."

"I know that, Father, and believe me, in my case your project is working like a charm. I am now completely and sincerely convinced that being totally deaf like Morag is a real tragedy. My own blindness is only a minor inconvenience in comparison... But having said that, I don't really know if Morag feels the same the other way round."

"Never mind... *you're* the one who needed to be taken down a few notches, Daisy."

"Well thank you, kind sir."

"And when I say there's more at stake, I'm thinking of Morag. We need to bolster her self-confidence; she's very shy and insecure; she's been traumatized by her disability."

"Really? To me she seems to be doing just fine."

"Well, yes, thanks to you. I shouldn't be scolding you, perhaps, but using this opportunity to praise you. You've been doing a great job, as I knew you would when Father Boudry told me about you. I don't' regret taking you on, believe me."

"Only, I didn't know what I was letting myself in for!"

"True, but if we knew everything in advance, we would never get out of bed in the morning."

"Also true. But can you tell me more about Morag, though? How so is she traumatized?"

"Well, try to imagine a child born deaf, who has no idea what's going on, and her own mother is so shocked and dispirited that she just gives up on her baby... Morag has had to come a long way... she needs a positive mother-figure to help her heal her wounds... she needs *you.*"

"I see... so that's why you're so angry that I've let her down today."

"That's right, but as I said, you're doing great. I appreciate your dedication. Type a nice letter for her tonight!"

This conversation was still on Daisy's mind when she met up with Morag at the back entrance of the museum a few hours later, at closing time. As soon as she felt her partner's presence, she mouthed the word "sorry", and the deaf girl stroked her arm in response. They hugged briefly: no hard feelings. Then Father Contini made his presence known.

"I have a car. Shall we drive over to your convent?"

And as soon as they were seated, all three of them cosily side by side on the back seat, the priest gave instructions in Italian to the driver. The brief exchange between "Claudio" and their host made it clear that this was not a taxi, but some kind of Vatican service car, and Claudio an employee

Contini knew well. The drive, inevitably, was short and brutal, as the convent was not far away, and Italians did not seem capable of driving calmly.

Then they were received by the mother superior in person, who was waiting for them at the top of the stairs of the main entrance of "their" convent. Morag nibbled at Daisy's earlobe, and Daisy smiled: they had never enjoyed such a reception before, not even on their first day. What was going on?

They only knew the mother superior as a stern old lady who was always frowning, as far as Morag could see, and always hectoring all the other nuns, as far as Daisy could hear. Now she cooed at them, all smiles, and she called her guest *Excellenza...* Aha.

They were led to an office where they'd never been before, Morag still tagging along, holding Daisy's hand. And once they were seated, the conversation suddenly turned to French, as by some clever manoeuvre Contini had determined that French was the only language the three speakers present had in common.

The priest—or whatever he was—explained their business as briefly as possible. "We were wondering, my dear Sister, if you could tell us more about the link between your Congregation and St Plautilla."

"*Eh bien, votre Excellence*, it is quite simple, really. The founder of our convent, Contessa Lavinia Barelli, was a great admirer of the saintly Roman widow. The Contessa was quite old when she finally inherited the wealth of her husband's family and could use it to establish this convent. And she had fond memories of worshipping at a chapel dedicated to St Plautilla when she was a little girl. The name and the fond memories stayed with her all her life, and by the time she was free to build the convent, she chose this name for us, and made sure our chapel was dedicated to her favourite saint."

"Fascinating! Could we take a peep around in that chapel of yours, dear Sister?"

"Of course, *votre Excellence!*"

All four of them repaired to the convent chapel, which Daisy and Morag had already visited, for prayers, in the first days of their stay. But they had somehow managed to winkle out of that obligation since then. The place was redolent of incense and burning candles, like Daisy remembered. Now the mother superior gave them a guided tour, proudly citing the name of the not-so-famous artist who had painted frescoes of St Plautilla's life-story on the walls. "I'm sure you're familiar with it, *votre Excellence*: here you see our saintly matron binding her veil over St Paul's eyes before his beheading."

"Yes, yes, and all this dates from around 1869?"

"From *before* that date, actually: everything was ready for the inauguration in 1869, but by that time, tragically, Contessa Barelli had already passed away."

"You don't say, *la pauvre!*"

Suddenly Morag came alive; she tapped on Daisy's shoulder, removed her cane from her fingers and put it down somewhere, and took both her companion's hands in hers. Then she used them like puppets to execute a little mime. She made Daisy write with her forefinger in the palm of her left hand, before making her right hand tap the lid of her handbag.

"Oh, right," Daisy muttered, "you want me to take out my notebook!"

She wondered if Morag expected her to write something about what was going on, but as soon as she'd retrieved the notebook, Morag took it from her and started writing herself. Then she showed her message to Contini, who read it out loud.

125

"This chapel is pure Baroque, but the rest of the convent is not. WHY?"

Daisy smiled and patted the deaf girl's shoulder. "Excellent observation from our art history student. This could be interesting. Have you any idea, *ma Mère?*"

"Well, like I said, Contessa Barelli had this thing about a chapel she used to visit as a child. I suppose she asked the architect to design our convent chapel in the same style."

"Interesting indeed!" Contini exclaimed, "because this could mean that around 1800, when the Contessa was a young girl, there still existed a chapel dedicated to St Plautilla somewhere in Rome, and it was a *Baroque* building. Have you any idea *where* it was situated?"

"Non, votre Excellence, je suis désolée."

"But how do you even know as much as you do? 1869 is a long time ago."

"The Contessa left us some papers. She wrote this autobiographical note—I can show it to you—to explain why our congregation should be dedicated to the Roman saint. That is all."

"Very well, my dear Sister, let us have a look at those documents!"

They went back to the mother's office. Daisy took Morag apart and mimed her intention of typing a letter to her, later. The mother superior retrieved a thin folder from a filing cabinet: "The Contessa's papers..."

Contini rifled through them, read some pages here and there, and muttered, "I see... yes... the lady was very much into the Catholic revival following the nineteenth century revolutions. But no *specific* details about that childhood chapel... *dommage!*"

"Mother," Daisy asked, "does the name 'Desiderata' ring a bell in any way?"

"No, child, I can't say it does. And believe me, I've studied these papers very thoroughly, and there are not that many of them, but the Contessa never mentioned anyone named *Desiderata*."

"And the 'Desiderata *stone*'?"

"No."

That night, after Contini had left, Daisy and Morag dined at the head of the table for the first time. The mother superior wanted to know what this visit from the *Monsignor* had been all about. So Daisy explained the whole story a bit more in detail: the blind woman from ancient Rome who was mentioned by Bishop Rorick of Trier, and her possible association with St Plautilla.

"I see! So it is this 'Desiderata' that really intrigues the man, not *our* patron saint as such?"

"I'm afraid so... but please tell me, Mother, is Father Contini an *important* man?"

"But of course, my dear child! You may not be aware of it because you're blind, but the Father, as you call him, is officially an archbishop. He wears purple. And he happens to be an important Vatican prelate, a member of the Curia, the governing body of the Church. In France, or in your own country, you would call him a cabinet minister or a secretary of state. A real politician! He is one of the progressive new men, very close to the Holy Father, Paul VI."

"Oh, and I thought he was only a modest scholar doing some research at the Vatican Museums, just like us."

"Yes, but that is something he does as a hobby, on the side, especially now, in the summer, when his agenda may not be so full... I wish *I* could relax somewhat in the summer, but we nuns never take holidays from our vows, and the children's hospital has hardly less work now than at any other time... Then of course *Monsignor* Contini also has a reputation for seeking the company of pretty women, on the

127

side, the old goat, although a blind one is a first, to my knowledge."

Later that night Daisy wrote a long letter on the typewriter, two full pages. From now on they had the blessing of the mother superior in person to use the machine. She'd said, "Oh, so *you* were making that racket! (*ce boucan!*) Did you really think you could use a typewriter at such hours, in a *convent*, and no one would *notice*?" Anyway, in her letter Daisy apologized again to Morag for her absence that afternoon, reported the findings of the day, and explained that she, Morag, had actually contributed a little piece of the puzzle herself with her remark about the chapel being in Baroque style.

Noz ze have reached a dead end; unfortunately: But still; dear ?orag; today I've been travelling back and forth through the centuries; it zas quite diwwying:

Love; Daisy

VIII   AD 64: The plot thickens

On their second day on the job, and in the following weeks, Desi and Feli at least had something to keep their minds busy while they worked at the baths. For Feli it was very hard to figure out who was who, whereas Desi could identify each individual by his voice and by how the others named him, and she could gauge his personality by what he said. Only, she had no idea what these men looked like, apart from their height and their heft. And for Feli, obviously, it was the other way round. But they worked out a method, based on the usual whereabouts of their customers within their private meeting room.

Desi briefed Feli regularly: "The general always settles down on the bench closest to the doorway, on the right. That's where he was lounging the first time, and he always goes back to the same spot if possible." And in the same way the other men had fixed habits. Humans are territorial animals. Thanks to this trait, while Desi reported the goings-on within the group when they had a moment alone, Feli knew who she was talking about.

When they got home at the end of the day, Sextus too would question his daughter eagerly, but there was not always anything new or interesting to report. Rufrius and his cronies had a tendency to repeat themselves, to rehash their grievances, and each afternoon's conversations tended to be a copy of what had been said on the first day. The Pomponius family soon concluded that they were not getting any closer to solving the mystery that Claudia had so brilliantly formulated. However, Sextus kept identifying more of his daughter's customers. He knew everyone who was someone in Roman politics.

Antonius was probably the equestrian Antonius Natalis, known to be a close friend of the praefect. Then you had Subrius Flavus and Flavius Scaevinus, who'd both been Tribunes of the Praetorian Guard, therefore old colleagues of Rufrius. And there were a couple of others that even Sextus couldn't place.

"A real clique," Desi commented.

"There's no harm in meeting good friends on a regular basis."

"And no point in staying on in sweltering Rome to do so."

Then, sometimes, Desi was able to report a more interesting conversation, which really had her father salivating because it concerned his favourite topic: politics.

"This afternoon they had a lengthy debate about the sense and nonsense of the vote. Why even hold elections, when the emperor has all the power anyway? They were complaining that the Senate, although an elected body, had nothing more to do than to stamp its seal of approval on every decision submitted by the palace. Someone joked, 'we will be stamping bread loaves and roof tiles next'."

"They have a valid point," Sextus sniggered approvingly, "it is a strange system, what we have nowadays."

"Yes, but they seem to think that if the people were allowed to choose their leader in a genuine free election, their candidate would easily win from the emperor... but that doesn't make sense: Nero is incredibly popular, am I right?"

"Yes, valid point too, my dear, but you forget one thing: every voting citizen is someone's client, but no one is Nero's client."

"Or you could argue that every citizen is Nero's client

before all else. After all, he gives *you* grain and money too, doesn't he?"

"Yes, clever girl, but I'm thinking of the system whereby I give my vote to Canio, and he gives that to *his* patron, who in his turn has another patron, *higher up*. Democracy is like the chain of command in an army, and I'm not sure this would benefit the emperor if things should ever come to a head... Could these men be contemplating a popular uprising?"

"I don't think so, no. They were just griping as usual, banging on about the fact that Nero is just a young upstart with no legitimate claim to power. It made me sick to my stomach to listen to them."

Desi had the feeling that the men at the baths were waiting for something, biding their time. As she rubbed their bodies with oil, scraped them clean with one of those wonderful brass strigils, she kept listening to the conversations and tried to figure it out. As it happened, the very first occasion when it became clear that something ominous was in the air, was when the subject of the Christians came up, one day.

The praefect (or ex-praefect) said to the poet (blackballed poet), "My dear Lucanus, the Christians have become the talk of the town this summer, and I was just thinking the other day: *you* were the first person who told me who they are, *ergo* I knew about them long before everyone else!"

"Yes, remarkable that," Antonius (the sycophant) said, "one moment no one has ever heard of them, then before you know it they're on everybody's lips, and everyone pretends to know all about them."

"That's exactly how it works, Antonius! And it is not a coincidence that you heard about them from *me* first, Rufrius, because *I* am the one who spread these rumours in the first place. If you have a gripping tale to tell, and you repeat it for a while on the Forum, talking to the right people, it's amazing how fast it will become public knowledge!"

"Why did you do that? Why didn't you tell us?"

"I wanted to wait and see if the rumours would catch on. Now we know they did. As for the reason I launched these stories, it's because it might hurt Nero's reputation. Believe it or not, there are quite a number of Christians living at the palace!"

Several men cried out, "How is this possible?" It seemed unbelievable that people with such vile beliefs could be tolerated at the palace, even by such a despicable upstart as Nero.

Lucanus burst out laughing, "Look at your faces, my friends! You don't understand, do you? I'm talking about *slaves!* This thing is looking to become the religion of choice of the slaves... So the first time I ever heard about the Christians was at court, when I was still welcome there. It turns out that quite a number of slaves from Nero and Poppaea's own household are Christians. The fool knows it full well, but he turns a blind eye."

"Typical!" the old praefect growled, "but maybe we could use this. Do you think we could get some Christian slaves to kill their master, for instance, in his sleep?"

"Possibly, yes... after all, they believe in nothing. The only problem is: how can I approach those household slaves, now that I'm no longer welcome at the palace?"

"That's not the only difficulty," someone remarked, "right now Nero is holed up in Antium, to escape the heat, and we are here in Rome. What are we waiting for?"

Desi thought, "Good question!"

But then, the very next day, she understood. They had been waiting for *someone.* She and Feli were standing by the

132

door, as usual, when the men came in from their workouts and wrestling matches. But for the first time the praefect addressed Desi directly as he entered the private meeting room.

"Blind one," he mumbled, "I want you to make haste today. Got that? Tell the deaf one."

Desi answered sluggishly, "Erm... very well... Sir," staying in her role as borderline retard. Then she signalled to Feli as unobtrusively as possible, "He wants us to hurry up!"

Soon the men were clean, and started putting on their toga's, apparently. Desi and Feli stood by the door, and the blind girl could hear it, as the men helped one another drape the ceremonial garments over one shoulder, under this arm and over that elbow in complicated folds. This was highly unusual; the men had always dressed very informally in light summer tunics. Someone muttered, "The fuss we have to make for the great Piso!" Another one remarked that a blind and a deaf slave were really of no use at all to help you get properly dressed.

"That reminds me," Rufrius growled, "blind one, you and deaf one can leave us alone now. Off you go!"

Desi bowed her head slightly, and taking Feli's hand, she left her post without a word. Her mind was reeling: what on earth was going on in there? As soon as they were out the door she wanted to stop, to discuss things with Feli, and to try to eavesdrop on what was going to happen next inside the room. But then Feli softly rapped her knuckles on top of Desi's head and pushed her along, so that they kept moving swiftly. Desi didn't resist: Feli always knew best. As they walked away along the echoing central hall of Nero's baths, they could hear a whole group of men approaching the door of the meeting room. The man they called Piso and his retinue, no doubt. "Darn!" Desi thought, "I'd so like to hear what's going on!" But Feli pushed her to the side, into a corridor, then they passed through a door and were outside in the open, hurrying along a colonnade. This was an inner court, a palestra with a peristyle all around it; you could hear the grunting and panting of the visitors wrestling, running, or working out. Then they turned off the arcade and took a corner, walking around a wing of the building, the sounds from the sports enclosure more muted now, and finally Feli stopped close to an outside wall. She made her friend crouch on the ground and placed her hand on the rough masonry right in front of her, and that was when Desi suddenly understood: a grate!

She could hear the men inside, speaking. There were probably some open windows high up as well, but they did not allow to distinguish any words being uttered. However, just one foot above the ground, gaps had been left open between the stones: a very simple airing grate made up of smaller building blocks. Maybe this also served to drain the water when the floors were flushed clean. The holes must have been at floor level inside the building. Lying down on her belly, Desi put her ear to one of the openings, and sure enough, she could hear everything.

"Well done, champion!" she signed to Feli, and then she listened intently.

Inside the room, the important visitor was still being introduced to the members of "our informal little group". Apparently he'd left his retinue outside, so Desi realised that it wouldn't have worked to linger by the door anyway. Then the newcomer, whose voice Desi had never heard before, started delivering a little speech. Desi could just picture the men, including Rufrius, standing at attention in their cere-monial togas.

"Gentlemen, I was very flattered that you asked me to be your candidate, and the champion of your cause, and I would be delighted to use my name and my reputation with the people to foster your plans. However, after thinking it through carefully, I've come to the conclusion that your plans would never work."

There was a hum of protestations from the men.

"Please, let me explain," the visitor went on. He spoke slowly, in a deep, booming voice. Ideal for eavesdropping.

"I could easily get the Senate behind our cause, and we could get some kind of challenge organized. But then what? Nero too is much liked by the people; we are not at all certain we could prevail against him... and how do you propose to get the Praetorian Guard on our side? I believe Tigellinus is fiercely loyal to the young emperor."

The speaker paused for effect and there was complete silence in the room. This Piso, whoever he was, could certainly speak like an old-school orator.

"Gentlemen, you may be certain of my sympathy and collaboration, but I want you to rethink your plans. We have to *remove* Nero, somehow, and Tigellinus, obviously. But then, if we succeed at that, we cannot expect elections: a *new emperor* will have to be put in charge. After all these years the people have come to expect that form of rule. It cannot be avoided. Only this time we will be talking about an emperor with *restricted* powers, completely under the control of the Senate. Such an emperor would be a *primus inter pares*, and the Senate would come into its own again."

Now there was approving applause from the men in attendance.

"Think about it, gentlemen, and let me know your plans... discreetly. I have great faith in your abilities; I have high hopes. Thank you. *Valēte!*"

And with that, apparently, the man left the meeting.

"Of course I know who they are," Sextus exclaimed enthusiastically, "Tigellinus Ofonius is the current Praefect of the Praetorian Guard. That makes him the most powerful man after the emperor himself."

"Really? No wonder this Piso character wants those men to 'remove' him!"

Desi had just reproduced the "important visitor's" little speech word for word for her father and mother. She was very good at that kind of thing, especially as the elegance of Piso's speech had struck her. On their way home she had already done the same for Feli in sign language, that went without saying.

"Now, as for Gaius Calpurnius Piso," Sextus went on, "he is a leading Senator. He was even Consul once, under Claudius, and he is a member of one of the oldest plebeian families of Rome. I've listened to his speeches on the Forum: he is indeed an impressive orator."

"But I bet that on the Forum he was not talking about removing Nero and becoming emperor in his stead."

"No, obviously not, but it is no secret that he wants more authority for the Senate, and some restrictions imposed on the powers of the emperor."

"You're sounding all star-struck again, PF, but I definitely heard this man encourage Rufrius and his cronies to plot against Nero and Tigellinus, and then please leave it over to him to become the new emperor!"

"You were eavesdropping on a highly confidential political meeting, dear girl, and men will say strange things in such a situation... but if Piso should ever succeed, though, wouldn't that be something? The *first plebeian emperor* in our history!"

"I can't believe I'm hearing those words from *you*, Pater. These men are just fantasizing about killing poor Nero! As long as I can remember you have told me I should honour the gods and the emperor. And now you are seriously saying that killing Nero might be a good thing? I don't understand!"

"Desi has a point, Sextus," Claudia intervened, "I find your attitude a bit disturbing too."

"Well I'm sorry, *cara*, but there's nothing we can do about this whole business anyway. And don't forget that Nero himself also had to 'remove' a couple of rivals to seize power. Or at least his mother did it on his behalf. Then *he* had his *mother* removed, and more recently his first wife, as everybody knows. So yes, we have to honour the emperor, but we need have no illusions about how mere mortals achieve such a godlike status... Desi is old enough now to understand that."

"Yes, but what do we *do* about this?" Desi wanted to know.

"*Nothing*, I tell you! It is out of our hands."

"Couldn't you at least talk to your patron, senator Canio?"

"He probably knows already... at least part of it. But it would be extremely dangerous for me to tell him more. Because then he would become *aware* of the fact that I know a lot of things that I shouldn't... I wish you hadn't told me... It would have been much better if you hadn't eavesdropped, too."

"That is also true, sweetness," Claudia said, "what you did today was foolish and very dangerous. Promise that you'll never do it again."

"Erm... sure, darling Mater. At least now we know why these men don't care much for summer holidays on the coast!"

Desi didn't need to do more eavesdropping, she could hear everything while she was working and follow the latest developments step by step. Rufrius and his men were desperate to "rethink their plans" and find a solution to the conundrums that Piso had so brilliantly exposed. They came in from the baths earlier and earlier and discussed the topic endlessly. They were racking their brains.

Lucanus the poet was the first one who came up with something new. "I think it would be a good idea to find some fresh recruits, but only people who can really contribute something specific to the task at hand." He explained that he was still on good terms with Petronius, the famous author, one of Nero's favourites at court, who could help him gather intelligence, and could be very useful for editing propaganda material, as he was a very witty writer. "The only problem is that he's utterly unreliable. Just like the Christians he believes in nothing! But if I handle him carefully, I can use him without him even realizing it."

"Excellent idea," Rufrius said, "I want you all to think hard along the same lines: do you know anyone who could serve our cause in any way, voluntarily or unwittingly?"

The next day Subrius and Flavius came in with good news. They'd heard from old comrades in the Praetorian Guard that Tigellinus's deputy, the Joint Praefect Faenius Rufus, didn't get along at all with his boss, but that he was quite popular among the elite soldiers. "Don't you know him from the old days, Rufrius? If you tried to recruit him discreetly, he might listen to you."

"Very good, my friends. I had rather lost touch with the man, but it is high time for me to renew our acquaintance, so much is clear."

Then Lucanus reported that Petronius was back in town, because he needed to see his publisher about a work in progress. "I arranged to run into him on the Forum, and we talked. The famous author complains that Nero is avoiding Rome more and more. He's not only staying in Antium to escape the heat, but he intends to spend the fall near Neapolis and the winter in Greece."

"Yes, that's going to be a problem," Rufrius said, "unintentionally Nero is making it very hard for us to get near him."

"Impossible, even," general Paetus growled, "as long as he's holed up in those far-flung palaces, in the middle of nowhere, we can't attack him, it's as simple as that."

There was a long silence as they all pondered this. Then Antonius piped up, "Wait a minute, I've just thought of something… remember the great fire, ten years ago? Claudius was still emperor; he coordinated the firefighting in person; he called on the citizens to assist the *vigilēs* and paid them from his own purse… Now, with that precedent in mind, what would happen if Rome burned again? Nero would have to hurry back, he would have to go out and attend to the firefighting, inspect the damage, console the victims. And there would be chaos and disorder everywhere."

"By *Jove!*" the others cried, "are you proposing to *set fire* to the city?"

"Gentlemen, please," Rufrius interjected, "let Antonius speak… You don't say much, ordinarily, my dear friend, but when you *do* speak, I must say that your ideas are quite out of the ordinary."

"Just think," Antonius went on, "what with the heat and the drought we've had in the past month, Rome has become a tinderbox, an accident waiting to happen… on the other hand, most people like us have already left, and those who are still here can be discreetly cautioned to leave as well."

"The advantages are clear," the general said, "Nero would have to go out and mix with the populace, like Claudius did at the time, and this would make him particularly vulnerable… that is when one of us—or anyone—could kill him and get away with it! And even if that didn't work at once, in the long term he would be staying on in Rome, right where we want him, in order to coordinate the *rebuilding* of the city."

"Yes, yes," Rufrius said eagerly, "the situation would be completely changed... to our advantage."

Desi thought, "I can't believe what I'm hearing! Once again. This is getting worse and worse: a complete nightmare!" She had to make a conscious effort not to frown fiercely; she knew all too well that she could barely hide her feelings, normally. "Oh Feli, you're not going to believe this!"

Lucanus said, "Wait a minute, if we go through with this ungodly plan, I believe we'll be taking a huge risk."

"How do you mean?" the others asked.

"How will the people ever accept a change of regime from a bunch of *arsonists*? It doesn't make any sense!"

"They will never know," Antonius said forcefully, "how could anyone ever find out? Besides, to make sure no one suspects us, we will have to come up with a convincing scapegoat... maybe Nero himself?"

"That doesn't make sense either. If he has just been seen by all doing all he can to help the victims, he will be more popular than ever."

"Yes, but still very vulnerable, as I said," general Paetus reflected, "but maybe you, Lucanus, have hit on the solution we need, when you told us about the *Christians*, the other day..."

"The Christians!" they all cried: that seemed to be an excellent idea.

"Yes, thanks to your own efforts, they've been in the news a lot lately; they make every Roman's skin crawl; the populace will be baying for their blood!"

Then, a few days later, the whole conjuration seemed to have come to a head. The men had been very busy meeting people and making arrangements, then reporting back to the others in veiled terms. But none of the new recruits ever showed up at the baths. It was still the same "informal little group" from the beginning; in fact Piso had been the only visitor from outside. However, it became quite clear to Desi that these men were now working on the crazy and criminal plans they had recently agreed on. Even Lucanus no longer had any misgivings.

It was also clear that they were paying some of their accomplices to do the dirty work for them. At some stage Rufrius remarked, "For the time being we'll have to pay these men ourselves, but don't worry about that: soon enough we'll recoup our investments with a handsome premium."

So, on that day, when the praefect announced it was time for everybody—meaning the group—to leave Rome, she understood what was coming: the plan was about to be launched, meaning that some henchmen would be starting a great fire.

"Go to your country estates, my friends, and wait for news and further instructions. Make sure you bring your loved ones and all your valuables in safety. That will be all."

He now stepped over to Desi and tapped her shoulder, which made her jump out of her skin, even though she'd heard him coming, but it was because he'd never touched her before; she only him. However, it was a good thing for her to act surprised, as if she hadn't followed the conversation at all, so Desi simply grunted, "Huh?"

"Blind one, your services are no longer needed, we're all going away to the country. Rome is getting too hot for us, heh-heh."

"Erm... very well... Sir."

Then the blind 'slave' raised her hand slowly and rubbed her forefinger against her thumb.

"Ah yes: the pay. I'll pass by the freedwoman on my way out and settle my accounts. She'll give you your due. Off you go, take the deaf one with you, yes?"

And so, all of a sudden, it was over. Cominia Gariliana

141

told them to go home, that it could take a while yet before the man came over to pay her, that she would bring the money after closing time. Desi wondered if she should warn the good woman about the fire, but decided against it. She must live quite near and this was outside the city wall; and even if the fire spread this far, Cominia would be all right if she sought refuge in this huge stone building, with all that water in it.

Then, as soon as they were on the street, at a safe distance of the baths, she started briefing Feli on the latest developments while they kept walking. "Can you imagine? They're going to set fire to the city! We must do something to stop them; if only we knew some more details!"

Feli pulled her friend aside, gave the signal that she wanted to say something, so Desi faced her and raised her hands.

"Maybe this can help? There is something written on it."

She placed a little piece of papyrus in her friend's hand. A label, of the sort they attached with a piece of string to book scrolls, to indicate which work it is.

"What is this? Where did you get it?"

"It's a message, I tell you. One of the men had a dozen of these labels on the couch by his side, and he was copying the same message over and over with a reed pen. They were all talking, and the scribe was not paying attention all the time, so when he was looking away, once, I managed to pinch this and hide it in my tunic, under my belt. I figured he would have lost the count; he didn't notice a thing."

"Well done, you're a real champion again!"

'Champion' was a new sign the two had recently thought up, when they were playing latrunculi, or at least that was how Desi translated it in her own mind. But more and more it was becoming clear that it always applied to Feli, never to her.

"This must be a message for the 'recruits', giving them instructions of some sort… Now the difficulty is for me to read it: will you be able to copy it on a tablet?"

"Sure!"

When they got back to their insula, Claudia was sitting in the courtyard as usual, doing some spinning with her cartel partners; the girls went upstairs without being seen by the matronae. Sextus, as expected, was not home either, so they opened the chest and went looking for some wax tablets they might use. There were a few belonging to Mater, but they were filled with accounts, apparently. Then they found the PF's booklet, empty, as usual; he never had any accounts or records to keep. (This was not the tablet hanging by the door.) The wax pages were as smooth as a baby's bottom. "Write down the message, Feli, quick!"

Feli took the stylus and painstakingly scratched into the wax every 'squiggle' she could see on the papyrus label.

Y K K K K L B M T F Y V K M K T

Then Desi just as painstakingly had to finger the grooves of each letter to make out its shape, but after she'd completed the task she put down the tablet and signed, "Is that all there is? It doesn't make sense! It must be scrambled."

"What is scrambled? Do you mean like telling lies?"

"Yes. You can write something in such a way that it only makes sense for those who know the lies that have been put into the letters."

"So even if you can read, you can never be sure if it is not full of lies?"

"Something like that, yes."

"Great! So much for the joys of reading. What do we do now?"

"Don't worry, I know the man who can help us. If *he*

143

can't, nobody can. We must ask the man who taught me to read in the first place: the schoolteacher!"

And off they went to seek out their old friend Tassos, slipping out of the insula without being spotted by Desi's mother. It was not that easy to find him, as his school was closed for the summer. But the two girls knew that most of the pupils were the children of local tradespeople and shop-keepers. They tried a few shops near the portico where classes were normally held, and sure enough, a friendly cobbler could give them the teacher's address. They climbed the stairs to the first story of an insula nearby, and ended up at the front door of the Greek slave's owner. The mistress of the house led them through the large, luxurious dwelling to Tassos's small private room, and as it happened he was glad for the diversion.

"Desi and Feli, it's been a long time! Have you finally come to pay the fee you owe my master for the lessons?"

"I'm afraid not, Tassos," Desi answered sweetly, "I'm not really grown up yet. But what if I tell you that you will live on at least as long as I haven't paid you?"

"Then I'm gladly willing to wait a little longer. What can I do for you?"

He put aside the scroll he was reading and took a look at the label his former pupil handed him. "What is this?"

Desi fingered the letters on her tablet and explained briefly where Feli had "found" the label, and why this could be very important information. "But obviously the message has been scrambled, and I figured that as you taught me to read and write, you have the best qualifications to crack the code."

"That is not an entirely unreasonable assumption, dear girl. Now let me see... ah yes, YKKKK is the giveaway... Hah!"

Tassos remained silent for a moment, then he mumbled something under his breath, and at length he said, "Yes... I want you to write down the alphabet on a fresh page of your booklet."

Desi did what he said, carefully forming the familiar row in the wax layer.

A B C D E F G H I K L M N O P Q R S T V X Y Z

"Good. Now if I say that YKKKK can only mean 'nine' or 'fourteen', what does that tell you?"

"Erm... wait... that it might be a date!"

"Yes, but what does it tell you about the code?"

"Oh, right, I've got it: VIIII or XIIII, so K must stand for I."

"Very good. Now look where K is situated in the alphabet."

"Oh, I get it: it's the *next* letter! And Y stands next to X, so the correct figure is XIIII."

"That's right: a very simple code indeed. Now you can figure out the rest of the message as well."

"Really?"

Desi started fingering the row of letters Feli had transcribed on the tablet, and probing the alphabet, she rapidly wrote down a new version.

X I I I I K A L S E X T I L I S

"Oh, incredible!" she cried, "As I said, it's a date: the fourteenth to the kalends of Sextilis!"

"Exactly," Tassos chortled, "and what is supposed to happen on that day?"

"A bunch of arsonists is going to set fire to Rome. Probably in the middle of the night. That is only three days from now!"

Tassos chortled again, "In that case you might want to pay me before then!"

"No, but seriously, Tassos, I don't have enough time to

explain all the ins and outs, but Rome is going to burn, and you'd better do something about your own safety... and maybe warn your master and your pupils' families."

"But what can I do, and what can *they* do for that matter? I'm a slave, and my master isn't going anywhere, because he has different business interests to attend to. My pupils' parents are tradespeople and shopkeepers; they can't just abandon their livelihoods because Tassos says so, based on information from a blind young girl."

Desi realized that her old teacher was right. What was needed now was to inform the authorities at the highest level. Time to talk to senator Antonius Soranus Canio; for once the PF's worthless patron might come in handy.

There was no time to lose. They rushed over to the bath-house were Canio and his retinue were most likely to hang out. They'd spied on Sextus often enough to know which establishment that would be. Not Nero's new baths, but the old second-class *thermae* on the Esquiline hill, close to where the senator had his domus. Moreover, Desi knew her father's patron was still in town, despite the heat wave. Canio was not a patrician; he was only a senator because he was rich, and he was rich only because he was a hardworking busi-nessman. No summer break for him either, just like the shopkeepers.

At this time of day the baths would be open for men only; the women's hour was either early morning or late afternoon, so Desi had to stay by the entrance and plead with the porter. "Is senator Canio in at the moment? I have an important message for him. I am Desiderata Pomponia, daughter of Sextus Pomponius Sacer. If the senator is ba-thing, my father is bound to be there with him, so could you please at least call Sextus Pomponius out for me? I'm pretty sure the senator will make it worth your while in the end: this is very important."

146

At length the PF appeared by the entrance, staying inside while his daughter stood in the street, across the threshold. He was still tying his tunica belt, dripping, and he grumbled, "What on earth do you think you're doing, Desi?"

His daughter showed him the label, explained what the message meant, and said, "What if I told you that Rufrius and his men intend to set fire to Rome on that date?"

Sextus became very angry, crumpling the little piece of papyrus and throwing it down. "Gracious *Iove*, this is becoming an obsession! You got me hauled out of the bath for *this?*"

"Listen, Pater, this thing is real! Rufrius told his men to leave town and bring their loved ones and valuables in safety. I really believe that Canio should be warned!"

Sextus said nothing; he was completely at a loss.

"Oh my father, please, have I ever made undue demands on you; have I *ever?* But this time I have no choice, I'm begging you to help me, because it is for the greater good."

"All right... all right. But listen: when you tell Canio what you know about this plot, don't mention Piso, do you understand? If you mention Piso my patron will clam up completely... and another thing: I'm taking you in to see him, but Feli stays *here*, outside. Got that? Enough is enough!"

At last Sextus escorted his daughter to the great man, and arranged for her to be able to speak to him alone. It was not the first time Desi met him; she knew that he didn't care much for her, probably because he found her empty eye sockets quite disgusting. But she used the opportunity to hold an impassioned speech, without mentioning Piso—only Rufrius, who she held responsible anyway—, and apparently he listened carefully enough.

"Rufrius... a big fish... yes. I've heard about this little club of his. And the fourteenth to the kalends of Sextilis, you say? That is only three days away... not much I can do to sort this out at such short notice."

"I was hoping that you could raise the alarm, Sir, some-how... talk to a tribune of the urban cohorts, or an aedile, maybe... I don't know."

"Neither do I; I'm only a small fish; I'm not on friendly terms with the high and mighty... but I can promise you one thing, though, I'm going to look into this story of yours at the very first opportunity. I'll have to do my own little investigation. Only, it will take some time."

"Well, Sir," Desi answered with a trembling voice, "if Rome is set ablaze in a few days, it will be too late for that."

IX   1964: The Seneca hypothesis

"Finding a church in Rome is like looking for a needle in a haystack," Vanetta said, "at least if its name has been changed… you know what I mean."

"Well," Daisy said, "I always tell myself that this needle-in-a-haystack business may be difficult, but it is not impossible. Just burn down all the hay and go through the ashes with a big magnet."

Contini burst out laughing. "That is what they call 'search and destroy' in the military!"

"Well, if the needle can take it, why not?"

Sister Liz, who was translating everything in sign language for Morag, sniggered, and the deaf girl pulled Daisy's earlobe in merriment.

The five of them were sitting in Contini's office, somewhere in the Curia building, and it was very cosy. The acoustics of the place suggested a well-upholstered room, the walls covered with books and the windows framed by heavy curtains. It was ten in the morning and Contini had just ordered a round of coffee for them from his secretary. Like Liz, his secretary was a nun, Sister Maria Tabitha; all female staff at the Vatican belonged to some order or other. Soon the office smelled of coffee and Italian biscuits (hmm… soft almonds!), which blended well with the sweet and spicy remnant odours of the cigars that the Curia bishop apparently favoured. When they'd finished their coffee, Vanetta started reporting his findings, and Liz interpreted for Morag.

"So, a needle in a haystack," the old man explained, "but thanks to human nature, this is precisely the reason why various scholars, experts and *cognoscenti* throughout history couldn't resist the challenge and tried to compile catalogues. Today we claim that there must be nine hundred churches in Rome; in Rorick's time already, there must have been a few hundred of them in the holy city. So, as a scholar, what did you do then, and what do you do now? You publish a list, and you try to persuade your colleagues that yours is the most complete: the ultimate, authoritative catalogue... So I went looking for these in the literature and in the archives."

The oldest lists dated from the early Renaissance, Vanetta said, so 14th century at the earliest.

"You always claim, Monsignor, that these things have been studied for almost a thousand years. Well, I say: make that six hundred and you'll be closer to the truth."

On top of that, he explained, there were a number of difficulties to overcome when you parsed these venerable documents.

Those who compiled lists of Rome's churches were seldom interested in their precise location, except to distinguish, say, *San Paolo alle Tre Fontane* from *San Paolo fuori le Mura*, or all those Santa Marias from one another, but even then such indications of location were rather vague. St Plautilla was listed a few times, but because there was only the one, no indication of location had been deemed necessary.

Some churches had changed names, for instance during the Counter-Reformation or the Enlightenment, and at other periods of Catholic revival, when Sacred Hearts and Holy Trinities became all the rage. To complicate matters further, the newer lists seldom mentioned the old name of a church, once it had been changed, and when a name disappeared and another one appeared, it was not always clear which old name had been replaced by which new one.

Then the few authors who did mention a St Plautilla could have done so simply because they had read about her shrine in Rorick's Compendium.

"In other words," Vanetta concluded, "my search was not very fruitful."

"Now I understand that we are dealing with a very complex haystack, sir."

"Exactly, and no way of burning it down! All I can say is that St Plautilla was last mentioned at the end of the 16th century..."

"So she must have been a victim of the Counter-Reformation."

"Very good, my dear, you know your history."

"But then this brings us back to the testimony of Contessa Lavinia Barelli, and to Morag's remark. As a child, around 1800, the Contessa worshipped in a 'chapel *dedicated* to St Plautilla', and it must have been in Baroque style. This would be consistent with a change of name due to the Counter-Reformation, isn't it?"

"Absolutely. The Baroque is the style of choice of that period. And before you ask: it could very well be that this chapel had been renamed in the 16th or 17th century, *but that it was still known by its original name among the faithful.* Such place names can survive for a long time through folklore and oral tradition."

"Incredible!"

"But what can you give us *in concreto*, my dear Vanetta?" Contini wanted to know.

"Well, Monsignor, I could compile a little list of my own and mark those churches on a map of Rome. Now that I know that St Plautilla is not an old church, nor a new one that has kept its old name, it narrows things down considerably. We need to focus on new churches with new names. By new, I mean Baroque, of course. Some of these will really be new, others will have replaced old ones under a new name. There is no telling which is which, alas."

"But Vanetta, you may still end up with a hundred items on that map!"

Then Daisy remarked, "Maybe we should start our search with the smallest buildings, as we know it must be a chapel rather than a church."

"Excellent idea, but you can't always tell if a church is big or small, nor at what point you would start calling a building a chapel. On the other hand, it is only a matter of ringing up the sacristans of those churches, if they have the telephone, and otherwise drop by briefly and ask if they have any Roman inscriptions on the premises."

"So you are confident that the Desiderata stone would still be there?"

"Oh yes, absolutely! In that respect I can reassure you: there is no reason why it shouldn't have stayed more or less where it has always been."

"Yes, I've always said that stones can't just disappear."

"And quite right you are. You see, you can go back all the way to when the very first churches were founded in ancient Rome. At the time you would have called them 'places of worship', mostly clandestine, in the cellars of private houses, as our faith was still being persecuted by the authorities. One of the distinguishing features of such places was that the worshippers brought in the funerary stones of their forbears and loved ones. The slabs with inscriptions were mounted on the walls of these informal 'temples'. It was a way of raising the numbers of the faithful from beyond the grave: the more the merrier. At the same time, when these first Christians were martyred, some remains or relics must have been carefully kept there as well. You can still see this

152

setup in the oldest churches that survive today, those based on original Roman basilicas, like, say, *Santa Maria in Trastevere*. And those are precisely the places Rorick would have visited in the 6th century."

"And there he would have seen the Desiderata stone. Not necessarily a *Christian* tombstone, right?"

"Not necessarily, no. The Quinctius stone you liked so much also comes from a church, I think."

Vanetta proceeded to explain what had happened throughout the centuries when these oldest churches were refurbished, or torn down and rebuilt. The relics and the Roman inscriptions would be placed back in the new building on the same site, especially if it kept its old name. But on the other hand, during the Counter-Reformation and later, when relics and miracles were no longer in demand, the old "souvenirs" wouldn't have been displayed in the place of honour, but they would never have been thrown out altogether either. You always had older people with a sentimental attachment to such things, who would make sure of that. So those same relics and ancient tombstones would have ended up in side-chapels, underground crypts, or even in the vestry.

"Oh, right!" Daisy exclaimed, "maybe that is why the Contessa never mentioned the stone: she went to the right chapel, but in the meantime the Desiderata stone had been spirited away to an inconspicuous hiding place within the new Baroque building."

"Possibly, yes."

"Isn't that something of a paradox, though? The name of St Plautilla survived, but the stone was forgotten!"

"Names often last longer than stones in that respect; names are not as easily hidden away."

Contini said, "Vanetta, if you prepare that map for us this afternoon, we can go looking for the chapel tomorrow.

But for now, let us repair to the museum canteen, shall we? I have an idea."

"Time for lunch already?" Vanetta chuckled, "I lost track completely!"

And off they went, all five of them, from one wing of the Vatican to another. In Vatican City you never needed to walk more than a few hundred yards, no matter where you were. It was also very quiet, with no traffic, except for the odd delivery van or official limousine. The birds in the trees around them were clearly happy with their surroundings and voiced it unreservedly.

That morning Contini had decided they should avoid the mistake of the previous day, which was why they had convened in his office for coffee. This time Daisy would not be late for their daily briefing after lunch. Therefore they arrived rather early at the canteen, the first ones served and seated. But as they were tucking in, the place started to fill up; it became more busy than on the previous days. "Exactly what I thought," Contini said, "it is Saturday; there are a lot more researchers coming in than on a weekday. Let's give them enough time to settle in, then we'll see."

Daisy smiled, turning her face to Morag, who'd just been signed what the Monsignor had said. Daisy's expression conveyed: aren't these scheming old gentlemen a riot?

After a while Contini muttered, "All right, time to mobilize the resources assembled in this room."

He finished eating hastily, and stood up. In the meantime the room resounded with the overwhelming hubbub of innumerable conversations. The dapper bishop stepped over to a lectern standing on a small platform at the front of the canteen. Apparently this place was sometimes used for larger conferences. Sister Liz described all this to Daisy *sotto voce*. Contini now tapped the lectern with a spoon he was still holding: "Erm... excuse me, brothers and sisters!"

154

The loud rap, combined with the purple sash and skull-cap of a bishop, no doubt, made the whole room go quiet at once. "*Scusate, fratelli e sorelle,*" he repeated, in fact in Italian, and then he proceeded to ask the assembled lunch guests if anyone had ever heard about "*la lapide di Desiderata*" from any *other* source than "*il 'Compendium Mirabilium Sanationum' del vescovo Rorick di Treviri*". He also asked about "*una chiesa o capella di Santa Plautilla qui a Roma.*" What a beautiful, singsong language, Daisy thought with a sigh of longing; she should definitely learn it one day. After Contini's little speech it was quiet for a very short while, and then a solitary voice piped up: "I think I do! There's a Church Father who mentions 'the inscription of Saint Desiderata'."

"Wonderful! No one else? Well, please join us at our table, my friend, and tell us all about it."

It turned out that the scholar who came over with his tray was German, "Kurt Morgenthaler at your service," and that he spoke passable English.

While he finished his meal, he told the little group about an obscure early Church Father, Aristobulus of Sinope, who mentioned "the inscription of Saint Desiderata" in a letter to his more renowned colleague Tertullian.

"They were arguing about the Seneca hypothesis," the German scholar specified, smacking a little.

"Oh, I see," Vanetta exclaimed, "Tertullian is the first author who mentions an alleged exchange of letters between St Paul and Seneca. Nowadays we think that these 'Epistles of Paul and Seneca' are a complete hoax."

"Yes, the existing epistles clearly are, but at the time, around AD 220, some authors claimed they had seen the *original* correspondence. However, the hypothesis these two Church Fathers were arguing about, was not whether there had been a correspondence or not, but whether Seneca had converted to our faith, and whether Stoicism could have influenced St Paul's thinking."

"Wasn't Seneca also Nero's tutor and advisor?" Daisy asked.

"Ah yes, your encyclopaedic knowledge again," Contini chuckled, "Very good! The New Testament also tells us about some Christians living at the palace, probably slaves. At the end of his Epistle to the Philippians, St Paul, who was in Rome, wrote: 'The brethren which are with me greet you. All the saints salute you, chiefly they that are of Caesar's household.' And at that time it was Nero who was the emperor; *he* held the title of Caesar."

"That's exactly what Tertullian argued as well: Seneca, a regular at Nero's court, must have known the first Christians, and Paul stayed in Rome for two years before Seneca's death in AD 65. However, Aristobulus argued that the two could never have been on friendly terms. 'I only need to remind you of the inscription of Saint Desiderata,' he told Tertullian in his letter. And that's all. He was assuming his correspondent knew exactly what he was talking about. It's a quirk letter writers often have, regrettably for us down the line of posterity, as we are no longer in on this insider information."

"So that is all there is to it?" Contini asked.

"Yes, I'm afraid so, Monsignor. It's not much, I know."

"Oh, but the interesting thing, here," Vanetta exclaimed, "is that in AD 220 these two authors were completely familiar with the stone and its location. Just imagine. The Christians were still a persecuted minority in the Roman Empire... Who's reign was this? Wait... Heliogabalus was the emperor! Now, Tertullian lived in Carthage and Aristobulus in Sinope, yet when these two gentlemen visited Rome, they would go and pray at this particular shrine as a matter of course. For some reason St Plautilla's chapel must have been very important indeed."

156

At the debriefing that day, Father Cadogan asked, "Can any of you recall the very first moment you realized that you were different?"

As no one else came forward, Daisy said, "Yes, I can. For me that's quite easy because I remember it exactly."

At the age of five or six, she started telling the group, when other children ask such questions as "How are babies made?" and "Where do people go when they die?" she'd once asked her mother, "What does 'blind' mean?" Her mother had been taken aback. "That's hard to explain, darling... Maybe you should ask your father when he comes home from work. Daddy is a lot better than me at explaining these things..."

"Now it was my turn to be taken aback," Daisy went on, "I said yes but, Mummy, are *you* blind too, just like me?— No! I am not!—Is Daddy blind?—No!—And how about Granma, Aunty Agatha, and Cook, and Nanny?—No, no, they're not blind either, none of them!—So it's only *me*?— Yes... well, there are other blind people in the world at large, but you don't happen to know them... And that is when it suddenly dawned on me that most people were *not* blind, and that they had been keeping this fact from me. I felt obscurely that I'd been taken advantage of, and this made me very sad... and a bit angry as well. When Daddy came home from the bank where he worked, at the end of that afternoon, he had a lot of explaining to do, believe me."

It was very quiet for a while after Daisy had finished telling her story, then at length Father Cadogan said, "Thank you ever so much, Daisy dear, your testimony is quite impressive, you seem to remember the whole conversation word by word... Now, does anyone wish to comment on this?"

"Yes," Morag said through Sister Liz's competent services, "I find it very moving, of course, typical Daisy too, but I also want to tell you this: you were so lucky! At least you could talk it through... your Mum and Dad could explain straight away what was going on. With me it took ages before I could communicate with anyone, and for years and years I was completely baffled... I had no idea what was going on, and there was no way anybody could tell me."

Daisy raised her hand and stroked Morag's arm, while the other deaf participants vied for 'speaking time' through Liz and expressed that they agreed, they too could only be jealous of how a blind little girl could *ask*, and receive answers.

"I know, I know," Daisy said when it was finally her turn again. "Only yesterday I told you, Father, that being blind, after all, is only a minor inconvenience. I had it easy, because in my case language and communication were never affectted, except for reading, maybe... but I understand now that the isolation of a deaf child must be a terrible thing. It must restrict your sense of self, I suppose... almost suffocate your very soul! At least I was spared all that."

"And your dad worked at a bank," someone said, "and you had a cook and a nanny."

"Yes I know, we had it good, but that is not *my* fault, obviously... On the other hand, it did mean that my dad could help his blind daughter in ways most people can't afford to. He hired a private tutor to develop my verbal skills even before I went to school, then he sent me to a special boarding school for the blind, no expenses were ever spared for my development. So it is true I was very privileged."

"Is your father still alive?" Father Cadogan asked.

"Yes, he retired recently, but he's still going strong: your typical, strappy Great War veteran, with pencil moustache and all!"

"Ah, we don't have those in Ireland, but next time you go visit him, please say hello from Father Cadogan from Dublin. Tell him I'm a great admirer!"

As they were walking back to their digs, that day, Daisy felt that the mood between her and her companion was different. Of course they were never very communicative during their walk, but Morag would always make clear that she enjoyed her blind partner's company in the way she held her hand or her elbow; sometimes even with an exuberant little dash up the street to the convent. But not this time; she was rather absent-minded; she seemed to be lost in thought. "Is it what I said at the debriefing?" Daisy wondered. Maybe Morag had been saddened by bad childhood memories, or put off by the fact that her companion turned out to be a banker's daughter who'd had a very fancy life... Surely she'd never had that, on top of how tough it must have been to be born deaf. Daisy made them stop and gave Morag a long tight hug; then they walked on; there was nothing more she could do.

A few hours later, when they had settled down for the evening, Daisy suddenly retrieved her notebook from the handbag on the nightstand, and wrote a message for her roommate: WHAT IS ON YOUR MIND, MORAG?

Then she took out the wax tablets she'd recently bought in a souvenir shop; the first set had been brought back to the educational service. She handed them over to the girl sitting on the bed next to hers. A moment later an answer came back, that she could make out with her fingertips.

N O T H I N G
J U S T   S A D

A new message was pencilled in the notebook: WAS IT SOMETHING I SAID AT THE DEBRIEFING?

                        A BIT
                       ITS OK

SORRY! MAYBE A BIT CONFRONTING? IT COULDN'T BE HELPED,
THOUGH.
                      WILL YOU
                     LEARN BSL

OH YES, I WILL, I PROMISE. BUT NOT NOW. THERE IS NOT MUCH
I CAN LEARN IN A WEEK.
                      YOU WANT
                       TO FIND
                     THE STONE

YES. WE ARE SO CLOSE NOW! WILL YOU COME TOMORROW?

                      NO NEED
                      YOU GO
                     HAVE FUN

X AD 64: The great fire

Feli woke up first, when the floor of the landing shuddered. Then she saw the glow coming from downstairs; she felt the heat and she smelled the fire. Like the oven at the bakery, but without the bread.

She shook Desi's shoulder, then prodded the next kid, sleeping on the straw mattress closest to them, and motioned him to wake the others, pointing at the glow from downstairs.

Desi understood at once that this was not a leisurely early morning wake-up call, at the side of Feli's warm, familiar body. This was the night of the fourteenth to the kalends of Sextilis; this was the fire! She could smell it and hear it crackling.

They all stood up in a hurry and girdled their tunics. Then Feli rapped her knuckles on Desi's head: from now on she was in charge and Desi would follow her unquestioningly, until her friend "gave back" her command.

The deaf girl motioned the others to follow her too, and opened the door of the Pomponius garret. The neighbours' children started knocking on their own doors, and then followed the two older girls into their apartment.

The smoke and the heat were just starting to overwhelm the landing as the other adults emerged from their homes. They saw their kids disappearing behind Feli and Desi, and as the smoke gripped their throats and the heat hit their faces, they realized there was no time to lose: the landing was going to burst into flame at any moment now, and the deaf slave seemed to have a plan. She was a clever one.

Sextus and Claudia woke up to find their humble home invaded by all their neighbours, and could see through the door and the smoke that the staircase had changed into a roaring whirlwind of fire; the flashing flames illuminated the room with flickering brightness. They too understood at once what this meant: they were trapped in their garret. Now that the stairs and the landing were burning, the fire would spread sideways and devour the dwellings, feeding on the wooden floors and the roof beams. They were caught like mice in a trap; they would burn like rats.

But meanwhile Feli was crouching in the corner, at the lowest point under the roof, between two beams, and she was pushing up the tiles. With quick movements of both hands she pried them loose one by one, pushed them out and sent them sliding down the eaves, crashing into the street below. Within seconds she had made a hole big enough for even an adult to go through. One of the men helped her break off the wooden slats that still barred their way.

Within minutes the whole company was emerging on top of the roof, the smoke billowing from the gaping hole. Feli made Desi crouch low, and stood up to take stock of the situation. There were fires everywhere, all around them in the neighbourhood. The moon was shining bright. In front of her the tiles above the staircase were smoking too, and the glare of the flames showed through the cracks that were starting to appear. They needed to move on, but they would have to move to the courtside of the insula first, and circle around the staircase. Then they would see.

They were huddling right by the edge of the roof; one wrong step would have you hurtling down to your death in the street below. So Feli went down on all fours, made Desi hold on to her ankle, and started crawling forward as fast as she could, keeping the safest course possible between the fire and the edge of the abyss. All the others imitated the two girls and followed them as closely as possible, single file. As they all set off, Desi cried out anxiously, "Mater! Are you there?"

"Yes, sweetness, I'm right behind you!"

Crawling along behind his wife, Sextus thought, "Desi is not asking for *me!*" But he knew all too well why his daughter was angry at him. She'd pleaded and pleaded. "Oh my father, please, please, we must leave, spend the night at an inn outside Rome! I'll pay for it with the money from the baths." But he'd rubbished the idea, calling it an obsession again, and pointed out that the money she and Feli had made belonged to *him* anyway. How stupid he'd been! Looking at the gaping edge of the eaves, Sextus felt cold shivers going down his spine, but then he felt how hot the roof tiles were becoming under his hands and knees. He focused desperately on his wife, moving on steadily in front of him. As always, Claudia seemed to be the epitome of calm and composure, a real Roman matrona.

Desi, and especially Feli, had spent the previous days preparing an escape plan. Feli told Desi about the rickety tiling above their heads. "We can escape right *through* the roof!" And she knew precisely where they needed to go. There were three adjoining insulae on their block, and the third one would have a chimney, because there was a bakery downstairs, at street level. Its staircase rose along an outside wall at the back. The layout of the three buildings was utterly familiar, as the girls had explored them and played all over the place for years. Growing up, they'd spent many rainy or cold winter days running up and down those staircases with their playmates.

Feli led the way for twenty people crawling one behind

163

the other, following her path like panicking ants. Eight adults and a dozen children, crawling as fast as they could, crawling for their life, between the abyss and the fires. When they crossed over the second insula by way of the courtside, the flames of its burning staircase were plainly visible over the top of the roof, the raging flames reaching for the night sky on the street side. They hurried on, and there it was: the chimney of the bakery on the third insula. That was where they needed to re-enter the dwellings.

As soon as they reached the last roof at the end of the block, Feli started uprooting the tiles again, sending them crashing into the courtyard. As she'd anticipated, this building was not on fire yet, because the bakery had a vaulted stone ceiling and the wooden staircase was on the outside and at the back, separated from the street by solid walls. The fire from the neighbouring buildings could not spread to this one as easily as that. Yanking off the tiles' supporting slats, she finally completed their escape hatch and could help Desi down into the room below. Before she followed, Feli looked back over her shoulder and saw the whole roof of their own insula collapsing in an eruption of fire and sparks. The others, just behind her, could hear the screams of the neighbours in their death throes, those from the other side of the landing, and from downstairs. Their group had made their escape just in time.

And on that night, Gattus, the cat who used to dart around the garrets, had also made his escape. He'd jumped right after the fugitives through the hole in the roof, then he'd darted ahead of them, waited patiently for them to catch up with him, and he'd been the first one to jump into the second hole they made, and disappeared.

They all emerged into the street soon after him, having crossed a dark and deserted garret room and found their way to the exterior staircase. So far so good. But all around them

164

now it was total chaos, people running and screaming, raging fires flickering everywhere; it was overwhelming. However, for Feli it was a *silent* spectacle of panic; she did not let the jumble of frantic movement disorient her, did not lose her focus. She took stock and decided which way to go. As she and Desi and their little group moved on down the street, she saw a dead woman lying on the pavement, killed by a falling roof tile, its shards still scattered around her body. People were just stepping over her while they fled. Maybe she'd been hit by one of *her* tiles, Feli realised in a flash… but on the other hand, she'd just brought twenty people down to safety, so better not dwell on it.

On that night, somewhere in those same streets, an eight-year-old boy was running for his life too, like everybody else. His name was Tacitus, and fifty years later, as a middle-aged man, he wrote down what he'd witnessed in his famous *Annals*:

"The blazes in their fury ran first through the level portions of the city, then rose to the hills, while they again devastated every place below them, outstripping all preventive measures. The calamity was rapid and had the city completely at its mercy, with those narrow winding passages and irregular streets which characterised old Rome.

"On top of all this there were the cries of terrified women, the feebleness of the aged, the helpless inexperience of the children. The crowds who sought to save themselves or others, dragging out the infirm or waiting for them, added to the confusion by their hurry in the first case, by their dithering in the other.

"Often, while they looked behind them, they were intercepted by flames from the side or in front of them. Or if they sought refuge in a neighbouring quarter, when this too was engulfed by the fire, they found out that even places which they had imagined to be safe, were involved in the same calamity. In the end, doubting what they should avoid or where they should go, they crowded the streets or flung themselves down, while some who had lost everything, even their very daily bread, and others out of despair for their loved ones, whom they had been unable to rescue, let themselves perish, although escape was within reach.

"And no one dared to stop the calamity, because of incessant menaces from a number of persons who forbade the extinguishing of the flames, because again others openly hurled burning brands, and kept shouting that there was someone who gave them authority, either seeking to plunder more freely, or obeying orders."

Things were slightly different with the little group of survivors from a certain attic floor of a Subura insula. Here the infirm were leading the able-bodied, hurrying them along. They were moving against the stream of fleeing crowds, down the Argiletum in the direction of the Forum. Sextus had the feeling they were going the wrong way, towards the heart of the conflagration. He stepped up to his daughter and asked, "Desi! Wouldn't it be wiser to go to the *Porta Esquilina* instead? That's the closest gate, the other way! Our best chance to escape!"

"Feli knows what she's doing," Desi answered coldly, "if she didn't, she'd *ask* me. As long as she's not asking, that means that she *knows*. You can go to the Esquiline Gate if you want, but leave Mater behind with me!"

Sextus looked at his wife, and saw her shaking her head ever so slightly, so he kept moving on with the two girls.

Feli suddenly veered off into a small side ally; they passed a public fountain, its spout still gurgling incongruously; then they reached a heavy wooden grate set into the flagstone street surface. She motioned the four men of the group to help her lift it up, and together they were able to remove it rapidly. A steep stone staircase became visible in the glow of the fires. The two girls led the way down. Soon they were all marching on through the filth, and Desi called out, "Hold on to the person in front of you! Follow me and keep moving; I'm not bothered by the darkness!"

The layer of human excrement clogging the sewer tunnel was even thicker now than the last time, the stench was worse than ever, but they kept moving on at a steady pace.

"You've done this before, huh?" Sextus called out to his daughter.

"Of course, PF, Feli and I are real sewer rats! But I understand the plan now: we're going straight to the Tiber; the riverbank is the safest place to be. If the Island and the Trastevere are not burning, we can cross one of the bridges to safety. Otherwise we'll keep moving along the riverbank until we're clear of the flames."

"Nero at this time was at Antium, and did not return to Rome until the fire approached his house, which he had built to connect the palace with the gardens of Maecenas. It could not, however, be stopped from devouring the palace, the house, and everything around it.

"On the other hand, to relieve the populace, driven out homeless as they were, he threw open to them the Campus Martius and the public buildings of Agrippa, and even his own gardens, and raised temporary structures to receive the destitute multitude. Supplies of food were brought up from Ostia and the neighbouring towns, and the price of corn was reduced to three sesterces."

And the Pomponius household, together with their attic neighbours, ended up in makeshift shacks on the Vatican Fields. These were the "structures" in the emperor's own gardens mentioned by Tacitus. They'd been erected swiftly by platoons of navy carpenters under the direction of admiralty engineers. But first the stranded survivors had spent several nights in the open air, and gone hungry for several days, while Rome went on burning on the other side of the Tiber, in plain view of the refugees. Sleeping out in the open had not been too bad, as the nights were still warm and the weather clear; hunger had been a lot more of an ordeal.

The fires would not come to an end, rekindled relentlessly by sparks swept along by a steady wind. The emperor—through Tigellinus—ordered the praetorian guards and the urban cohorts to join the regular *vigilēs* firefighters. Twenty thousand extra men were mobilized. But it was still not enough, volunteers were recruited among the refugees, and Sextus was among the first who applied. He now spent his days clearing the rubble of burned-out insulae that were blocking the narrow streets. This also involved extricating dead bodies from the ruins, the charred remains of the victims, entire families that had been trapped in their homes. He also helped with the demolition and excavation of undamaged buildings to create firebreaks. At strategic locations in the city, broad swaths of the urban fabric had to be razed, after the 'uniforms' had forcibly expelled the inhabitants. When he came 'home' at nightfall, dirty and exhausted, Sextus would feel like he'd just spent another day on a battlefield: Rome had become a disaster zone, a moon landscape, a nightmare. And still the fires started all over again in the most unexpected corners.

"At last, on the sixth day, the conflagration was brought to a halt at the foot of the Esquiline hill, by the destruction of all buildings on a vast space, so that the violence of the fire was met by clear ground and an open sky.

"But before people had laid aside their fears, the flames

returned, with no less fury this second time, and especially in the spacious districts of the city. Consequently, though there was less loss of life, the temples of the gods, and the porticoes which were devoted to enjoyment, fell in a yet more widespread ruin.

"And this outburst was tinged with greater suspicions because it started on the Aemilian property of Tigellinus, and it looked like Nero was aiming at the glory of founding a new city and calling it by his name.

"Rome, indeed, is divided into fourteen districts, four of which remained uninjured; three were levelled to the ground, while in the other seven only a few shattered, half-burnt remains of houses were left."

When he reached the part of the shacks where he lived, a strange and soothing sight awaited Sextus. Claudia, Desi, Feli and a dozen other women were standing or sitting on makeshift stools in the shade of a tree and they were carding and spinning wool. Nero's gardens were still quite attractive, with their shaded lanes, although they were now full of shacks and crowded with refugees. Looking at his wife spinning and chatting with the other women in the peaceful evening, Sextus couldn't help himself, he still had to see it as a quaint hobby, a fad that kept them amused and whiled away the idle hours. It made him smile and relax: such a charming tableau!

Most remarkable was that even Desi was participating. Apparently, carding the wool between two bats was a mechanical process that didn't require eyesight to perform correctly. With her fingers she could feel when the fibres were aligned smoothly enough. As for Feli, she seemed to be very adept at spinning, and obviously there was nothing wrong with her eye-hand coordination.

Claudia had revived the cartel with the money she'd

salvaged from the fire. In the few moments between waking up and escaping through the hole in the roof, she'd had just enough time to open the familiar old chest and grope around under Sextus's toga and her best stola for the leather purse containing the cartel's capital, fifty-six denarii and forty-five sestertii. She'd retrieved it and tied its strings to her waistband before making her escape. In the first days, when they'd gone hungry, she'd used some of the money to buy food from local farmers. The small-time producers from the countryside showed up at the makeshift camps where the refugees spent their nights, and they tried to cash in on the survivors' deprivation. Claudia didn't begrudge them their windfall and paid with a smile. After all, part of the cartel capital, her own share, was hers to spend as she saw fit. This was when Sextus had found out about it. He'd been furious: so she'd made lots of money with this spinning business and had never told him?

"Well, what do you expect, Sextus? You're always banging on about how everything in our household belongs to you, only you, by rights... But this money belongs to a cartel of housewives and none of us is going to let our husbands take control of it. So I kept it hidden to avoid fights, that's all."

Claudia had been unexpectedly fierce about this; harsh words had fallen, along the lines that he, Sextus, had never earned a single *quadrans of an as* with honest work in his entire life. "Even Desi and Feli have done more to provide some income for the Pomponius household!" This had stung, and goaded Sextus into applying for a job as a temporary firefighter.

On the day the markets should have been held, Claudia, on a hunch, had gone out to the *Via Flaminia*, not far from where they were camping out in the park, and sure enough, her usual supplier had arrived from the north with his cart.

So she'd bought a bale of fleece, some carding bats and spindles from him, and 'the housewives' cohort' had been back in business. The three other women from their landing were in, of course, and a couple of other survivors of the original club, but there were also new recruits from the camp. And Claudia saw prospects for some good business opportunities ahead: many people had lost their wardrobe in the fire, few would be producing yarn or cloth in the immediate future. And the survivors needed something to do, urgently. Now that the authorities were providing food and shelter, the refugees had less worries, and more time for productive work.

The exhausted firefighter was warmly welcomed by the whole company. Claudia dropped her spinning at once and hugged her husband tightly, even though he was rather grungy. He'd washed up a bit by the Tiber on his way home, but his clothes were still streaked with sweat, soot, and dust. They all missed the bathhouses terribly.

"How was your day, *carissimus*? We can still see smoke rising from the city centre; what's going on?"

Everybody wanted to hear his news, assuming that he knew more for having been on the spot. But Sextus realized all too well now that the foot soldiers on the battlefield are not always better informed about what is happening.

"I don't know, *carissima*, there are rumours about looters relighting the fires so they can search for valuables undisturbed. The whole place is a huge mess."

"Have you had any news from Canio or his clients?" Desi asked. She'd also hugged her father warmly. They had made up, and probably the hard work Sextus was putting in was a way of atoning for not listening to his daughter before the fire. Now she was simply very curious to hear the latest news when he came home, but she was careful not to talk too openly about 'the plot', as it still put the PF's nerves on edge.

"Actually, I met Canio himself today. He tried to stop us when we were tearing down some of his properties for a firebreak. He protested with the uniforms in charge, but they gave him short thrift: orders are orders; if you have complaints, go through the proper channels… So I went over and said hello to him. He told me that his domus on the Esquiline is unharmed, and that I'm welcome to visit him there at the usual time if I want."

"Some things never change… but I'm glad for him, especially as I need to talk to him again."

"Are you still going on about that?" Sextus asked wearily, "I know that Canio and I should have listened to you *before*, but now it's too late and you should let it go."

"Well, I'm still concerned for the emperor's safety, that's all."

But it was no use. With a tired wave of his hand Sextus put an end to the discussion. "Let's all get us some grub. I want to go to bed early, I'm exhausted."

Rumours went round that Nero was indeed following in his stepfather Claudius's footsteps, getting personally involved. He'd made appearances at the hardest hit locations, inspecting the damage and consoling the victims. Rufrius and the others had been correct: the emperor wanted to be seen taking a personal interest in his people's plight, and he must have been very vulnerable. Even if the most elite praetorian bodyguards never left his side, "one of us—or anyone—could kill him and get away with it." Someone had to warn the authorities, Desi thought.

She would have liked to venture out into the ruined city on her own, or rather with Feli, obviously, and try to find someone who would listen to her. It was urgent to raise the alarm about the plot. But her 'twin sister' refused to help her. She refused to budge from the spot.

"You already tried to talk to this politician who owns your father: he didn't listen. But he knows everything now, so it's *his* problem. We stay out of it, it's too dangerous."

"I'm not sure I really mentioned the plot against Nero to Canio: I only warned him for the fire; I was being cautious. Besides, we could go looking for any *other* uniformed big shot... you know?"

"I say let's keep out of it. This is none of our business. Why should we care if they kill this emperor? Then we'll get another one; it's all the same to me."

"No, Feli, no! This is a *good* emperor; I care about him because he's a good man."

"Are you in love with him? How can you fall in love with a man you've never met? And I can't even tell you if he's good looking or not!"

Matters of the heart were very serious matters for both girls. Desi was always asking Feli whether a boy was good looking when they would run into some neighbourhood youngster who sounded attractive to her. Then they would discuss his merits and drawbacks endlessly, and enjoy themselves very much doing so. That is why Desi had an idea, at this stage of the discussion. She asked her mother to lend her a coin—any coin—with Nero's likeness on it, then she handed it over to Feli, and said playfully, "There, that's him: the man I love! How does he look?"

Feli considered the question for a moment, fingering the tiny profile.

"Bah... ugly face, I'm telling you."

"Well I don't care: I'm blind!"

But it was no use. Feli could be very stubborn. She kept saying it was too dangerous to interfere with this business. And that is why they had stayed at the shacks and learned to card and spin under Claudia's guidance.

After another three days the fires had finally been extinguished for good, and Sextus decided he could take a day off and go pay a visit to Canio with his daughter. Claudia had even managed to clean up the only tunica he had a bit; it was decided that Feli would stay back with her. And off they went.

They crossed Nero's bridge and walked down the main thoroughfare across the Campus Martius, hand in hand. Sextus described the damage to Desi, and concluded, "You know the *Via Triumphalis*, right? Well you wouldn't recognize it anymore."

"I *know* this street all right, dear PF, but I've never *seen* it, really, so I can't tell the difference, no."

"My point exactly, you'll just have to take my word for it."

"It *sounds* different, though."

"There are a lot of people camping in the ruins of their houses. Maybe that is what you hear."

"Yes, and they are awfully subdued. You don't often hear Romans talking so softly."

At the *Porta Carmentalis* they had to pass a checkpoint. The urban cohorts were making sure no looters could enter the city through the Servian wall. But Sextus had a firefighter's tag on a string around his neck; he was guiding a blind girl; they let him through without asking too many questions. As they went on across the Forum and into the Subura, he told his daughter what he saw: the badly damaged public buildings and temples; the narrow streets like their own that had been levelled by the fires. On every corner, public slaves were still busy pushing aside the heaps of rubble. Finally they went up to the Esquiline, where the nice houses of the rich had not been much affected by the conflagration. As they wound their way to Canio's place through shaded alleys, Sextus cautioned Desi once more: if

174

she was given the opportunity to talk to the great man, she should not mention Piso.

As it turned out, the great man wanted to see his client's blind daughter immediately. They were led through to his private office as soon as they arrived, and the senator greeted them warmly, before getting down to business at once.

"Desiderata! tell me, do you really think this disaster was caused by arsonists, like you said?"

"Yes, Senator, now I'm sure of it. You've probably heard the rumours about people throwing burning torches and shouting that they had the authority to do so, that they were obeying orders. It is also very suspicious that for days on end the fires kept coming back from the most unexpected places."

"Yes," Sextus added, "I've really wondered about that. It makes you think, doesn't it?"

"And I can tell you what happened on our own block on that first night," Desi went on, "Two of the three insulae went up in flames *simultaneously*. It was not a question of the fire *jumping over* from one building to the next. There must have been gangs of arsonists throwing burning torches into the staircases of entire streets in one go, in the middle of the night, when the slave porters were dozing and the *vigilēs* patrols were few. By the way, the only reason the *third* building on our block did not catch fire is that the staircase was at the back, behind the bakery. I don't know if it is still standing now."

"Yes, it survived; it belongs to me as well. But how do you know all these details? I mean: you being blind."

"Our slave girl Felicitas, who managed to get us out alive, told me what she saw."

"The same slave girl that is deaf and dumb?"

"Yes, but we're very good at communicating by sign language."

175

"I can see that! Now: do you think we could have prevented the fires, somehow?"

"Maybe, maybe not... Don't you agree it would have made a big difference if the *vigilēs* had at least been on the alert, that night? Of course, with the dry summer and the wind blowing, it would have been hard to prevent the fires entirely, but still..."

"Hmm... if only I had acted! I was planning to retire and leave my business interests to caretakers. Now I've lost almost everything and I'll have to start all over again. I certainly owe you an apology, my dear girl. I should have listened to you."

"That's the thing: you can listen to me now! I'm very concerned for the life of our emperor. What I didn't tell you last time is that the same men I overheard at the baths were planning to assassinate Nero and seize power."

"What!?"

"Yes. The fire was only meant to force him to come back to Rome. Now that he's here, taking care of things personally, mingling with the people, he is in great danger of being attacked. I want to raise the alarm with the authorities... urgently."

"All right... this time I believe I might be able to act on it more effectively. My standing with the high and mighty is much better at the moment... I did myself a pretty good turn as I was the only higher official present in town from the very beginning of the calamity... Yes, I can take you to the senate building on the Forum, or what remains of it, where the current consul, Gaius Licinius Mucianus, is holding court."

"The consul himself, Sir? That sounds good!"

"Yes, he has just arrived from his summer residence; he has taken charge of everything now; the tribunes and aediles of the different forces and districts are all reporting to him directly. And he reports to the emperor on a daily basis."

Desi thought, "A consul! That means: appointed by the emperor himself, so certainly interested in what I want to tell him."

Canio thought, "This girl, although a disgusting cripple, gives me another opportunity to show my face at the consul's office. Let's hope he's interested in what she has to say."

The roof of the senate building, the Curia Iulia, had burned down and caved in; the rubble had been pushed aside, and the consul was working from a makeshift office under a canopy of poles and salvaged draperies.

When Canio and his retinue arrived at the door of the Curia, his clients and bodyguards were told to wait outside. Only after some negotiations with the two praetorian guardsmen barring the entrance could he go inside with Sextus and Desi in tow. Of course the purple stripe on his toga identified him as a senator, but it was normally not allowed to take a retinue along into the building.

The consul had a retinue of his own in attendance, men standing or sitting on folding chairs all around him in the shade of the canopy, frowning earnestly at the proceedings. Canio and his two guests had to wait endlessly for their turn in the blinding sun, but then he was very gratified when the consul recognized him at once, and exclaimed, "Senator Canio! Step forward and state your business concisely, my friend, you can see how busy I am."

Canio explained that here was a girl—the daughter of his client Sextus Pomponius Sacer—who had known three days in advance when the fires would break out, and who wanted to warn the authorities that the emperor's life was in danger.

"The emperor's life is *always* in danger, Canio, that's what the praetorian guards are for. Besides, the girl is blind, I can see that."

"Still, Consul Mucianus, I ask you to listen to her, it will only take a moment."

Desi hated it when self-important men like these talked about her as if she wasn't even present, just because she was a girl and a cripple. But this Mucianus apparently gave Canio a nod, and Canio pushed her forward and said, "Go ahead, Desiderata Pomponia."

Once again Desi held an impassioned speech, explaining the ins and outs of the conspiracy to kill the emperor and seize power. But immediately she realized the difficulties of telling what she knew: she didn't want to dwell too much on the fact she had been eavesdropping shamelessly on the men she was accusing—and she couldn't mention Piso by name. Instead she insisted on the fact that the great fire that had raged these last ten days was only the first phase of an elaborate plot, and that the emperor was in great danger, because he was especially vulnerable at the moment.

"That was the intention all along, Consul. Like General Lucius Caesennius Paetus said: 'one of us—or anyone—could kill him and get away with it'."

"General Lucius Caesennius Paetus, eh? Careful what you say, girl, these are very serious accusations indeed, and the general is not here to defend himself against your allegations… I'm afraid I have to insist that you tell me exactly how you happen to know all this."

Now Desi had to tell the consul about her job at the baths.

"Oh, but my dear girl, men will say all kinds of crazy things while they're relaxing at the baths! But still, I find your story very disturbing, and a bit vague, by the way, except for the fact that you are quite carelessly tarnishing the names and reputations of some very important men!"

All right, Desi thought, the big fish doesn't believe me. She squared her shoulders and declared, "Well, I have said what I wanted to say, Consul Mucianus. The information is in your hands now, and we shall leave you to your duties."

"So you stand by your statements?"

"Yes, absolutely, Consul."

"Wait a minute," Canio now intervened, "Mucianus, this girl tried to warn me three days beforehand that Rome would be set on fire. She knew the exact date!"

"That only makes her a prime suspect as an accessory."

"A *blind* girl? Hardly! No, no, believe me: if she were an accessory, why would she have tried to warn me? She had no particular reason to come to *me*. If only I'd listened to her!"

Once again they were talking about her as if she was not there. Desi frowned, and stepped forward, probing for the table in front of her, then she walked around it and bent over. By the sound of his voice she knew exactly where the consul was sitting, but before she could whisper something in his ear, she needed to probe his face lightly with her fingertips. With a mixture of fascination and revulsion he let her touch him, and stared at the horrible slits of her withered eyes. Then finally the blind creature whispered very softly, right into his ear "Shall I tell you the name of the *real* mastermind? I mean the man who intends to become *the new Emperor of Rome*? His name is Gaius Calpurnius Piso."

"Really?" the consul muttered, sounding quite shocked.

"Mark my words, Sir."

"All right. You can go now… Don't worry, I'll take care of this."

As Canio was leaving the ruins of the Curia building with Sextus and Desi, Consul Mucianus turned around and addressed two men standing right next to him in the dark shadows of the makeshift dais.

"Did you hear that, Piso?"

"Yes, quite a contrived and preposterous yarn, don't you think?"

"No, I mean the last part, what she whispered in my ear. She said that you, Piso, intend to become our next emperor!"

"What!? The cheek of the girl!"

"And you, Rufrius, what do you have to say to defend your name and that of your friends?"

"I admit it, Mucianus, I employed this blind girl at the baths, but I was told she was *retarded*. Unfortunately, it turns out the little minx is no such thing, even quite the contrary: very good at spinning a clever yarn, after all."

"Yes, quite so."

When Sextus led his blind daughter back to their camp on the Vatican Fields, along the *Via Triumphalis*, he said to her, "It's a good thing you didn't mention Piso's name, Desi. Because you know something? He was standing right next to the consul under that canopy. Can you believe it? I recognized him at once!"

"Oh no! No, no... Oh my father, I *did* mention his name, when I whispered in the consul's ear!"

"What!? Oh *nooo*... I only hope the man will keep this to himself."

"Yes, I hope so too."

They walked along in silence for a while, Sextus wondering about the *second* man who'd been standing right next to Piso, exchanging whispered remarks with him, apparently very chummy. Most of the conspirators he knew quite well by name, but except for Piso he'd never met any of them in person, so he had no idea what they *looked* like. In that respect everyone had the same disadvantage as his daughter: you knew many people and things only by a name or a word...

"Sextus?"

"Yes?"

"I should have listened to you; I'm sorry."

"Too late for that, my poor girl. But let's hope for the best."

The emperor had lost his palace, and a few days later, so had Tigellinus. The Praefect of the Pretorian Guard suspected that some occult forces were lined up against him and his master. But even the intelligence apparatus he had at his command was not functioning properly: in the chaos that prevailed at the moment, his network of spies and informers was in complete disarray. For the time being they were blindsided.

They had retreated to the Guard barracks outside the city. The imperial court, reduced to the closest intimates and a barebones staff, plus the security apparatus protecting them, were holed up in the fortress of the Praetorian Guard. Tigellinus had to assume that they were under siege. The place was not as bad as it sounded anyway: the *Castra Praetoria* was more like a huge castle rather than a camp. It was situated on a plateau outside the walls, to the east of the northernmost tip of Rome, because tradition dictated that the army was not allowed to stay inside the city. But it had very comfortable accommodations for just such emergencies as this, when the emperor needed to be kept safe.

"*Divus Imperator!*" the current praefect said forcibly to his master, a rather wan and shy-looking young man, "the whole thing is so *infuriating!* When *your* palace burns down, rumour has it that you did not come back from Antium *until* you were personally affected. Then when *my* property is destroyed, they say *I* lighted the fire *myself* to make place for a more valuable development... I would like to know who is responsible for such vicious misrepresentations. They are using our own losses, our own suffering *against* us!"

The young emperor looked up at his right-hand man with big, anxious eyes. He hated it when the incredibly strong and self-assured praefect gave every appearance of being at the end of his tether, of losing his grip on the situation. Worrying about these problems, these threats, was the last thing Nero wanted to be doing. They were sitting at a desk in one of the inner offices of the fort, high up in a defence tower of the outer wall, just the two of them, consulting confidentially. Through the narrow windows they could see black smoke still rising over Rome.

The older man stared stonily at the little pipsqueak sitting in front of him. Tigellinus was in his early fifties, lean, well-trained, the epitome of traditional Roman fortitude. He reflected that his young charge, at least, was back in Rome, where he belonged. There was no question now of moving from Antium straight to Neapolis before spending the winter in Greece! This whole crisis had the advantage of focusing the emperor's mind on his duties, away from his pleasures and from his hobbies. Writing and declaiming poetry! Theatre performances, with himself in the leading role! Endless orgies lasting into the small hours of the next day! He even liked to fantasize that he was a great chariot driver, dreaming of races and circus glory like some vulgar, pimply youngster! And now he was withering under his stare. Tigellinus forced himself to smile at his young master, although it felt as if it might crack his lips.

"Why do you do it, Tigellinus?" Nero suddenly asked with the brusque boldness of the shy, "Why do you put up with me? Why do you keep looking out for a miserable wretch like me with such dedication?"

The old patrician swallowed hard. "I'll tell you exactly why, Divus. As commander of the Guard you can make or break an emperor any time, that's a fact, but you can never become one yourself. Such are the dictates of our most sacred traditions... So I'd rather serve a man like you, who lets me do exactly what I want. Keep that in mind, always, and we will remain the best of friends. And as long as I'm in charge, nothing bad will happen to you."

"So what do you want me to do?"

"You must carry on with the good work. Show your face in public, even if you hate it; you must be seen to be caring for your people. That's the best antidote to the vicious rumours."

"Very well, Praefect. I like doing good things for the people, just like Seneca always taught me."

"Yes, well, Seneca had better keep out of all this; *you're* in charge now... And another thing: there are rumours going round that the Christians are somehow responsible for the great fire. I don't know where that absurd story comes from, but I intend to encourage it and to act on it, also as an antidote to all the slander against you."

"But I *like* the Christians! They're so friendly. My best slaves are Christians."

"I know. That's why I'm bringing this up beforehand. But it can't be helped, you'll have to sacrifice them. I'm going to have them all arrested and fed to the lions."

"But I have *forbidden* public executions, Tigellinus!"

"Well, believe me, Divus, the moment has come to offer the populace some old-fashioned entertainment. The Romans will soon be baying for blood, and I want to make sure that it is not *yours* that will drench the arena's sand."

Desi was worried sick after her interview with the consul. She realized it had been a big mistake. She should have known in advance that if she went to the highest authorities, some member or other of the conjuration was bound to be there; it was no coincidence; the higher you went, the more chances you had to run into them. If you'd just set fire to Rome, you would need to stay close to the centre of power, watching for opportunities to finalize the planned takeover. Then Desi would reason, "I only *whispered* Piso's name in the consul's ear," trying to reassure herself. But it was no good: even if Mucianus kept this information under his hat and acted on it later, Piso had been standing right there while she exposed the whole plot! Now the conspirators *knew* that she knew everything... infuriating!

"You should have listened to me," Feli said, as they discussed the situation endlessly, "I told you it was dangerous."

But Feli also pointed out that their enemies wouldn't be able to find them that easily in the masses of refugees scattered all around Rome. "I say we're safe in this camp; we keep our heads down; at all times we must stay where there are a lot of other people around." Feli could always be relied on to remain calm, and try to cope.

What they couldn't possibly know, though, was that Sextus and Desi had been followed on their way back home, on that fateful day, and that Rufrius had an agent spying on them all the time.

When they'd left the senate building, they'd had to spend some moments right in front of the entrance, taking their leave from Senator Canio and thanking him for his help. Rufrius, meanwhile, had taken leave of Piso and Consul Mucianus as soon as he decently could, but as it turned out he had plenty of time to give instructions to his most trusted agent, who was waiting in front of the building.

"Did you see the firefighter and the blind girl that just came out a moment ago, Mendax?"

"Of course, boss. I've been keeping tags on everyone going in or out."

"Did you see which way they went?"

"Yep. They took their leave from that senator and went off in the direction of the Campus Martius... they can't be far ahead."

"Perfect! Follow them and find out where they live."

After that, Rufrius started making plans. He was fully aware of the fact that the blind girl knew *everything*, each and every detail of the whole plot, all the names... how could he have been so careless! And how she'd fooled him! He would have to plan her destruction and his revenge with utter care.

And so, a few days later, a platoon from the urban cohorts turned up at the camp on the Vatican Fields. This caused a sensation, obviously, but even more so when they made a beeline for a blind girl sitting in front of the shacks, in the shade of a tree, carding some wool with a whole bunch of women around her.

"Desiderata Pomponia?" the leading officer said, "You are under arrest. I have orders to take you into custody."

Of course there was a huge outcry. Claudia stepped forward and literally threw her own body in the path of the armed police officers. Other women joined her and surrounded Desi. A few of them darted off to go looking for Sextus, who would hang out with the other men when he was not working. Feli clung to her friend as if her life depended on it, looking on with wide eyes, trying to understand what was happening. But poor Desi was in no position to communicate with her; everything was going very fast.

"Step out of the way, lady: I have orders. If you have any complaints, go through the proper channels."

"But this is ridiculous! She's just a child, and she's blind!"

"Yes: fifteen-year-old girl; blind; name of Desiderata Pomponia. That's the person we're looking for."

"And where are you taking her?"

"I'm not allowed to tell. She will be heard by the proper authorities as soon as possible."

"But can't you at least tell me what she's being accused of?"

"Again I am not allowed to say, but as a courtesy to you, lady: I heard something about arson and slander... now step aside."

"But this is ridiculous! This can't be right!"

It was no good. The officers were already making for their swords, closing their fingers around the grips and preparing to unsheathe the short, broad blades from their scabbards, eyes set on the people blocking their path. They knew from experience that this little pantomime would be enough to make the members of the public give up their resistance. As the women stepped aside, two uniformed men grabbed Desi by her arms and they started to drag her along with them.

"Just one moment," Desi said, and pretended to be tightening her girdle. Then she raised her hands and signed over to Feli, "Follow us at a distance. Find out where they're taking me." The men grabbed her wrists to prevent her making secret signals like that, but already the blind girl was walking along without putting up any further resistance.

"Desiderata!" Claudia screamed.

"It's all right, Mater! I'm sure I'll be fine!"

As they set off towards the bridge, Desi's mind was racing, and she concluded that her situation looked grim. Piso—or maybe Rufrius—had made his move. If he could get the urban cohorts to arrest her, this only showed that his plans must be going well; he must have acquired a lot of power in the aftermath of the great fire. It was very unlikely that anyone would let her tell her story to the authorities again. "The bastards! They're getting away with it!" She wondered if Nero was still alive.

Desi was also feeling extremely uncomfortable without Feli at her side. Being arrested and facing an uncertain fate was nothing compared to being separated from her "twin sister", her eyes, her champion tactician. Now she really felt totally blind. She focused her mind on the fact that Feli must be following them discreetly, gathering information about what was happening to her. But what could Feli do with that intelligence if there was no one she could communicate it to? Oh well, she would surely find something. And Desi concentrated on where they were going; the route seemed familiar; they were heading for the Forum again, so they were probably taking her to the old jail there, the Mamertine prison close to the Curia, the ruined senate building. Wait and see.

They walked for quite a while, as she now expected, and the uniformed men refused stubbornly to engage in conversation with their prisoner. These were highly disciplined professionals. Then they reached the Forum, still recognizable by the sound of serious business being discussed all over the place, and the delicious smells coming from high-end food vendors. Some things never change. And at last they stopped in front of a building that indeed had to be the Mamertine, and Desi was handed over to the warders: "Another one for you guys. Be careful: she may be blind but she's not stupid."

"When will I be heard by the urban praetor?" Desi cried to the officers, but they did not reply and their footfalls receded. The warders dragged her inside the prison building and through an echoing corridor. "No urban praetor for you, dirty Christian," one of them growled.

"I'm not a Christian, I'm the daughter of a free citizen of Rome!"

The man punched her shoulder, in a perfunctory way, just so she'd understand that discussions were useless. "Ouch!" Desi cried crossly. Then a lock rattled, she was pushed into a cell, and the door slammed shut behind her. The place smelled like the vaulted stone cellar of their insula used to, including a whiff of pee, and Desi found that reassuringly familiar.

"You are not a Christian, I think?"

The voice of the woman sounded a bit like Mater, only much older and rather more polished. "No, certainly not! Are you?"

"Yes, most of us here have that privilege."

Addressing another woman standing next to her, the posh lady added, "Can you believe it, Hosidia? Now they have arrested a *blind* young girl as well."

"It only goes to show how muddled they are!"

The two of them took Desi to a quiet corner and sat down with her on a bed of straw. The place was very crowded; the other prisoners muttered among themselves under their breath, which created a strange, subdued atmosphere. Many of the women around them were wearing chains, which rattled softly from time to time, but not those two from the 'reception committee'. Desi concluded that only the slaves were chained.

"You're not an escaped slave either, are you?" the first woman, the posh one, inquired.

"And who are you, if I may ask?"

"You may. I'm the deacon of the Christian women and children that are locked up in here. The men and the *real* deacon are locked up elsewhere. And what's *your* name, by the way?"

"I am Desiderata Pomponia, but you may call me Desi. I am not a slave: I'm the daughter of a free citizen of Rome."

To prove what she was saying, Desi retrieved the lunula hanging from a thin cord inside her tunic.

"A double moon crescent? Real silver! Quite unusual: beware of thieves!"

"Are the Christians thieves?"

"No, silly! The runaway slaves, the purse-snatchers. There are all sorts locked up in here with us."

"Well, my mother makes me wear my lunula on a long

188

string, so that it's always hidden away, inside my tunica."

"Very wise."

"Do you happen to know if Nero is still alive, my lady?"

"Are you concerned about him? Well, only this morning he was alive enough to have us all arrested!"

"*Nero?* The emperor? No! He's a good man!"

"Maybe, but he doesn't always listen to the right people."

"You speak as if you know him. Are you very posh?"

The old matrona chuckled, "Yes, I suppose I'm posh all right, and I know Nero well enough to conclude that our arrest was not his own idea."

"What's your name again? Or did I already ask?"

"You did. I am Plautilla, but most of us just call me 'deacon'."

"Plautilla! What a pretty name! I hate 'Desiderata', you know."

XI   1964: A Sunday quest

On Sunday morning the participants of the project had the opportunity to attend Holy Mass in St Peter's basilica. Seats had been set apart for their group, right next to the central aisle, where Sister Liz could stand before them and sign for the deaf without disturbing any other worshippers. The blind would have to make do with Latin.

In theory the Pope himself could have been saying Mass, but they'd heard he was staying at Castel Gandolfo, his summer residence. It took some time for the celebrants to enter the church in procession while a choir was performing beautifully. But when at last the booming, crisp sound of the first words of the ritual came out of the fancy loudspeakers, Daisy was not too surprised to recognize the voice at once: "Contini!"

"In nomine Patris, et Filii, et Spiritus Sancti..."

This was even better than hearing the Pope; to get to know another side of her new friend, in his capacity as a priest. He sounded boldly grumpy, a bit blunt, exactly like on the day they had bumped into one another. Saying Mass at St Peter's was not a joke. Maybe it was not the bishop's favourite part of the job, either, poor thing. At least, Daisy reflected, she also knew a more friendly side of the man now, humorous and quite tender in a reserved way. Mother Superior had called him an old goat; well, a very sweet old goat then.

She soon lost the thread. After all, she was not a Catholic, although a Latin Mass was not that different from an Anglican service with its specific, outdated, liturgical language. You lost the thread because it was only too familiar. Growing up in England in the twenties and thirties you had to go to church an awful lot, whether you wanted or not; whether you liked it or not; it had been part of public life. And you always kept to your own religion of course. Then, when she went to school, there had suddenly been a hodge-podge of denominations thrown together, Catholics, Non-Conformists, Presbyterians, even Jewish girls. The Anne Sullivan catered to blind girls only, so they couldn't afford to discriminate; there had been just enough blind girls in all of the United Kingdom and the British Empire to keep this one modest school going... And at school they'd learned to deal with other religions. The Catholic girls—a tiny minority—had told them they were not *allowed* to participate in the Holy Communion together with the Anglicans, because it was one of the *seven sacraments*, and was only valid if administered by a "real" priest. The Anglican girls had been scandalized by this highhandedness, but their teachers had told them they should learn to respect each religion's "sensitivities". The Catholic girls had insisted it was not just a matter of *sensitivities*, but that the *salvation* of their eternal *souls* was at stake. Oh, how they had debated!

The Holy Mass in St Peter's was a solemn occasion, and Daisy was thrilled to be there. But it went on and on. Endless chants, prayers, readings, hymns; the congregation responding swiftly to the prompts in liturgical dialogues that were unknown to her. Sometimes you had to kneel down, then sit up again, and when Morag prodded her she did the same as her friend next to her. The Irish youngsters around her were good Catholics all, no doubt; it was Daisy who could no longer say the same about being an Anglican. Not that she'd ever consciously decided this should be so, or even given it any thought. Things had just petered out, precisely because they went on and on. If you didn't pursue your faith actively, apparently, it all too easily slipped away... Until the end of the fifties she'd still accompanied her old neighbour to church from time to time, when she was in the mood. And Mrs Maurois had been so glad to have her by her side when they went together... but as a motivation this was not enough, it turned out, and since the sixties had started she'd stopped going altogether. "Still, at least I can't say I'm a complete *unbeliever* either... I think."

When she'd heard Contini's voice on the loudspeakers, Daisy had assumed they would not go looking for the stone after all. "It must have slipped his mind that today would be Sunday." But as soon as Mass was over, and the congregation started to file out, their group was accosted by Sister Tabitha, who reminded Daisy and Morag that Monsignor was expecting them in his office, and she offered to escort them there. Daisy told her and Sister Liz that Morag had decided not to come along, and that she would be off on her own now. "All right, dear," Liz said, "have fun!"

And that is how—next item on the agenda—in due course she ended up in the bishop's executive-sounding office again. "I have not forgotten our little plan," Contini cried as soon as he arrived, sometime after his secretary and his guest, "and Vanetta has been true to his word: I have a list and a map with the most promising churches marked down on it. I prefer not to count them, but there are quite a lot."

He then explained that Sunday, right after Mass, was actually the ideal moment to start the search. "That's when the sacristies with a phone will be manned, ready to answer our queries."

It was funny to witness how the bustling bishop seemed

to have already forgotten the extensive and demanding rituals he'd just performed in the biggest and most important church in all of Christendom.

At first Contini himself made the calls, sitting at his desk. Sister Tabitha looked up the phone numbers in a directory of some sort, and Daisy sipped the coffee she'd been served. There was not much she could contribute as she couldn't read the map, nor speak Italian. She listened intently at the conversations all the same, enjoying the language again: *"La lapide de Desiderata…"* But after a few calls the priest told the two women that it was no good. "No luck so far, and when they hear they have an archbishop on the line they clam up and want to put me through to their superior… Tabitha, you do the talking and I'll keep the records."

He pushed the phone over to his secretary and she started dialling the numbers he gave her and made the inquiries in a clipped and business-like manner. Daisy wondered if she was pretty, this Sister Maria Tabitha who sounded so youthful. She sighed wistfully. She would never know.

An hour or so later, Tabitha had canvassed almost fifty churches. Nobody had ever heard of St Plautilla as a church or chapel. Only fifteen of the people she'd interrogated had declared there were no old inscriptions, none whatsoever, on their premises. The rest did have some, but none of them had ever heard of the Desiderata stone.

"Which is no guarantee they don't have it," Contini commented, "they just don't know. Still, we can eliminate definitely those fifteen who are sure they have nothing of interest for us. Now I've written down a dozen names and addresses of churches without a telephone. I propose we pay them a little visit in my car, my dear Daisy. That should keep us nicely busy for the rest of the day."

"And how many churches are left to investigate after that?"

"I still haven't counted, but we're not even halfway through yet, not by far. Still, we've made a good start; we'll carry on like this for a couple of days; what else can we do?"

"And how do you propose to go about it? What is your method?"

"Well, for the moment we're concentrating on the city centre and the Vatican area: those parts of Rome that certainly existed in Rorick's day."

"All right, that makes sense."

As they left the office, Contini instructed his secretary to carry on calling any churches that had a phone, "Please write down the results, if you don't mind, my dear. When you're done you can go back to your convent."

"Very well, *padrone*, but I'll be taking a day off later in the week, just so you know."

Again they made use of a chauffeured car, but this time it was not Claudio at the wheel, but one Paolo. Daisy understood that the priest instructed him to drive calmly, as it was Sunday. At any rate the drive started smoothly, and they entered the first church on their list, quite close to the Vatican. Daisy followed her companion inside, holding closely on to his arm. Visiting a church was an utterly familiar experience, entering a space of echoing acoustics, of spacious sighs, muttered prayers, and scraping feet, with whiffs of old stones, polish and incense in the background. And immediately as they got hold of the sacristan, there was a lengthy exchange of respectful greetings—"*Excellenza!*"—and Daisy could feel her guide's arm moving forward as he offered his ring to be kissed by his underling. Then a lengthy exchange of subdued mutterings, in Italian, about the business at hand. The man was awfully sorry that he could not be of more service to his excellency. They left as quickly as was decently feasible.

And so it went on for another hour. In the next couple

of churches Contini did check on a few old inscriptions that were still on hand from a distant past, but none of them had anything to do with Plautilla or Desiderata. Then it was time for lunch, he pronounced. They drove straight to a restaurant he only needed to name to his chauffeur—*Il Livorno*—and as they alighted he instructed Paolo to pick them up again in a couple of hours. If you knew a bit of Latin and French like Daisy did, it was amazing how much Italian you could second-guess. After entering the establishment the bishop went straight to the phone and called up his office for the latest news. Still no results on Tabitha's side, and she was about to call it a day.

Anyway. A moment later they were sitting in a charming backcourt under a vine-covered pergola, the almost inaudible whisper of the leaves in the almost imperceptible breeze suggesting the words "dappled shade" to Daisy's mind. Contini read out and explained some dishes he could recommend from the menu card, and the waiter took their orders.

"They seem to know you well in this place, sir, no *Excellenza* and kissing of rings here."

"That's right, the proprietor has become a real friend; he's a closet communist and a professed atheist… so refreshing."

"I can imagine! It must be tiresome to be treated with such deference all the time. Speaking of which, why don't you drop the purple sash and skullcap on occasion? You could pretend you're just a 'normal' priest."

"Oh no! I'm not *allowed* to do that. Once ordained, always ordained."

"I see: it's one of the seven sacraments!"

"Exactly. Holy Orders, just like Holy Matrimony, once established, cannot be undone on this earth. Having said that, when we bumped into each other last week, I also found it quite refreshing that you couldn't see my 'rank', although you knew from the start that I am a priest."

"Yes, funny, that: on the second day of the 'project' Father Cadogan introduced you as 'our scholarly priest, Father Contini'. Then, when we bumped into each other, I could feel the buttons on your cassock."

"And when did you guess that I might be a little more than an ordinary priest?"

"Also funny: Vanetta calling you 'Monsignor' should have given away the game, but I thought he was only joking, because he is always so familiar with you. But when you drove us to the convent in a chauffeured car, and the mother superior called you *Excellenza*, I understood. I interrogated her as soon as you'd left, and she told me all about you. That you're a member of the Curia, and close to the Pope."

"And yet your attitude didn't change; I'm still simply 'Contini' to you."

"Maybe that's because I'm not a Catholic."

"I thought as much. Are you even a believer?"

"During Mass this morning I was wondering about that. If you don't pursue your faith actively, it slips away; I confess that I've let it lapse, rather. But I did conclude that I am not a complete unbeliever."

"Like so many people in our modern world... what a pity!"

"Mother Superior also told me you're a ladies' man, that you have a taste for pretty women."

"Ah, nasty gossip, who could resist it? But I plead guilty as charged... and why not? I *like* the wonderful creatures God gave us together with the ability to enjoy their company. As long as I keep my vows, there's no harm done."

"Indeed. If you *didn't* keep them, I would be the first one to punch your nose."

As it was Sunday, there was no debriefing on the a-

196

genda. When Paolo picked them up after lunch, Daisy and Contini went on with their quest, running through the different locations on Vanetta's map. They still had no luck, but they both enjoyed themselves very much, visiting all those churches like a pair of inscriptions-obsessed tourists.

For dinner the 'project' had an appointment at one of the convents that hosted the participants. Daisy was dropped off by the chauffeured car, in grand style, and escorted by a nun into the fragrant gardens of the convent, past a gurgling fountain to the place where the whole group was lounging in wicker chairs, having drinks in the mellow shade. She had to tell about her adventures, a kind of debriefing after all. Father Cadogan remarked, "The Desiderata stone, eh? My dear Daisy, this could be the title of a very exciting novel!"

Finally they went inside, where a table had been set apart for them in the refectory. As the group was settling in, Daisy knew that the deaf youngsters would cluster as far away as they could from Liz and Cadogan, delighted to be able to chat among themselves in sign language. The blind kids would do the same right next to them; and that for her the best thing to do was to orbit towards the "adults". The priest noticed the manoeuvre and was kind enough to facilitate it. "Daisy dear, why don't you join Liz and me?"

And that is what she did. This was an ideal opportunity to question her hosts about the background of the 'project', something she'd been wanting to do for some time.

"Yes, yes, I can imagine that by now you must be intrigued by all this," Father Cadogan said amiably, "and believe me my dear, there are no secrets here."

While they were being served by the nuns, and the younger participants tucked in without paying any attention to them, the Irish priest told his story. It had all started with a couple of colleagues and himself, who'd noticed how deaf kids were taken to Mass by their parents, and made to attend holy rituals they could not understand.

"Does it make sense at all to celebrate Mass for people who can't hear it?"

"Obviously not."

"Well, for some in the Catholic hierarchy the answer is not that obvious, alas. You may have heard about the debate going on about the Latin Mass, Daisy, even in that Anglican Britain of yours. It is one of the subjects being discussed right here at the Second Vatican Council these days. It looks more and more likely that we will soon be celebrating Mass in the vernacular tongues of the faithful, instead of Latin, the idea being that people should be allowed to *understand* what they are celebrating."

In Dublin a small band of crazy parish priests had decided that the deaf too should be able to follow Mass, and they set out to learn ISL and celebrate in hand signs for the deaf. They had gone looking for sign language interpreters like Sister Maria Elizabeth, who could teach them. Most of these teachers worked at specialized institutions for the education of the deaf. "But little did we know that we would be opening a Pandora's box of pent-up sufferings and frustrations!"

The Dublin priests were unwittingly catapulted in the middle of a protracted trench-war between specialized educators, a war being waged over the heads of the deaf pupils.

"You know, some of the people who decide about these things have a disturbing tendency to think that deafness is just a slight impairment, easily resolved. The only thing their charges need to do is to learn to read and write in English, lip-read and speak, and become normal members of the community. And we should all be grateful to them for making this possible. Well, thank you very much!"

During the Mass celebrations for the deaf, the priests had discovered the vital importance of sign language, the true mother-tongue of their target audience, the only medium that allowed them to be themselves. The ISL teachers and interpreters had told the priests how sign language was being repressed in the official schools for the deaf. It was time to find a fresh angle to illuminate this problem, and that is when he, Cadogan, had come up with his 'project'. As a priest he was also confronted with the problems of the blind; why not bring them together to gain new insights on the issue? So the idea for the scheme was born. This was the third year that he and Liz had organized a summer outing to the Vatican Museums for their charges, and it had never yielded better results.

"When we go back to Dublin next week, I'll be writing reports and publishing articles in the Catholic press about what we've discussed here, on the 'project'. I'll be trying to convince people that they need to take the deaf more seriously. So I'll be telling the public about this very smart and wise blind woman—totally blind since birth—who spontaneously came to the conclusion that her impairment was a mere *inconvenience* compared to what her deaf fellow-participants were suffering. And I'll be telling about these deaf girls who at some stage complained that they had to use *English* all the time, and asked to be left alone, so they could just relax and use sign language instead. And other stories like that. So now you understand why what we're doing here is so important for us."

"I see, yes... You know, you remind me of Mister Gantz, one of the teachers at my school for blind girls."

"And what was his angle? I'd be really interested to know."

"Well, he taught us to *focus*, to form a clear picture of our surroundings in our minds, and to keep track of our position on a mental map. That way we were taught to be less dependent on others."

"Sounds good! Was he a Catholic?"

"I don't know; he was from Latvia, I think."

"Ah. A Baltic German. Lutheran."

"So doomed to the eternal fire?"

"I'm afraid so, yes."

"Now you're being silly!"

"I know. Sorry."

"What a *polite* religious fanatic you are!"

"Yes. They can put that on my grave."

The next morning, when Daisy arrived at Contini's office, she was quite excited. She'd had an idea. In fact she'd had a strange dream that night. She explained to her friend and his secretary that the blind often have these nightmares, where the whole world seems to be slowly closing in on them. "Very disturbing of course, but last night, for once, the same kind of dream gave me a sense of pleasure, of discovery... I don't know; it was a relief that the world around me had come within my grasp, easier to touch. Anyway, when I woke up, I understood why I had felt so elated. It suddenly hit me that the Contessa who founded our convent still holds the key. It may not seem logical, but there you are."

Daisy explained that there was one piece of information they needed urgently if they wanted to find St Plautilla's chapel: *where* had young Lavinia spent her childhood? Where had she lived *before* she married and became Contessa Barelli? Because if she had such fond memories of the chapel, it is likely that it stood in her neighbourhood, that her mother could easily take her there on a regular basis.

"Of course my dear Daisy!" Contini cried, "why didn't we think of this before? It could narrow down our search quite nicely."

"So this morning at breakfast, I had to pester our mother superior again, but it was no good: she has no idea where the Contessa lived, not as an old lady nor as a child; she doesn't even know her maiden name. It is not mentioned in the Contessa's papers!"

"All right, but it should be easy enough to find that out from the public records, or in fact the *church* records. She must have been married by a priest, so the marriage records entered then will give us her maiden name. Knowing that, we will be able to find her birth certificate, or at least the church record of her baptism… That's the first thing we're going to investigate right now!"

Once again Contini manned the phone and spoke in rapid-fire Italian, while Tabitha brought in their first coffee. This time the bishop didn't mind the obsequiousness of his underlings. On the contrary, he seemed to relish giving orders to people working for the local diocese, who had access to the parish records of Rome and immediately looked up the references he required. From time to time he had to wait while they did what he'd asked, then, when they came back on the line he would scribble the results on a pad. Tabitha had retired to her own office next door. Finally Contini announced proudly, "This was not so easy, but fortunately I know a man at the ministry of the Interior, an old classmate from school, who likes to stay at his post in August because it gives him the feeling he is running the whole country on his own."

"Just like a certain archbishop who seems to have the run of the Vatican right now."

"Oh no, that is not the same thing at all: no one can take over from the Pope! But anyway, my old friend tapped his contacts at the public records so my information could be cross-checked. The Contessa was born Lavinia Rossi in 1789 in the San Lorenzo district, and she was a butcher's daughter. She must have been very pretty and charming, and her father must have made a fortune selling meat, because by the age of sixteen, when she married a young nobleman who was ten years her senior, the Rossi family lived at a fancy address in the city centre. The address of her childhood home, however, still exists and is situated in what was then, and still is now, a very ordinary neighbourhood. It is known as the San Lorenzo-Tiburtina neighbourhood. It is right behind the Termini station."

"And how many churches has Vanetta marked on his map in that area?"

"Erm… let's see… only four of them."

"So we can visit those in your car and be back in time for Cadogan's debriefing."

XII   AD 64: Thrown to the lions

On that first day in the Mamertine prison, Desi was in a funk, and she was racking her brains to understand what was going on.

First and foremost on her mind: what was Feli doing? She missed her "twin sister" and helpmate terribly. And she wondered anxiously how she was coping without any means of communicating with anyone: if only she'd learned to write in Latin!

And then she kept wondering why she was here, locked up with all those Christians: it did not bode well. This 'deacon' Plautilla seemed to think that it was Nero who'd had them all rounded up, but Desi was assuming that Piso was ultimately responsible for *her* arrest. And blaming the Christians for the fire was part of Rufrius's plot. It didn't seem to add up: how could the emperor and his enemies be carrying out the *same* plan now?

She would have liked to discuss this with Plautilla, but the deacon was very busy "tending her flock", as she called it. Some of the women and girls cooped up in the dank prison cell were having crying fits and nervous breakdowns, which brought in the warders, who started beating up the "noise-makers". Then Plautilla pleaded with them, asking permission to "lead prayers", arguing it was the only way for them all to stay calm. With her polished accent and her authoritative matrona's voice, she could be quite persuasive. So, reluctantly, the guards allowed the Christians to invoke their "sacrilegious deity".

"Oh our father, you who are in the sky," they all intoned softly, "you who created the earth and the sky, let your reign begin. Let your will be accomplished here on the earth, just like it is in the sky…"

Desi pricked up her ears: this was just some silly mumbo-jumbo, obviously, and although she didn't understand a word of it, somehow it didn't sound aggressive in the least. It was not like these people would want to start sacrificing babies any time soon. What struck her particularly was a line to the effect that this "father in the sky" should forgive his followers' mistakes, *just like they forgave others*. Now that was a strange petition, coming from people who had just been rounded up and locked away by their enemies!

Eventually Plautilla had a moment for herself and she came over. She settled down next to Desi, and stroking her shoulder in a maternal way, she asked softly, "Are you holding out, there? You're looking *so sad!*"

Desi swallowed hard. "That's because I can't weep, matrona, and I can't hide my feelings either. I miss my parents terribly, and especially my best friend, Feli."

Desi explained about this deaf girl, Felicitas, who always guided her and looked out for her; and that she, Desi, was the only person in the world Feli could talk to. "She's my eyes and I'm her ears and her voice."

Plautilla found the whole thing rather confusing: she could imagine a blind girl miming some simple instructions for a deaf one, but how could the deaf one ever reply? And what's more: "Your friend spends all her time with you? How so? Doesn't Feli have a home of her own? Or is she your sister?"

"No, actually she's my father's slave."

"Oh… So you have your personal slave, eh? How many slaves do you have at home?"

"Just the one... You misunderstand; it's not at all like it sounds; we're very poor. Feli is more like a *twin sister* to me, I can give you my word!"

"All right... And now you're missing her terribly."

"Yes! I'm no longer *whole* without Feli!"

After a short silence Desi said, "Plautilla? I have so many questions to ask!"

"I can imagine. Go ahead, ask away."

"What's going to happen to us, do you know?"

"They won't say, but I fear the worst. This whole operation doesn't make sense unless the emperor, or rather his deputy Tigellinus, intends to have us all publicly executed."

"Thrown to the lions!"

"Something like that, yes, I'm afraid."

"So that's why the guards let you pray: we're going to die anyway."

"Yes, maybe. They must know something."

"And that's why the others are so distressed!"

"Yes, of course. Even for us Christians it is hard to take. But I tell my sisters that as long as we're allowed to die together, it will be all right."

"But that's the thing: I'm not a Christian and not a slave! You and I are Roman citizens: they're not supposed to throw us to the lions, it's against the law. What are the two of us even doing here?"

"Don't ask me!"

Desi now told Plautilla what she'd heard at the baths. She had to whisper, as they were not allowed to make any noise, and she explained that it had been Lucanus's idea, originally, to blame the Christians.

"Lucanus! Well I never! From Rufrius I wouldn't expect anything else, but from our good friend the poet, no... He seemed to take a genuine interest in us; I had high hopes of converting him."

"So you know these people, Plautilla?"

"I know all of them, yes. And I've known Nero since he was a baby; I'm one of Poppaea's godmothers, too. When she married Rufrius at the age of fourteen, I knew it would only mean trouble."

"Really!? So you belong to the inner circle of the imperial court!"

"Yes, and quite a number of our fellow-prisoners are slaves from Nero's household."

"Of course: Lucanus said so! But how come the plotters are the ones who've spread these rumours first, and then it's Tigellinus who's had you all arrested?"

"I think that's quite plain: both sides find it expedient to use the same scapegoat."

Desi reflected for a moment, and she thought she now understood: Piso—and Rufrius—must have persuaded people in high places—like Consul Mucianus himself—that she was not only an arsonist and a slanderer, but a Christian too.

After darkness came, they were told to go to sleep, and they all settled on the straw. It was very painful for Desi, because for the first time in her entire life she was alone at night. Feli was not there, sleeping right by her side, her body heat always present. Other bodies were pressed against hers, Plautilla was lying next to her, with her arms around a little slave girl, an orphan. The blind girl and the orphan were both aware of the privilege they were receiving. The floor was hard and the straw was scratchy, but those inconveniences were nothing compared to Feli's absence. At length they all fell asleep and passed a fitful first night in prison.

And the next morning, a few hours after they'd received some stale bread for breakfast, something wonderful happened. The door opened and the warders pushed a new prisoner into the cell. "Another recruit for your gang, matrona," they told Plautilla, sniggering, "a thieving runaway slave girl!"

"Feli!" Desi thought, as she'd noticed the total silence coming from the new prisoner. She waved her arms and opened them wide, and the newcomer, her chains rattling, rushed towards her, and they fell into a tight embrace. They had never before hugged like this; they adored one another but took that for granted; they were not in the habit of expressing their feelings so freely. So it was with a little shudder of embarrassment that Desi finally disengaged herself and started signing with her hands.

"Feli! How did you get here!? What happened?"

Then she held up her hands to receive an answer, and Feli's signing was constricted by her chained wrists and produced rattling sounds, but she managed to communicate anyway. "I've just been arrested! I snatched the purse off a toff right in front of the prison. I made sure they caught me; the police patrol was just coming our way; I figured they would throw me in here immediately."

"Champion! So yesterday you followed me and found out where I was?"

"Yes, and then I waited for a long time to find out what they intended to do with you. I was hoping you would be brought over to the tribune of the urban cohorts or something: then I could have alerted your father."

"But how? How did you intend to do that?"

"I would just have dragged him along to the tribune's office, double-quick! But nobody came to fetch you. What I did notice were groups of people, youths mostly, who stopped in front of the prison, laughing, miming wild beasts. You know: with their fingers spread and crooked like claws, baring their teeth. They mimed how beasts attack their prey, and pointed at the windows of the prison, and then walked away, laughing... Then I knew that they were going to throw you to the lions, most probably... Sorry for springing it on you like this."

"It's all right, I already knew: the matrona and I had figured it out. And then what did you do?"

"I went back to our new place and I repeated the mimes to your mother. She understood. She was very upset, but at least now somebody knows what is going on. Then I went to have a look at the circus near our camp, you know the one. And sure enough, the same men who erected our shacks, the people from the navy, they were working on the circus near the emperor's gardens, preparing it for a big event."

"So that is where it will all end!"

"Probably. I've looked around in town: the great circus on the other side of the palace hill is completely destroyed, and the smaller ones outside the walls are badly damaged, and only a pile of charred wood is left of the new amphitheatre. So I'm sure, now: they will throw us to the lions right there, near our new home."

"But Feli, why did you make them arrest you? Now you will die too!"

"That is what I want. If they kill you and I live, I will be alone. That wouldn't make any sense!"

"Oh Feli, if only you'd let me teach you Latin!"

The two girls fell into one another's arms again.

Plautilla had witnessed their interaction with growing astonishment: so this was Feli and this was how they communicated. Like two little girls absorbed in elaborate hand games! "Good Lord in the sky," she thought, "thank you for letting me witness this before I die."

Desi turned to the deacon and told her the news: they were definitely going to be thrown to the lions, in the Caligula Circus by the Vatican hill. "Workers from the navy have already started preparing it."

"So Feli has been telling you all this? All right. Now we

know. Did she try to alarm your father? Will he try to get you out?"

Desi asked her friend, and Feli answered, "I tried, yes, but unlike your mother, your father does not understand me."

"But Mater will explain this to him! Surely the daughter of a real plebeian cannot be fed to the lions!"

"Your father is not always very effective."

Desi reported these remarks back to Plautilla, and the deacon said, "You know, Desi, you and I are going to be executed regardless. You, because you were framed. Me, because I volunteered."

"What!? You're here of your own free will?"

"That's right. I did it for the same reason as Feli. I refused to be separated from my flock. If they are killed and I stay alive, that wouldn't make any sense."

Plautilla explained that as long as their enemies were only executing a bunch of hapless slaves, they'd learn nothing from it. But if *she* joined the slaves and if they all managed to die with dignity, then it would make these people wonder. Or at least, that's what she was hoping. "We have to die like true Romans to make it count."

Having said that, Plautilla went back to the others. It was clear now that she had serious work to do. Discreetly she moved around, from one woman to the next, and one by one they heard the news: it was confirmed; public execution in the arena; the Caligula Circus near the Vatican hill. The deacon consoled each woman, tried to rub some courage into them with a comforting hand. She even did this with the purse-snatchers and the runaway slaves. Then she organized what she called "a special worship" for the Christian women, to prepare them all for their ordeal, and Desi and Feli did not participate. They sat to the side with the 'common criminals' while the faithful huddled in the middle of the cell, whispering prayers.

And life went on; they waited for their fate to unfold. When she was not busy, Plautilla and her special helper, Hosidia, liked to sit in a corner and chat with the girls. Plautilla was very curious about Feli, and Desi about Nero, so they exchanged stories. The matrona was thrilled to hear how the two girls had grown up together and developed their language so early and spontaneously, that they couldn't even remember doing it. "I always thought Feli had taught *me*, but recently she told me that she'd always assumed *I* had taught *her*. So we *really* don't know how it happened!"

Desi wanted to know what kind of man Nero was. Oh, Plautilla replied, he was so sweet as a child! But as a youngster he'd become very difficult; don't boys always? It was hard for the poor kid to have such an ambitious mother. She'd been obsessed with making an emperor out of him, but she never realized that he was not at all cut out for that kind of thing: too shy and weak-willed. He was always very serious about his poetry, though, you had to give him that. "And then, when he came to power at the age of seventeen... well, that would be enough to drive any boy crazy. Still, he did quite well, considering... Thank God he listened to the advice of some good people like Seneca and Burrus."

"When you say thank God," Desi asked, "do you mean the god of the Judeans? They're always preaching that there's only *one* god."

"That's right: we Christians believe in the Judean god, the creator of the world and of all that is in it. But he is also our father in the sky, who cares for us like every father cares for his children."

"But that doesn't make any sense! How can there be just one god? Only recently the emperor has built a temple for the worship of his dead baby daughter: new gods are added to the pantheon all the time!"

"Well, I know Nero and Poppaea. They're also supposed to be divine beings, but believe me, they're only human, too human."

Until then Plautilla had not tried to convert Desi or even explain her faith to her, but she clearly delighted in engaging this lively young girl in debate, as soon as she showed an interest and came up with questions. At another time, for instance, the blind girl asked, "Tell me, matrona, what is this thing about a Messiah? A Judean peddler on the Forum told my father that you Christians believe the 'Messiah' actually came, and went, and that no one even noticed!"

Plautilla and Hosidia had a giggling fit when they heard this. "Sorry, Desi, blame the nerves... The Messiah, absolutely. But the Judean peddler was probably thinking of a king who would take over and rule the world..."

"Yes, I even wondered if *Nero* could be the Messiah, in reality."

"You're a great fan of Nero, eh? He would like that... No, but the thing is, we believe that a man called Jesus was the Messiah, indeed, the son of God, the first-born, the one-and-only Son. But he did not come to rule the world, he came as our saviour."

"That I don't understand."

Plautilla took her time and made an effort. "Just imagine that the creator of all things decides one day to come down to the earth, as a human being... just imagine. Would he appear at Caesar's court? How boring! And who needs another king, raising yet more taxes and armies? No. God would want to meet ordinary people like you and me, simply become one of us, a member of the millions, embracing us with all his heart. That is what the Messiah came for; that is why Jesus was just a carpenter."

"A *carpenter*? The Messiah? You're not making sense!"

"Well, that is what we Christians believe. We're not claiming that it makes sense, but Jesus Christ came, and went, and no one even noticed, that's right, but he was our saviour. He gave his life for our salvation. You have to understand—this is the core of our faith—that God decided that he himself, as the Son, had to become a sacrificial lamb. He was crucified by the roadside just outside Jerusalem, thirty-something years ago."

"Crucified! Like a slave! What did he do wrong?"

"Nothing, really... it's a long story... and don't forget: they're going to throw *us* to the lions too, and did *we* do anything wrong?"

During this whole conversation Desi kept signing for Feli, frowning with the effort. The deacon looked on and marvelled: the blind girl seemed to be able to speak Latin with her mouth and... something else with her hands *simultaneously*. Astonishing.

"Does Feli understand what you're telling her about our faith?"

"Yes, yes, Feli and I are always mighty interested in religions, you know."

Desi told her new friend about the temple of Asclepius, how its forecourt used to be the marketplace of the religions in Rome.

"Yes, well, that's the problem," Plautilla grumbled, "our faith is not some fancy new thing you can take on next to your other gods."

"Is that one of your *rules?* That all the other gods have to go?"

"Not a rule, no, but a consequence. Once you've embraced Christ, believe me, all that other business no longer makes any sense."

"Feli says: if that's the case, no wonder becoming a Christian means trouble!"

"Well, tell her it's the *others* who have problems with *us*."

"Feli says she likes your religion already! But what *I* can tell you is that your faith is really hard to swallow for a true Roman."

"Don't I know it!"

A few days—and nights—went by. The death that awaited them was too horrible to contemplate. The two girls tried not to think of it; they lived in the moment, enjoying one another's company. The Christian women and children, on the other hand, kept praying to the Father and the Son, and asked what they called the Spirit to give them strength. And each morning, when the guards brought in the stale bread to feed the prisoners, the Christians would perform some kind of ritual, breaking a small piece off and eating it very slowly, to start with. Still complete mumbo-jumbo, Desi concluded, and Feli agreed. The only thing they approved wholeheartedly was the idea, that Plautilla kept repeating, that they would die together and give one another the strength to bear it. Desi said to Feli, "That's true. As long as you and I can hold on to each other, let the lions do what lions do... I'm so grateful you came to me, Feli, it's the greatest gift I've ever received!"

"You're welcome, blind one. You're my twin sister."

"Wait..."

Desiderata fumbled with the cord around her neck, pulled it over her head, brought out her silver lunula from inside her tunic and hung it around her friend's neck.

"There, deaf one, it's yours. Now you're a freedwoman."

"The greatest gift I've ever received!"

And then, on the fourth night, the guards burst into their cell with a detachment of uniformed police, and they were rudely roused from their sleep and bundled into an oxcart waiting in front of the prison. They were all chained together, even the real citizens, and the cart trundled off, leaving the deserted Forum, the uniforms marching left and right with lighted torches. Every precaution to make sure no one tried to escape. Behind them, at a distance, they could make out another cart, containing the men, with another torch-bearing escort.

After a long trek through the darkened streets, in the middle of the night, they arrived at the circus near the Vatican hill. They were led down a narrow stone tunnel into the vaulted basements under the stands of the racing track. Straight away, they could hear and smell the lions—who'd already been brought in—even before they could see them. It was awful.

Cages had been erected in the dimly lit dungeon, and the prisoners were herded into a holding pen, separated from the beasts only by iron bars. "That way they can get to know their next lunch," the guards joked, "stay clear of the barrier, you hear?"

And indeed, the lions, more than a dozen of them, showed great interest in their new neighbours, the tiny flames of the oil lamps reflected and multiplied in their staring eyes. The guards—different from those of the Mamertine—took away the prisoners' chains, joking again that all that iron was not good for the teeth and stomachs of their "darlings". And then, very suddenly and swiftly, they grabbed a couple of young girls and started to drag them off. The girls screamed and their mothers tried to tear them loose from the guards, but they were mercilessly beaten back with truncheons. The men slipped out with their catches, slammed the door of the cage shut, and locked the others up.

"Hey!" Plautilla shouted, "what do you think you're doing?"

"Just lend us those two, boss. It's for the gladiators. We'll bring them back later. You're all gonna die anyway, so it would really be a shame to let such a pair of lovelies go to waste."

Plautilla scolded and pleaded, "Have you no human decency at all?" But it was no good; the guards persisted stubbornly, and the two girls wailed in desperation as they were dragged away. The guards led them through the access tunnel to the makeshift barracks on the Via Cornelia, in front of the circus, where the gladiators were staying on their last night before these games. Some of them, they knew, would not live through the next day. The sobs of the girls died off as the outside door was shut on them.

Desi realized that they sounded quite young; their mothers kept wailing pitifully. "Poor Christian girls," she thought, "it could just as well have been me!" How lucky she was that men were always so put off by her blindness; she'd been told often enough that she was an attractive girl too, in a way, but that the ghoulish slits of her eyes were just too horrible to look at. A Gorgon mask. Desi thought, "If only I could put off the lions the same way, tomorrow!"

"You rapists!" Plautilla screamed very unceremoniously when the kidnappers returned without the girls, after delivering them to the gladiators. She was trembling with rage. "Now we know who the *real* wild animals are!" And Desi reflected that it is not always possible to *forgive others their trespasses*.

And then the male prisoners were brought in, and were herded into another cage next to theirs. The Christian women and children rushed to the barrier separating them from their men, and they all started to cry out at once. They grabbed the men's hands through the bars, and held on to them; the same emotional reunions played themselves out over and over again. The mothers of the two abducted girls told their husbands about what had happened, they wailed again, and the fathers wept with despair. Plautilla was also talking to a man, an old chap by the sound of it, but she was speaking in a foreign language Desi did not recognize. Probably not even Greek, but some Judean dialect. The only thing she could make out was the man's name: Plautilla called him "Cephas". The two seemed to be very close, but more like siblings than spouses. The old man must have been the "real" deacon.

After a long while things settled down a bit, and the Christians started to pray and sing softly, standing close together by the barrier that separated them. Desi and Feli moved over to another corner of the pen and started to converse silently with their hands.

"Tell me, Feli, those lions, do they look fierce... or not?"

"No. They look very puzzled. If they weren't so big and dangerous, it would almost be comical. They all seem to think that we're a bunch of awfully excitable monkeys!"

"Exactly! They're not used to so much noise. And you know why? They must have been brought in from the zoo in the gardens of Lucullus. They're used to people who laugh and are relaxed. Nero has forbidden executions by beasts for so long, that these lions have probably never done this before. And do you remember what the men at the baths said, on that very first day? It's not so easy to get big cats to attack human beings. You have to train them for that. I'm pretty sure these goons, here, haven't had the time to do that properly."

"So what do you have in mind? I can see that you're starting to make plans!"

"Yes. It's a remark the matrona made a moment ago: she said those goons are the real wild beasts. And now I'm just thinking: she could be right, and these lions could really be quite domesticated."

"Good! Carry on; I like it when you start using your head again; it's been a long time!"

216

"Very funny... Now tell me: do you remember what happened to the cat on the night of the fire? How he followed us to save himself?"

"Yes. I'm the one who told you about that. He must still be chasing mice all over our old neighbourhood right now. Why do you ask?"

"I was just thinking... Do you remember how I used to make sounds with my lips, when the cat was torturing a mouse? Tell me: how exactly did the cat react when I did that?"

"It's funny that you should mention it: when you did those things with your lips pinched so, the cat would look very puzzled, exactly like the lions are looking at us right now. Why are you asking? What is the idea?"

"There are two things. They always say that cats are not obedient like dogs, but I think cats are smart enough to look up to us humans and follow our lead when they need to. That is what saved the life of our attic cat on the night of the fire. The zoo lions could well be domesticated enough to do the same thing, in a way, tomorrow. When they'll be sent out to devour us during the show, they might look at us, and go like 'What's for lunch, humans? What are you going to feed us today?' They might be a bit confused for a while, look at us like *carers* and not like prey, and while they think it over, I want you to walk us back into the lion's pen, real calmly, and then right to the exit. What do you think?"

"It could work! And what is the second thing?"

"We might confuse the big cats further if I whistle like a bird. And also: we might make ourselves less appetizing for them if we use the same stratagem we used as beggar girls. There's a slop pail in here, I heard and smelled, so in the morning, before it all starts, we'll have enough stale pee at our disposal... is there any white powder growing out of the stones?"

217

They were standing in front of the only wall in their prison; the other three sides were barred off. And Feli signed, "There is some, higher up, where the vaulted part begins. You'll have to give me a leg up."

"All right. And I need you to study the lay-out very carefully, see if you can figure out an escape route."

"Well, your idea of just walking out through the lion's pen could work: the door of their cage doesn't have a key lock like ours, it's bolted shut with an iron latch secured by a wedge. Even from inside the cage you can easily open it with your hands through the bars."

"Excellent! So that part won't give any trouble... now about the escape route... how about the tunnel we took when we came in?"

"I can see it through the bars... but it's closed, and anyway it leads to the road. Tomorrow there will be guards outside."

"That's true. Keep looking; keep studying the lay-out."

They now slowly crept along the barriers, the ones without lions, and Feli looked intently through the bars, scrutinizing the vast stone vault under the circus stands, lighted only dimly by some oil lamps, and she reported what she saw to her friend. The Christians had finished worshipping and had settled down on the straw, huddling close to the bars that separated the men from the women. They were trying to find some rest, some sleep or some peace of mind if they possibly could. But the two girls were wide awake, investigating, excitedly planning a purely hypothetical escape as a way of keeping their hopes up just a little while longer. Desi suddenly stopped in her tracks, turned her face to the outside space, and stayed completely still for a long moment.

"Feli! I can feel the air *moving!* And it smells funny. Does the tunnel towards the street have an open lattice as a door?"

"No. It's a massive one, I can see it. A heavy, iron-clad

door, and it's shut."

"Can you see any other opening out there?"

"Wait a second, there's something strange... this basement has been *flooded*... that's why the white powder is only
present at the top of the wall. The rest has been washed clean
by streaming water."

"Streaming water! Of course! Do you remember what I
told you once about the *naumachiae*, the naval fights? They
flood the arena of a circus and stage battles with scaled-
down warships. One of the few spectacles the emperor still
approves of, although they're no longer as deadly as they
used to be... Now, Nero had this place *refurbished* a few years
ago..."

"Blind one, you're a champion! I can *see* it now: the
flames of the lamps are flickering in the airflow all the time...
of course! And the smell you just mentioned, I can make it
out too: a slight whiff of *mud.*"

Desi crouched, patted the ground, rooted under the
straw with both hands, and came up with some sticky sand
on her fingers. Then she signalled, "Silt from the river! They
must have built an underground channel from upstream to
flood the circus arena with river water when needed. And
when they do that, the river flows right through these basements."

"Bingo! So when we're out of the lion's pen, you take the
lead and just follow your nose... and that way we can find
the entrance to that channel."

In the end everybody did fall asleep, even the two girls.
The last exchange they had before they drifted off, was Desi
promising Feli that if they ever got out of this alive, the first
thing they would do was to buy a slab of marble, and Desi
would write down their story in an inscription.

"And we'll tell the whole world that Piso did it, and then

we will hide the stone in such a way that we'll always know where it is, but Piso will never find it…"

In the morning they all slept late; they were exhausted, and the daylight did not reach into the dungeon much. But then they were rudely woken up by all the guards coming in at once and banging on the metal bars with their truncheons.

"Rise and shine, convicts! Showtime!"

The two girls that had been taken away that night were brought in and shoved back into the women's cage. There were tearful reunions with their parents; the mothers took them in their arms and tried to console them. In between sobs the girls then haltingly told them that they'd been given the choice: stay with their captors, those of the gladiators who would survive, and become their "companions", or return to their parents and share their fate. So they'd chosen to be mauled by the beasts instead of becoming their rapists' mistresses. Desi was impressed: for these Christian girls it really counted for something to die together with their parents and with the other faithful.

"I wonder what Mater and the PF are doing right now?"

Then the head of the guards—one of the kidnappers—rapped with his truncheon on the iron bars again and called out, "Hey, you, the blind one! Come over here, we want to tell you something."

Desi moved forward, towards the front barrier, and Feli followed close behind.

"Only the blind one!" the guard snarled, "are you deaf?"

"Yes, she's deaf all right," Desi told him, "you can bellow as much as you like, she can't hear you. What do you want from me?"

"There's a gentleman here who wants to talk to you, that's all. Go ahead, Metellus."

"*Avē*, girl, I'm the *editor* of the show today, on behalf of

220

the emperor. You know: I'm like the stage manager at the theatre, who gives directions to all those involved... Now, blind one, are you willing to die first? It's a huge privilege to be the first one to go, you know."

"Yes, I can see that. I'm willing to be the first victim, but only together with my deaf companion, here. We've already agreed we want to die together."

"All right, I can accept that, it will even add an extra pinch of spice, but you will be the one who plays the *star role...*"

"What role? What do you want from me, editor?"

The man, Metellus, what slightly taken aback: this strange girl sounded so *eager*. Well, he was eager too. "You know what my biggest problem is? You don't want the execution to go *too* fast... you want to add some suspense, a little twist that makes the thing just a bit more... interesting for the audience. You know?"

"Yes, yes, so what is it; what is your great idea?"

"Well, when I heard there'd be a *blind* convict today, and about twenty women and children too, I had this wonderful flash of inspiration, based on the fact that big cats always *walk off* with their catch and take it to a quieter place to devour it at their leisure."

Metellus explained enthusiastically what he envisioned. They had built a *collapsible* cage, see, and placed it right in front of the imperial box. The women and children would be placed inside the cage, and then a *ribbon* would be tied around it, knotted in a bow, holding it together like a big gift-wrapped parcel. You know?

"Sounds interesting. And what is my role in all this?"

"You will be standing in front of the cage, facing the entrance of the tunnel through which the lions will arrive. You will have a cord attached around your waist, a cord linked up to the bowknot of the ribbon holding the cage together. When the first lion, the leader of the pride, comes out, she will seize you, drag you off, and the bowknot will unravel. The cage will fall apart, releasing the other convicts, and the rest of the pride will start helping themselves."

"I see, yes. Interesting concept."

"It wouldn't work if you just bolted right away, the moment they let go of you. I need someone who volunteers to stay put. And when I heard there would be a blind girl on board, I thought, 'Aha, that's the solution I was looking for!' You won't even *see* the lions coming, right? Surely it won't be asking too much for you to stay where you are, you know?"

"No worries, Metellus, I'll be glad to oblige."

"Good, good!"

There was little time left for the girls to rub themselves with urine, to put it in their hair and on their arms and legs. They had to give up on spicing their concoction with salt-petre. Then they were all herded out of their prison and ga-thered in front of the tunnel leading to the arena. The guards with their truncheons made sure they stayed in line. Desi and Feli were standing right at the front of the group of women and children, with Plautilla just behind them.

"Why did you do that?" the deacon sniffed, "rub your-selves with pee?"

"Psst! It's part of our plan," Desi hissed, "don't give the game away!"

"Oh."

The older woman marvelled at this. She'd been impres-sed by the blind girl's conversation with that awful editor a moment ago: how calmly she'd volunteered to die first, and how casually they'd discussed her impending death! But now it turned out the girl had cooked up some half-baked plan of escape, probably together with her deaf friend. What a strange phenomenon: until now she'd appeared incredibly mature for her young years, but suddenly it turned out she could be incredibly childish as well. She was no different from the little boy who'd just asked her, "Deacon, tell me, is God going to save us at the last minute?"

"Maybe; let's hope so," Plautilla had replied. Oh well, as long as they all died with some dignity, that was all she was praying for.

It turned out they had to wait in line for hours, while the gladiator fights took place. In the end Desi couldn't help nudging the deacon again with her elbow, and she whispered as softly as she could, "Plautilla, I've always wanted to ask: how many Christians are there in Rome anyway?"

"Not many. If Feli can count, ask her to look around and tell you how many we are."

"You mean *all* the Christians are *right here?* There are no others?"

"No. Apparently Tigellinus kept tabs on all of us."

"Really!? But that's terrible! If the lions do attack us, none of you will be left!"

"Don't worry, Rome is not that important for the Church. There are a lot more of us in Jerusalem and in Judea; there are even a few communities in Greece and Asia Minor, in Corinth and Ephesus."

"Shut up, convicts!" the head guard growled, "Prepare to die."

In the meantime Feli was observing with growing concern how the guards were handling the beasts. They were standing in the women's cage, alongside the lion's pen, armed with long and sharp-looking pikes. One of them was holding a big chunk of meat and walking up and down with it in front of the hungry animals. They followed him back and forth inside their cage, licking their chops. At least some of them did. Feli noticed that the meat was tied to a rope, and she could imagine all too well how the game would be played.

Soon the men would start harassing the beasts with their pikes, exasperating them into a frenzy. Then, when they opened the gate of the tunnel leading to the arena, they would dangle the meat in front of the entrance and the beasts would rush out, and the dangling meat would be pulled up and out of reach in a flash. Then the lions would devour the convicts in a burst of rage. These men were not stupid, Feli concluded. They might not have had the time to train the beasts properly, but that didn't mean they couldn't handle them.

She decided not to report these observations to Desi: let her count to the very last on her hopeful theories. They waited some more, feeling hungry in spite of the fear gripping their stomachs. But obviously you didn't feed prisoners who were going to die in a moment anyway.

Finally Metellus gave the signal to start their part of the show. The convicts were pushed through the tunnel and emerged into the open, where other guards were waiting. It was early afternoon and the summer sky was deep blue, the sun beating down on the white sand of the arena, blinding them, who had just come out of the gloom of the dungeon. Desi didn't notice it; only felt the warmth on her skin; and Feli closed her eyes until they were accommodated to the glare. But for those who could hear it was the roar of the crowd that was even more overwhelming: it kept surging, and continued unabated.

The women and children were herded towards the collapsible cage. After they'd stepped over the grilles lying flat on the ground, these were quickly raised around them and tied up together. Meanwhile a helper tied the other end of the "ribbon", the ripcord, tightly around Desi's waist, pulling the knot solid and smearing some sort of grease on it so that she couldn't possibly untie herself.

Desi thought, "What's wrong, Metellus, don't you trust

me?"

She and Feli were left standing in front of the cage, facing the tunnel of the lions' pen. Feli crept away behind her friend, putting both her hands on Desi's shoulders so she'd know she was there. Desi wouldn't see the beasts coming and wouldn't be as afraid as Feli now was. Besides, deep down Feli just knew, somehow, that her "twin sister" wouldn't mind dying first. She'd volunteered. And if the leader of the pride dragged Desi off, and the other lions left them alone, so she herself could get away, her friend wouldn't even mind being the only one to die, surely.

Desi stood erect and the crowd kept roaring. Most people found the blind girl hilarious, and the other one cowering behind her even more so. There was much laughter and applause, to the editor's great satisfaction. Some plebeians on the back seats high up on the stands started chanting, "Run, girl! Run, girl! RUN!"

Desi thought, "You bastards, I won't give you that satisfaction!"

Then she heard the first angry howls of the lions, coming from inside the tunnel, as their handlers prodded them viciously with their sharp pikes. She squared her shoulders a little more, and put one leg in front of the other to secure her stance.

She thought, "I will die like a true Roman."

But it was not like anyone had even bothered to respect her citizen's rights, either.

She thought, "Silly me!"

From the women's cage the deacon cried out to her, "Desi! Be brave! We will meet again at the end of time!"

She thought, "Oh, Plautilla!"

The lions were coming.

XIII 1964: Finding Desiderata

The search was not very successful. First of all, it was Claudio again who chauffeured them from the Vatican to the San Lorenzo neighbourhood. He drove like a madman.

"Can't you tell him to behave, my dear Contini?" Daisy remonstrated.

"I've tried, believe me, time and again, but it's no good. He just can't help himself. The only reason I put up with it is that he's a good Catholic, with eight children to feed at home. And he's clever enough to remind me of that when needed."

Claudio had no idea they were talking about him.

They started with the church closest to the street where Lavinia was born. It turned out to be "new" all right, Baroque, with no old relics, not even an antique inscription of any kind. And the priest who happened to be present had never heard of a St Plautilla chapel nor of the Desiderata stone.

"No luck so far. Still, my dear Daisy, your hypothesis is sound, we must carry on."

And as he could see on the map that the other churches they had to visit where within walking distance, he decided to let Claudio wait for them in front of the first church, and to proceed on foot. They spent a few hours making a little round along the churches in Lavinia's old neighbourhood, further and further away from her place of birth. While they strolled from one church to the next, Contini told Daisy about the district.

"It's very popular with students nowadays, because *La*

Sapienza University is nearby... although the San Lorenzo campus would not have been built yet around 1800, when little Lavinia lived here."

"And did this area already exist in Rorick's day?"

"Excellent question, my dear! But I think I can reassure you: yes, probably. Although this neighbourhood lies *outside* the Aurelian wall of ancient Rome, the Via Tiburtina leads right through it; the highway to Tivoli. A new residential area would have appeared along that road long before the fall of the Roman Empire, and some of it would have survived in Rorick's time."

As they were roaming the streets, Daisy hanging on to her companion's arm, they were suddenly heckled by a cheeky passer-by: *"Ciao, Monsignor, ciao Doris Day! La donna è bella e il vescovo è cornuto!"*

"Typical Roman *esprit*," Contini grumbled, "I won't even attempt to translate, it is not suitable... but who is this *Doris Day* I keep hearing about?"

"Oh, just a Hollywood actress who's all the rage at the moment. We're exactly the same age and apparently I look a lot like her."

"Very flattering for you, no doubt."

"You're such a scholar, Contini, and you've never heard of Doris Day! Don't you ever go to see a film?"

"God forbid... If I went to a cinema to watch a Hollywood film, that would immediately become front-page news in the communist press!"

Then, as they completed their tour of the local churches, still with no results, Daisy started to have some misgivings.

"Contini, we've run out of churches! If this really is the neighbourhood where we should be looking, then we have to wonder: does the St Plautilla chapel still exist at all? For example, you mentioned that the present-day *La Sapienza* campus was built *after* Lavinia Rossi's time: couldn't it be that *our* chapel was torn down to make place for the University buildings?"

"Yes, you're right, I was thinking along the same lines. There's another part of this area that did not exist in 1800: the Termini station."

"Of course! The first railways weren't built before the Contessa had become an elderly lady."

"Exactly. And though I'm not too worried about the University site, on the other hand, if the chapel was situated where the station and the tracks are now, then we're in trouble. There wouldn't be a *trace* of it left."

"So we need to check the records on that point."

"Yes, time to call Vanetta. Therefore, time to have lunch, so I can get to a phone. But first I must give some instructtions to Claudio."

The bishop led Daisy back to the street where his limousine was waiting, and he told his chauffeur to go home for lunch, and come back over an hour and a half. That way they could get their blind guest back to the Vatican in time for her daily debriefing. Then he picked out a small restaurant nearby, hoping for the best, and as they went inside he asked the *padrone* if they had a phone. Daisy was led to a table and her companion into a back-office. The owner of this modest establishment and his whole family were very honoured to have a bishop as a guest, and after Contini had come back from making his call, some time went by as the owner, his wife, and three sweet little boys made a genuflexion and kissed his ring. He gave them his blessing one by one. Finally he settled down and ordered the plat du jour, "Nothing fancy or special for us, please, my son."

"Did you speak to Vanetta?" Daisy asked eagerly.

"Yes, no worries, my dear. I know exactly where he hangs out and how the Vatican telephone exchange can get in touch with him. I gave him our assignment and he'll call back this restaurant's number with an answer as soon as possible."

As she tucked in on a portion of delicious spinach *tortellini*, Daisy told her companion that she was feeling a bit worried. "I had such high hopes when I woke up this morning and realized we had to focus on the Contessa's childhood neighbourhood... but so far we've been drawing a blank. It's not looking good."

"I know, my dear, the results are discouraging; there's a good reason why the Desiderata stone is not in the Corpus; it is not that easy to uncover an inscription that has been lost for centuries. But I'm sure our approach is still sound... I'm trying to picture the Contessa's life in this area around 1800, and Rorick's visit to Rome in the 6th century, and I'm trying to focus on what would have stayed the same up to this day."

"Not so easy, I guess, and I can't help you much. Like Du Bellay said, '*Nouveau venu qui cherches Rome en Rome, et rien de Rome en Rome n'aperçois...*'"

They remained silent for a while, enjoying the food and taking a few sips of the house wine, then Contini continued, "No matter what Vanetta tells us, there is one place I want us to visit later this afternoon: the basilica of *San Lorenzo fuori le Mura*. As its name indicates, it is a prominent feature at the limit of this district. No matter what, it would have played an important part in the life of a Catholic family such as young Lavinia's, and it was definitely there in Rorick's day too, because it is one of the seven 'pilgrim churches' of Rome. That is also the reason why it is not marked on Vanetta's map: very old, Romanesque in style, not Baroque."

"Lavinia would have gone there on a regular basis, I see. Only, it can't be the 'St Plautilla chapel' of her youth, can it?"

"In principle, no, but you can never be sure... I'm just thinking... what if there is some little *side-chapel* there,

229

somewhere, that is dedicated to St Plautilla?"

"I see! And what if that side-chapel happens to be in Baroque style? That is certainly worth investigating, then!"

A moment later the *padrone* came over to their table and told the bishop that he was wanted on the phone. When the latter came back a moment later, he announced that there was no problem: the on-campus churches of old were still there, still on the same spot. As for the railway station and trails, Vanetta had consulted a couple of old city maps, and it was plain that although they'd torn down a fair portion of a residential area, no churches had been affected. "At the time the Pope was still in charge in all of Rome, and they wouldn't have dared!"

"Great! That's a relief, anyway... You know, Contini, your brainwave about the San Lorenzo basilica has rekindled my hopes a bit. Clever how you thought up a thing like that."

"Well, Rome is a wonderful place for someone with a sense of history, and as a priest, I have that more than most people."

While they finished their meal, they discussed this topic further. Daisy's companion gave her the example of the Tiber Island, where you have the *Fatebenefratelli* Hospital. "Just an ordinary hospital, nothing remarkable, but the fascinating thing is that it's situated just across the street from a church, St Bartholomew, and that the church is situated on the very same spot as the temple of Asclepius in ancient Rome, Asclepius being the Greek god of medicine and healing. The temple was established in the 3rd century BC, so you could argue that the Tiber Island has been dedicated to medicine for more than two thousand years."

"Really? So what you're saying is that apart from the obvious *monuments*, like the Forum or the Pantheon, you also have *functionalities* that survived in Rome over millennia."

"Indeed, very well formulated, my dear!"

"Well, that's fascinating... any other examples you can think of?"

"Erm... let me see... surviving functionalities... well, take the Villa Borghese gardens, one of the biggest and most popular parks today. In antiquity you had the gardens of Lucullus on the very same spot. It probably already had some kind of zoo, too. And in ancient Rome, of course, you had *cemeteries* along the main roads just outside the city gates. I've already mentioned this. Today, the biggest cemetery of Rome is the *Campo Verano*, near the San Lorenzo church we'll be visiting later. But the remarkable thing is, it lies right next to the old Via Tiburtina, on the site of ancient Christian catacombs, so in that sense you could say that this cemetery too has existed for almost two thousand years."

"Another reason to check out the place! And how about the Vatican? Were there any important temples on the Vatican hill in ancient Rome?"

"No, actually. The Vatican is a real upstart! The first basilica wasn't built before the 4th century. In earlier times the Vatican plains were just an area of market gardens and private parks outside the city. The official story is that the 'Circus of Nero' was also there; that's where St Paul and St Peter are said to have been martyred."

"And St Plautilla would have been present too, for moral support, before she was martyred herself, sometime later."

"Precisely. So the current basilica is reputed to stand on the tomb of the apostle Peter, but the exact location of the circus is unclear: it would have been situated along the Via Cornelia, outside the city, on the other side of the Tiber."

At the debriefing, that day, Daisy was feeling nervous and impatient to go back to the search, understandably. She told the group she could no longer report about art appreciation, as she and "Father Contini" were still looking for the Desiderata stone: "We've gone into the field now, that is to say, we've been searching all over Rome."

The others reacted with remarks along the line of, "Oh, that again, haven't you got enough of it already?"

Daisy reflected that it was only the second time she told them about this, so: "Excuse me if I'm boring you!"

On the other hand, it was the first time Morag reported extensively on her activities. After she'd taken stock of all the treasures the museums had on offer, she was now concentrating on the examples of cross-over influences between antiquity and the Renaissance. "After all, the artists of the Italian Renaissance must have been very familiar with the Vatican collections, and the Greco-Roman art on display inspired them tremendously. That was the whole point of the Renaissance, right? So, looking at the collections, you can find all sorts of very concrete details from, say, antique sculpture, and find them back in details of anatomy in the later Italian paintings... I was never much interested in sculpture before, but now I'm comparing statues and paintings all day long! And the funny part is: I don't even need English for that, not until I write up my results. For the moment I'm only using my eyes and my brain."

Daisy was glad to hear that Morag was having a good time on her own; that she really didn't mind them pursuing different interests; that there were apparently no hard feelings between them.

Then, at last, she and Contini were chauffeured to the *San Lorenzo fuori le Mura* basilica. The bishop had announced his visit over the phone, and they were received by a very knowledgeable priest, Father Formenti, who spoke good English. He led them on a grand tour, after kissing the ring and all that, first through the echoing main hall of the ancient basilica, then he showed them around in the cloister. This was literally packed with tombstones, slabs of marble covered with Latin inscriptions, "All from antiquity, and well-documented, of course." There were also beautiful Roman sarcophagi that had been recuperated by Catholic prelates like Cardinal Fieschi for their own burial. This last one, from the second century AD, was a real jewel of classical sculpture. Daisy would have liked to don her rubber gloves and investigate, but she let the man lead them around and talk for a while, before she made use of an opening to explain their mission to him, and the facts of the case. Fortunately, the man could listen too, and was very willing to help, but also very apologetic when he told them there was not much he could offer them.

"The story of the young Contessa is charming and fascinating, no doubt, but I wouldn't know of any Baroque chapel within this church complex that would answer your description. A *Baroque* St Plautilla side-chapel? I think not!"

"Well, it probably went by another name, officially. It was only called St Plautilla in the popular, oral tradition."

"Even so, it doesn't ring a bell, and the Baroque part is out of the question! Now for the other part of your story: Bishop Rorick's reference to the stone in his Compendium, and the mention by Aristobulus a couple of centuries before that. This is interesting, because you *did* have a lot of Christian catacombs around here in those early days..."

"Yes, yes, but all the catacombs are well-documented too," Contini interrupted, "please remember that we are looking for an inscription that is *not* in the Corpus."

"Even so, *Excellenza*, I have a suggestion. A place that would have been familiar to the Contessa in her childhood, and that might have been a remnant of a Christian shrine from the earliest antiquity... yes, it fits the bill quite well, except for one small detail."

The chatty priest was silent for a few seconds, to heighten the suspense, then he asked rhetorically, "Did I mention that our church was badly damaged by Allied bombs in 1943?"

"No, you didn't," Contini growled, "but I'm well aware of this fact. It has been beautifully restored, I must say."

"Well, there used to be a charming Baroque chapel on the Via Tiburtina, a few hundred meters down the road from here, in the direction of Tivoli. It would have been there around 1800, officially known as the *Sacro Sangue dei Martiri*, the 'Sacred Blood of the Martyrs'. During the same bombing I just mentioned, it suffered a direct hit. It was completely destroyed."

"Oh no!" Daisy cried, feeling very guilty. She was married to a former bomber pilot, and preferred to keep this painful truth under her hat. But she quickly calculated that Richard, her current husband, or Ralph, her first one, could never have been involved. They had both been stationed just north of London: Rome would have been way out of range for their Lancaster bomber, *D-Daisy*.

"So what are you telling us, Father Formenti? Could the Desiderata stone have been *destroyed* by an Allied bomb?"

"That I cannot say, my dear lady, but a new chapel has been built, sometime around 1950; it is a modern, concrete and glass little building. You see, *Sacro Sangue dei Martiri* had always been very popular with the visitors of the *Campo Verano* cemetery: that is why they decided to rebuild it after the war. I'm only suggesting that you might want to check it out, because for the rest, as I said, it fits the bill."

"And is there a sacristan, or anyone to show us around?" the bishop asked.

"Oh yes, there is always a caretaker present. I happen to know him well: old Bertini."

As they walked down the busy road, Daisy holding on to her companion's elbow, they were both in a state of great trepidation.

"Contini, this is such an unexpected development, it is completely outside of the plan we hatched with Vanetta."

"Yes and no, my dear. Like you I'm of two minds about this. It seems a long shot, but the one thing that gives me hope is the *name* of the place. 'The Sacred Blood of the Martyrs', that's exactly how you would rename a 'St Plautilla', now that I think about it..."

"Yes, I can see that, she being an early martyr and all that... but what if the stone has been destroyed by a bomb?"

"Unlikely. If it had been displayed plainly in the Baroque chapel, it would have been mentioned in the Corpus, including the date of its destruction. The fact that it is not on record gives us some hope for its survival... we'll soon find out."

When they reached the modern chapel and went inside, the bishop gave a brief description, talking under his breath so as not to disturb the worshippers. The building was a plain concrete cube, basically, closed off on the side of the busy thoroughfare of the Via Tiburtina, except for some small square windows high up in the wall. On the side of the cemetery, however, the whole wall was made of glass, with huge windowpanes set in a framework of thin steel pillars. This glass wall afforded a beautiful view on the graves and the greenery on the *Campo Verano*.

"There are few ornaments, all of them in a modern, abstract style. The altar and the crucifix on the wall above it are also simple and austere... Now, I am rather critical of modern architecture in general, but this is really done in very good taste, I must say."

"It doesn't smell like a church at all, except for the burning candles."

"Yes, they have votive candles that the visitors can light themselves... Now, where is the caretaker we were told about?"

Scanning the chapel, the bishop soon spied an old man who was clearly not there to pray for a dear departed, but kept himself discreetly busy tidying things up, although the place was already spotless.

"*Signor Bertini?*"

"*Excellenza!* To what do we owe the honour?"

And of course he had to kiss the ring, and the archbishop gave him his blessing, and the worshippers spotted an opportunity and half a dozen people came forward, and Contini blessed them one by one. Then, when he could finally state his business, he first asked the old man if he had already been the caretaker before the war, to which the man answered yes. The two were speaking Italian, but never had Daisy listened more intently, trying to follow or to guess what was being said with deeper longing.

"So you've known the old Baroque chapel well, my friend?"

"Certainly, *Excellenza.*"

"And do you remember if there was an ancient *lapide* with a Latin inscription?"

"Certainly. A strange inscription, like a message scratched on a wall."

"Excellent! Did the message start with the word 'Desiderata'?"

"That I wouldn't know; I never really *studied* the stone that closely."

"All right... but now listen carefully: what happened to the scratched stone when the bomb hit the old chapel?"

"Nothing. Is it this old stone slab you are interested in?"

"Yes, of course! Where is it? Can we see it?"

"Well certainly. I can show it to you… and the blind lady can touch it."

Contini put his hand on Daisy's shoulder and told her, "The man says there's a stone here with a scratched message!"

"*Where?* Where is it?"

Signor Bertini did some guessing of his own, and chuckled, stamping his foot down on the concrete floor several times, *"Sotto terra! Sotto terra!"*

And as the old caretaker chuckled some more, the bishop translated: "Under the ground."

"Really? Is the stone *buried* here?"

"È sepolto?"

"No! No! Vienite con me!"

The old man led the way to a small door in the back wall, on the side, behind the altar. They entered a cramped vestry with an office corner and many racks with supplies: cleaning products, candles and all kinds of leaflets. Bertini tapped with his foot on a closed trapdoor in the middle of the cubicle's floor: "This is the entrance to the crypt."

He retrieved a big electric torch from a shelf, and stepping over, he pulled the heavy steel door open, switched on the torch and shone the light down a steep stone staircase, its steps gnarled by age and chipped by bomb damage. "For as long as I've worked here, our crypt was never open to the public. You can see why. Even without the bomb damage, it was always a bit tricky, and the vault downstairs is very, very narrow. The three of us can hardly fit in there."

Contini translated for Daisy, and added, "I'm sorry, but I don't think you can get down those stairs…"

Without a word Daisy opened her handbag and retrieved her collapsible cane, its segments folded up along an elastic string. She fitted the pieces together, and with a flourish she produced a thin white cane. Sweeping the floor in front of her she found the opening, and stepping right up to it, she stopped and prodded the first couple of steps.

"With this in my hand I can negotiate any stairs just as well as the sighted. Let's go."

"I'm impressed once again, my dear. In fact *I'm* the handicapped one now, as I'm wearing a cassock."

Daisy liked the man for saying that, but what she couldn't see was how he unceremoniously pulled up his robe, revealing the lower part of his manly legs, with old-fashioned calf-garters holding up his pure-silk socks. Bertini chuckled appreciatively.

"Seguitemi!"

He led the way down the narrow stairs, shining his big, powerful torch, followed by the bishop holding up his robe with one hand, and the blind Englishwoman tap-tapping with her cane. The old caretaker was having the time of his life.

At the foot of the stairs they followed a narrow corridor that wound a complicated path through sheer rock. As they probed their way forward, they had the feeling there was no end to it; even old Bertini, who was not doing this for the first time, remarked, "Isn't it spooky, Monsignor? It's been ages since I visited our crypt!"

"What *is* this place," Contini asked, "is it part of the Christian catacombs?"

"I don't think so, no, it is not a burial site as such. In fact, in the thirties a German archaeologist came here to examine our crypt, and get this: he concluded it must have been the cesspool of a public latrine! He could even tell that the latrine had been built under the reign of Vespasian, the emperor who came after Nero. Meant for the travellers on the Via Tiburtina, obviously."

"A *German* archaeologist, eh? In the *thirties*? Why on earth didn't he *report* the inscription to his colleagues in

Berlin?"

"Oh, he was not interested in the inscription at all. He was only sounding the walls and digging holes in the floor. And he could hardly believe his luck: an *authentic* Vespasianian latrine cesspool... all right, this is it; we're there."

They had just emerged into a vaulted space that was no bigger than a bus-stop shelter, and there, on the sidewall, a white marble plaque glittered blindingly in the torchlight, the thinly scratched letters of the inscription barely legible in the glare. Contini stepped forward and squinted at the first word.

"Daisy! *This is it!* The Desiderata stone!"

"Wonderful! Fantastic! What does it say? *Read it!*"

And then...

Then the electric torchlight went "poof" in Bertini's hand, its bicycle lightbulb exploding, like such tiny bulbs were wont to do at the most unexpected and inconvenient moment.

The two men cried, "Oh!" and *"Accidenti!"*

"What's going on?" Daisy asked.

"The light just went out; we're standing in pitch darkness!"

"Oh, poor things!"

"It's so strange, I feel like I'm already suffocating."

"Welcome to the world of the blind."

"And how will we ever get out of here? We're completely lost!"

"Not me, I'm not. Don't worry, I know exactly where we are and how we came here. I'll bring you two back to the staircase in a moment, but first I want to read the stone with my fingertips, if you don't mind."

Daisy knew exactly where the marble slab should be: Contini had looked at it and turned around to tell her "this is it". So it had to be right behind his back now, more or less at the height of his head. She stepped around him and probed the wall.

"Here it is. I'll read it out loud, and then I'll write it down in my notebook so you can have a look at it later."

She retrieved her rubber gloves from her bag, put them on, and started fingering the network of slight, scratchy lines, making out the letters and the words. It was no more difficult than making out the script on a wax tablet. What was different, though, was the fact that Desiderata herself had painstakingly carved these lines in the hard marble. Daisy already knew that stones could speak and had a mind of their own, but now she felt the unique thrill of connecting with her doppelgänger from ancient Rome, directly through her fingertips.

"So here goes: *Desiderata... Pom... caeca nata... sibi et Felicitati... ser... surdae... vixi cum ea... feliciter an XV... donec vitam sacrificavit... Urbe a G Pisone incensa.*"

"*Urbe a G Pisone incensa?* Really!? Are you sure?"

"Yes. That's what it says. I'll write it all down."

"*A Pisone!* Incredible!"

Daisy finished writing down the inscription, then she led the way back to the stairs, probing with her cane. She'd told the bishop to put his hand on her shoulder, and the caretaker behind him held onto his. He kept muttering, *"Piano, piano, per favore."* He sounded very nervous. When they finally emerged into the modern chapel building again, it was time to say goodbye. Contini thanked the old man for his kind assistance. Then Daisy had a thought.

"Ask him if people called this place St Plautilla once. Was it ever known by that name as far as he can remember?"

When the answer came, Contini translated excitedly that in the old Baroque chapel, before the bombing, there had been some frescoes of the saint binding her scarf over St Paul's eyes before his beheading, and of the apostle's apparition to give it back to her. So yes, before the war, a lot of

240

people had referred to this place as St Plautilla. But unfortunately the architect of the modern chapel had not seen fit to commission new frescoes: he liked stark white walls better.

"Now that explains a lot, Contini! And the frescoes you saw at my convent must have been copied from the ones they had here. You should ask the mother superior to let Mister Bertini have a look at them. He will be able to confirm this, and if it is true, he will surely be delighted to see copies of those old frescoes again."

And then they were back at *Il Livorno*, in the courtyard with the dappled shade, the dappled sounds and smells, sitting at the same table as the day before. Only this time it was late afternoon, the worst of the heat was over, and they were enjoying some well-deserved cocktails before they ordered their dinner.

When they'd arrived, Daisy had asked Contini to bring her to the phone and to please get Father Cadogan on the line for her. She'd told him the good news about finding Desiderata's inscription, that she wouldn't be back at the museums at closing time, and would he please tell Morag and transmit her love.

Once they were seated, and after they'd clinked with their glasses of Aperol and taken a first celebratory sip, Daisy dug the notebook out of her handbag and laid it open on the table, so that the inscription was visible.

DESIDERATA·POM·CAECA·NATA
SIBI·ET·FELICITATI·SER·SVRDAE
VIXI·CVM·EA·FELICITER·AN·XV
DONEC·VITAM·SACRIFICAVIT
VRBE·A·G·PISONE·INCENSA

"Now, at long last, my dear Contini, you're going to tell me what it says."

The bishop leaned over and stared at the notebook for a while. "Ah Daisy, I still can't believe how neatly you managed to transcribe all this in the pitch darkness."

"The darkness was neither here nor there, and I also learned the text more or less by heart. The first line says: 'I, Desiderata Pom, born blind'... Now, Pom stands for Desi's family name, I guess?"

"Yes. She did not find it as important as her given name, which tells us she was probably not married. Otherwise she would have given us the genitive form of her husband's name in full. Her maiden name could have been Pompeia, Pompilia or any other surname starting with 'Pom'."

"We will never know for sure, how tantalizing these ancient inscriptions can be!"

"Indeed, we just don't have the needed context here... Now, the next line says 'for herself and for *Felicitas*, her deaf slave'."

"Her *slave*? How can you be so sure? Couldn't Felicitas have a surname starting with 'Ser'?"

"I don't think so, no. Traditionally 'Ser' stands for 'slave' in inscriptions; here it would be *servae*. And it is the *next* line that makes me conclude that this is indeed the case. 'I lived happily with her for fifteen years.' You can imagine that in ancient Rome a relationship between two women would not be publicized on a tombstone. So it can only be a 'living together' of unmarried sisters—who would have had the same surname—or of a mistress and a slave."

"All right... a blind mistress and a deaf slave! Morag and Cadogan will be thrilled when we tell them."

"Yes, a remarkable coincidence, that. And it makes you wonder how they could have communicated at all. But note the charming wordplay: *'feliciter'*, 'happily', deriving from the name Felicitas itself."

"Doesn't that suggest a level of intimacy? I'd like to believe that Desi and Feli could actually communicate with one another."

"We will never know for sure. Now the following lines tell us a quite dramatic story about this 'Felicity': 'I lived with her for fifteen years, until she sacrificed her life, Rome having been set on fire by Gaius Calpurnius Piso.' *Urbe*, in this context, refers to the city of Rome. You have to conclude that we're talking about the great fire of AD 64, as Piso died in 65. That is exactly a thousand and nine hundred years ago! Well, according to Tacitus Rome started burning on the 19th of July, and we are now in the middle of August, but still."

"And Felicitas died then, sacrificing her life for the sake of her mistress and perhaps the rest of her owner's family."

"Apparently, yes."

"And when Desiderata buried her, she scratched this inscription onto a slab of marble. Just like Quinctius, apparently, she intended to be buried in the same grave herself."

"That could be, but here I foresee some difficulties. If Felicity died in the fire, there may not have been any remains left to bury. Desiderata does write that the stone is also intended for herself, 'sibi', but why did she have it placed in the cesspool of a public latrine on the Via Tiburtina? This is very puzzling, to say the least... We will have to investigate the crypt some more in the coming days, to see if there are any remains buried there, or an urn with ashes maybe, but as Signor Bertini already told us: the place is not really a burial site."

"Oh, you must take me down there again, Contini! I want to probe that marble slab once more with my fingers, it gives me the feeling I'm connected directly to my doppelgänger from ancient Rome."

"Yes, quite so, I can see how that must appeal to you... Now there is also the question of Piso... Gaius Calpurnius Piso, the leader of the famous conjuration against Nero. The plot failed and the man was ordered to commit suicide. Desiderata claims that he set fire to Rome. Now that is sensational news indeed! To my knowledge, no other historical source has ever made such a claim before."

"And this is not just some idle story after the fact: Desiderata was there, she lost her beloved slave, she must have had valid reasons to carve this claim in stone."

"Absolutely. As I said: sensational."

Presently the "closet communist" appeared with a couple of waiters and served them a dish he'd highly recommended: *Triglie alla Livornese*. Red mullets with herbs in tomato sauce.

"This smells delicious!" Daisy exclaimed, draping one napkin over her lap, tucking another one in under her chin—she'd asked for three napkins, as she didn't want to sully her summer dress and still needed one for cleaning her hands.

"Promise you won't stare at me, Contini, I'm going to make a terrible mess."

"That's all right, I will look at your beautiful face only, like I always do... I can see that you are very happy."

"Yes. There is nothing in the world I like better than to solve a nice, wholesome mystery."

"And you are very good at it!"

"Provided I can team up with the right man. You didn't do so bad yourself."

"Thank you."

"The strange thing is, there was no corpse in this mystery, although thousands must have died in the fire. And thanks to Desiderata, we have unmasked the culprit effortlessly: Piso. Now what else can you tell me? You're so good at extracting information from almost every word!"

"Well, I still have some comments to make on the *location* of our find. That can also tell us a lot."

"And we need to look into the relationship between Desiderata and St Plautilla."

"Exactly... but perhaps both things are connected. We heard that the crypt was part of a latrine built in Vespasian's time. I'll have to find out who this German archaeologist was, and how he came to this conclusion, but let us admit he found reliable clues—some coins, maybe?—and his assertion is correct. In that case we have Desiderata alive and well in 64, aged at least fifteen. Then she has Felicity's stone placed between AD 69 and 79, under Vespasian's reign. This tells us that Felicity's remains were never found, by the way, unless she was *reburied* five years after her death. Anyway, the records of the saints tell us that Plautilla, on the other hand, was martyred in AD 67, so she and the two impaired women were *contemporaries*."

"And that is almost a proven fact; wonderful! Are you eating at all, Contini?"

"Only nibbling... Now, what I find even more interesting is that this crypt was already a *Christian shrine* in the time of Aristobulus, around AD 220, and still remained so in Rorick's day in the 6th century. Just *imagine*: a public latrine becoming a Christian shrine! And believe me, in those days the pilgrims must have been *queuing up* to go down into that stinking cesspool! Although after a century or two it must have been cleaned up. Then we learn that around 1800, the crypt was probably no longer open to the public, but the chapel was still called 'St Plautilla' because of its frescoes; fascinating."

"Yes, and what's more, when the Germans launched the Corpus project in 1853, the Desiderata stone simply missed the boat. Everything is clear now."

"You're right, my dear... very astute... you're quite good

at extracting information too."

"But why did the pilgrims pray at the Desiderata stone? Officially she is not one of the saints. Was she even a Christian?"

"Excellent question! Now that you mention this, let's have another look at a line that could enlighten us: *'vitam sacrificavit'*. Felicity sacrificed her life. But it doesn't say for whom: for Desiderata only? For her family as well? Could this mean that she sacrificed her life for the Christians? Could it be that the two women were members of the early Church? After all, the cripples of Rome had a hard time; they were universally despised; people found them loathsome. So the Christian ideals of mercy and brotherly love must have greatly appealed to them."

"But still, why were they *honoured* so in this clandestine shrine?"

"We'll never know, again. The stone only suggests Felicity's self-sacrifice. But the strange thing is that this inscription does not have any Christian formulations at all: no reference to Christ or to the eternal life. It could just as well be a pre-Christian tombstone. And yet the two women were honoured like saints; the early Christians preserved this inscription in its strange shrine and honoured the memory of Desiderata and Felicity for quite a few centuries after they'd gone."

"And in the end, maybe, they hardly could remember *why* they had to honour them... Yes, I like that; I like that very much!"

"Also interesting: there is no reference to Seneca. Not directly. But it makes complete sense that when Aristobulus read that 'Piso lighted the fire', he should have concluded that Seneca was not a friend of St Paul's. That is because the Christians were persecuted after the great fire of 64. Seneca is supposed to be one of the plotters in the Pisonian conspiracy, together with his nephew Lucanus, the famous poet. If Piso set fire to Rome, he was also, supposedly, responsible for the persecutions afterwards. Hence Seneca could never have been a great friend of the first Christians, including St Paul. Not a very straightforward line of reasoning, I admit, but that is how Aristobulus must have seen things anyway."

"Yes, but now that we know that Piso was an *arsonist*, who caused the death of thousands of people, you can hardly believe that Seneca, the Stoic philosopher, could really have been his friend."

"Ah… I hadn't thought of that yet… maybe you're right."

"Gosh, all this is so *complicated*, but also absolutely fascinating."

The proprietor of *Il Livorno* came out to ask if they needed anything, and he exclaimed, "Signor Contini, you have hardly touched your food!"

"I know, my friend, I have been distracted. I will need more time, but la Signora Hayes has clearly finished eating."

"Yes, clearly. Will you allow me to clean your hands, Madam?"

Delicately the man retrieved Daisy's napkins from her lap and bosom, then he lifted up one sauce-covered hand, and the other, and wiped them clean with a wet cloth he had brought out with him. He handed her a fresh napkin to dry her fingers. Finally he poured some of the wine they'd ordered in a clean glass and took away the old one, smeared with tomato sauce.

"Did you see that, Contini?" Daisy said as soon as the man had departed, "even a 'professed atheist' can be incredibly sweet!"

"Oh, I have never doubted that for a single moment. And I can tell you I've met some faithful Catholics who were mean, selfish bastards!"

247

"I can imagine."

"Having said that, what impresses me most is how difficult it must be for you, to be constantly at a disadvantage like this... when I think back to how dark it was in that crypt—I was suffocating!—I don't understand how you can put up with it."

"Well, being blind is not exactly the same thing as being plunged into darkness. While you and Bertini were paralysed by fear, all my senses were wide-open, wide-awake, including my sense of orientation. But on the other hand, that is exactly the point: I can never allow myself to *put up* with being blind. I have to make a conscious effort to push back the 'darkness' all the time. That takes a lot of energy, and sometimes I feel very tired."

"You are so brave, you poor thing!"

"But then again, isn't this what most people have to do, one way or another? To push back against what is *limiting* them? Take your own case: you have to keep pushing back the walls of spiritual inertia pressing down on you on all sides, because you're a man of the cloth. I can imagine it takes constant effort on your part. Nowadays most people can't be bothered to make that effort, but you have to keep working at it all the time."

"Yes, I believe you're right. My faith is the fleeting result of constant vigilance... How well you understand that! My dear Daisy, when you return to London at the end of the week, I'm really going to miss your company."

Daisy took a sip of wine, and put her glass down cautiously.

"Well, you know, my poor Contini, if only priests were allowed to marry, you could have a nice wife to fulfil that role in your life."

XIV AD 64: Finding the light

Nero was feeling queasy. When he'd entered the royal box, under a gold-tasselled dais, it had been all right: the crowd spontaneously erupted into cheers and applause, some people even chanting, "Divus Caesar! Divus Caesar!"

Tigellinus, who followed his master like a shadow, smiled with satisfaction: this whole thing was looking to become a great success. But he had to remain vigilant, everything depended on that. The retinue surrounding them was composed entirely of guardsmen, heavily armed under their white togas. They looked like normal clients on a day out, but formed a living redoubt around the emperor.

Before they sat down, Nero on a gilded, throne-like armchair, and Tigellinus on a bronze folding chair next to him, the praefect hissed into the emperor's ear, "Wave at the people, Divus, wave with dignity and condescension. Can you do that for me?"

And with a big, childlike smile, Nero did what he was told. The crowd purred with pleasure. The people still loved him! But you really had to prompt him all the time, Tigellinus grumbled inwardly. The little pipsqueak was *not* a born politician.

The Circus of Caligula was packed. At least the bend of the racing track closest to the Tiber: that was where an arena had been cordoned off for the games. The people of Rome had come out in great numbers to the Vatican hill, because they needed their minds taken off their sorrows. Their mighty city was in ruins; they'd all been affected one way or another, losing loved ones, or their homes, or still suffering from burns. It would be a welcome change to have a nice old-fashioned show like this, with acrobats, and gladiators fighting to the death like in the good old days, and a traditional execution by beasts. It was only a small event, an extra, improvised do, not your usual day-long festival. And the executions would be last, to underline the guilt of those vile Christians. The convicts everyone held responsible for the calamity deserved to die in gruesome pain! Those Christians were all arsonists and slanderers, accusing the emperor of lighting the fires, to hide their own heinous crimes.

When the gladiators started drawing blood, Nero nudged his neighbour with his elbow and whined, "Tigellinus! I'm going to be sick!"

"Just close your eyes, Divus. And no matter what happens, don't walk away. You may puke on my shoes if you have to, but remain seated!"

"Oh, I hate this... I hate this!"

"Just you wait," the praefect thought, "what will you do when the lions start shredding those poor Christians to pieces?"

Another person was pondering that exact same question only a few dozen seats to the side and half a dozen tiers higher than the royal box, also feeling queasy. Thanks to Senator Antonius Soranus Canio, Sextus Pomponius Sacer had an outstanding seat, just a couple of rows behind his patron. He had an excellent view of the arena, but the gladiator fights were not engaging his attention. He was biting the knuckles of his forefinger and fretting, worried sick. What if it were true? What if Feli had been right and Claudia had actually understood that hysterical miming correctly? Of course his wife was bound to fear the worst, as women were

250

wont to do, but still. With some help from Canio, Sextus had done all he could to find out more about Desi's fate, but to no avail. They had run up against a wall of official obfuscation, they had lost themselves in a maze of administrative evasion, and the fact that the authorities were in complete disarray because of the great fire hadn't helped either. No one could give them any news of Desiderata Pomponia... But surely they would not just throw her to the *lions*, like Claudia claimed that Felicitas had told her? And *where* was Feli anyway; where was his slave; had she bolted?

Nearby, but a lot closer to the royal dais, Gaius Calpurnius Piso and Rufrius Crispinus were sitting next to one another, with the rest of the conspirators scattered inconspicuously around them. You had to be careful, although not a soul seemed to have cottoned on to their plot. They were still respected members of the highest classes, sitting very close to the emperor. Only the blind girl knew their secret, but she would be executed shortly, and they were looking forward to witnessing her grisly end. However, the two leaders felt frustrated: their plans had hit a snag. They had Nero exactly where they wanted him, but they could not get at him: Tigellinus was just too crafty and cautious. And he had put all his eggs squarely into Nero's basket, to his own advantage, that much was clear, so there was no swaying or coaxing him. Rufrius leaned forward and waived at the current Praefect of the Praetorian Guard, sitting by the emperor under the dais, further down the front tier. They exchanged amiable smiles, from an old to a new commander. The fit-looking young men all around Nero and Tigellinus were guardsmen, no doubt about it. It was so infuriating: the praefect had no idea who his adversaries were, yet he'd managed to thwart them completely!

Finally the gladiators were done fighting, and half of them were dead. A good show. Time for the executions. After the arena stagehands had carried away the bodies and strewn some fresh sand on the blood, the condemned were brought in. Sextus looked up, squinted at the arena, and his breath faltered, his face turned white. Desi was there! She was the very first convict to emerge through the tunnel right beneath him, under the stands where he was sitting. And Feli was walking close by, next to her, holding her arm lightly like she always did. Then there followed a group of about twenty women and children. The crowd went wild.

Something started to scream inside the father's shocked mind as well, "Desiderata!" As she was positioned and turned around right in front of the royal box by her handlers, everybody could clearly see the hollow cavities under her brows. "Poor Desi!" How could they *do* this? She was a citizen's daughter; she was entitled to a fair trial first! She seemed very calm; Feli was the nervous one, cowering behind her mistress. Sextus marvelled: Desi seemed resigned to her fate, you couldn't escape the impression that she wanted to die like a true Roman. Then he thought, "How about me? Will I be able to stand this?" He had the disturbing feeling that Feli had already spotted him, that she was staring at him reproachfully. "No, I can't stand it!" he concluded, "I'm going to be sick..." And in contrast to the emperor, nobody was preventing him from leaving his seat. He stood up brusquely and started to make his way to the end of the tier, brushing along the other men's legs. Then he made for the exit a few tiers up and disappeared into the closest exit tunnel. As soon as he was inside the vaulted passage, he leaned over and vomited against the wall, feeling a deep sense of shame on top of the overwhelming nausea. As it happened, a tunnel like this was called a *vomitorium*.

Meanwhile Nero was nudging his neighbour again, insistently: "Tigellinus! Tigellinus! Isn't that aunty Plautilla? You know: one of Poppaea's godmothers?"

"Yes, yes, Divus: Dame Plautia Petronii is a Christian too. She's the daughter of Aulus Plautius and the widow of Publius Petronius, who used to be our legate in Syria and Judea. That is where she picked it up."

"But she's a Roman citizen! Of noble birth, even, like you say. She can't just be thrown to the lions; what were you thinking? Get her out of there at once!"

"No can do, Divus, and don't blame *me*... Dame Plautia *volunteered* to die. I pleaded with her, believe me, but she was adamant... I guess a Roman lady is entitled to die as she chooses; an undignified way to go for sure, but we have to respect her choice."

"But Tigellinus, this time I'm *really* going to be sick!"

"As I said before, Nero: close your eyes. And think about this: you're the commander in chief of all the legions of Rome, so you *must* show your people that you're a man."

The emperor looked on in wonderment as the stage hands erected a collapsible cage around the women and children; his wife's friendly godmother was standing at the front of their group, looking up at him.

As the angry howls of the lions reached her from within the dungeon, Desi tried to start whistling. She pursed her dry lips and blew too hard and no sound came out. It was not that easy after all. The crowd was making too much noise and she was too jittery to control her breathing. The lions would show up at any moment now. She concentrated fiercely, focussing on that part inside her head where she knew that her ability to whistle resided. "Wake up, oh you *daemon* of my whistling, I need you badly at this very moment!" She moistened her lips and suddenly regained control of her breath, and started twittering and warbling.

Desi could not see how the man in the first row of the stands dangled a chunk of meat at the end of a rope in front of the tunnel entrance. But when the first lion came out and the handler lifted the meat just in time, Feli tapped her shoulder, and she knew: here they come!

The lions were rearing for a fight. After they'd been taunted and tormented viciously by their handlers, they were bent on revenge, baying for their blood, but when they emerged into the blinding sun behind their leader, the men were not there. Only women and children, they could smell it while they blinked with their blinded eyes. The leader of the pride, an old and experienced female, even marvelled at the fact that the two young ones standing at the front, in particular, were smelling to high heaven of female human pee... Where were the men? Where were the cowards hiding? Did they think lions were stupid?

The animals now deploying around Desi and Feli were very hungry, obviously, but they were also feeling out of sorts, somehow. Their carers from the zoo could have told the arena handlers that, but they hadn't bothered, because their "babies" had been requisitioned highhandedly, and taken away from them on orders of the emperor himself. Well, dear emperor, good luck with these traumatized poor creatures. The gardens of Lucullus had not been affected by the fire, but the lions and the other wild animals in captivity had been through Hades while Rome was burning. All their instincts told them to flee the fire, but they were stuck in pens and cages, and had gone through a frenzy of panic night after night. One of the consequences was that they'd lost their appetite. Even after the fires had stopped, the beasts had been eating very little, and only after much enticing and coaxing with the tastiest morsels... and as Desi had already theorized, these lions had not been trained to see living human beings as meat, anyway.

The old female lion, the queen of the pride still standing in front of Desi, turned her ears forward. The crowd was making a lot of noise and she wanted to hear the strange warbling sound coming from the young female human facing her. Was she really singing like a bird? How charming! Immediately she was transported back to happier days, before the fires, when cheerful crowds had strolled past their cages and marvelled at them. One day a young female just like this one had serenaded them. She had a beautiful voice; she sang a melodious hymn to Venus just in front of their cage to see what effect that would have on the beasts. Well, they'd all closed their eyes and purred; it was the most enchanting sound they'd ever heard! The females of the human species were fascinating creatures, the old queen thought, although she didn't care much for the males... She stretched her forelegs and eased herself to the ground, then she turned her head left and right towards the others, who started following her example one by one. They all lay down and focused on the birdsong from the girl with no eyes.

All this happened in only a few moments, within a couple of heartbeats, and the way the crowds witnessed it made it appear nothing short of miraculous. It looked like the lions burst forth into the arena, panting with rage, then stopped, and saw the blind girl standing erect and fearless, apparently indifferent to death, her little slave cowering behind her. And instead of attacking and tearing those two to pieces, the lions kneeled down in front of them one by one... The crowd went very quiet, and suddenly they could hear that the girl was whistling like a bird, and they thought that they understood: she was hypnotizing the beasts like some oriental snake charmer!

Then they heard a thin, solitary voice coming from the highest tiers, at the back of the stands, where the women and slaves were confined.

"That's my baby! Desi! I'm here!"

"Mater!" Desi thought, but she carried on with her

whistling. Claudia had probably been crying all along, but her solitary wails had been drowned out by the roar of the crowd.

And again the crowd went wild. "Let her go! Let her go!" they started chanting.

In the royal box Nero rose to his feet without even thinking. This was extraordinary! Tigellinus tried to pull him down by the folds of his purple toga, but the emperor just pulled his arm up and ignored him. He raised his right hand and silenced the crowd.

"Citizens! Let us pardon the Christians today. Let us put this calamity behind us and start rebuilding Rome, better than ever before... That is my will!"

The crowds roared their approval, and Nero sat down again, smiling extatically.

Tigellinus hissed and scoffed by his side, shaking his head, no longer bothering to hide his contempt.

"What?" Nero demanded, turning to him, "you're always criticizing. Didn't I just give my people what they wanted? Didn't I make a nice little speech?"

"Yes, Divus, but how do you propose to *implement* your pardon? *Who's* going to round up those beasts without the Christians getting hurt, eh? At any moment now they'll start attacking everything that moves, and then you'll just look like a fool!"

"Oh... I hadn't thought of that."

"Precisely!"

Inside the cage Plautilla had come to the same conclusion. Even if young Nero had just pardoned them publicly, he'd done it a bit too late, and they were still in a very sticky situation. It was too early to thank the Lord. It was more like that moment when the Christ himself had said to the Father, "Not what *I* want, but what *you* want." Nevertheless, no matter how it all turned out, the events that had already taken place here today would make a huge impression. Thanks to Desi and her childish bravery, they would not die for nothing.

But even before Nero had risen to his feet, Feli had come to a decision of her own. She did not hear Desi's birdsong; she did not hear Claudia crying nor the crowds chanting, but she was scanning the whole scene and analysing all the details of what she could see. The emperor himself was there, she could recognize him by his purple toga, but also from the portraits on the coins. Then, not far from the emperor, she recognized the men from the baths: their leader was sitting right next to the man who wanted to become the next emperor. She'd seen him only once, at a distance, walking down the great hall of the baths with his retinue, but she recognized him all the same... bad news, that! They were the ones responsible for Desi's arrest, so if the two girls managed to escape, they'd have to make themselves scarce in order to keep out of these men's clutches. Then there was the whole setup with the cage and the cord tied around Desi's waist. Desi had explained the nasty little game that the strange-looking little man had thought up for their execution. It didn't matter: if the lions didn't attack Desi straight away, they could even use this to their advantage. Feli intended to yank the cord at a strategic moment, so the cage would fall apart. The other convicts suddenly becoming available to them would surely not fail to distract the beasts and divert their attention, long enough, maybe, for the two of them to make for the exit like they'd planned... Feli was already gripping the ripcord in her hand.

As soon as the first lion had stopped in front of Desi, and then lain down, Feli had concluded that they were in business. She prepared her move carefully, like the champion latrunculi player she was. She quickly counted the beasts lying in the sand left and right. They were all there! She'd counted and re-counted them inside their underground cage the night before, so she knew exactly with how many they were… Time to make their move.

Feli rapped her knuckles on top of Desi's head, in a way that signalled "let's walk away calmly." At the same time she yanked on the cord, and without looking back she started to steer Desi towards the entrance of the tunnel, that was still open, luckily, although they had to swerve between a few reclining beasts to reach it. The animals, understandably, became restless, some of them stirring, making to stand up. But their leader didn't move, eyed them all insistently, and they understood they should stay put. Feli looked at the last lion lying closest to the tunnel suspiciously. The beast, a big male with a dark mane, looked back just as suspiciously, but let them pass without stirring.

And that is how, just as Tigellinus was telling Nero what a sticky situation he had now created, the problem seemed to solve itself spontaneously. The two girls just walked out of the arena; the cage collapsed and the women and children followed them in a single file; in an instant they were gone, leaving only the lions behind. That is what everybody thought they saw. Oh, how hard it is to get to the truth! How to convey exactly what came to pass, when so much was going on in such a short time, and so much of it was so contradictory? But it happened all the same. Or it appeared to. Nero turned to Tigellinus again and smiled smugly. "Do we still have a problem?"

"No, Divus, everything is hunky-dory now."

And everything went according to plan. Through the bars of the barrier Feli unlatched the lock of the cage from inside and pushed open the door. The Christian men had already been herded in front of the other tunnel leading to the arena, waiting for their turn, but when the guards saw the women reappear inside the lions' cage, and when Feli opened the door, they immediately started to flee. They only had the enraged beasts on their minds, the ones they themselves had been jabbing with their pikes, and they bolted, without a sound, without a word. Never did such toughs disappear so fast through every available exit!

Now Feli turned around towards Desi, because her friend had to take over, to help them find the entrance of the under-ground channel to the river. But immediately she saw there was an unforeseen problem: as the others streamed past them, out of the cage, Desi stayed put, pulling on the cord tied around her middle. It was stuck. It was stretched tight and Desi couldn't move, no matter how hard she tugged.

"Oh no!" Feli thought. Stepping over to her friend, she gave her a rapid signal, "I'll fix it!" and disappeared inside the tunnel, following the tight rope. And as soon as she emerged into the arena again, she understood. The big male closest to the entrance had put his paw on the very end of the ribbon attached to the cord... Never, in the history of the world, had any cat, large or small, been able to resist the urge to paw a loose piece of string, or anything like that, dangled in front of its nose, appearing to move with a will of its own. In fact the big male had shown great restraint while Desi and Feli had walked past him and he'd watched the cord and then the ribbon snaking right in front of him through the sand. But in the end, as the very last length of ribbon passed by, wriggling tauntingly, he couldn't help himself anymore. He'd pounced at it. He'd whipped his paw down and caught it, pinning it to the ground. And he stubbornly refused to let go. Enough was enough.

Feli knew exactly what she needed to do. She stepped

right up to the big brute, bent over, and blew into his nose as hard as she could. It worked like a charm. The lion let go of the end of the ribbon, and gave Feli one mighty slap with his paw, breaking her neck and killing her instantly. As her body hit the ground, her head swung into an impossible angle with her nape.

Inside the cage, Desi fell back as the cord came loose, then she pulled the cord and the ribbon in and collected them in her arms as fast as she could. If only they'd thought of doing this right away! She waited for Feli to join her, but she was not easy in her mind. She'd heard a slap, and Feli had uttered a strange squeal. Then Plautilla grabbed Desi's armpits and pulled her up and through the open door. "She'll catch up with us if she can!"

"No! Feli! No!"

But the men had already spotted the beginning of a tunnel, and they were pushing the women and children inside, telling them to just walk on. "You can see the light at the end," someone said, "just walk towards the light, all of you!"

When they were all in the tunnel, stumbling forward in the dark, another man said, "I hope they're not going to give chase!"

"No they won't," Plautilla said, "Nero has publicly pardoned us. You men didn't hear that..."

"Are you saying there's no need to flee, then?"

"Well, Cephas, better not to trust the Romans right now. I don't know where this tunnel leads, but let's keep moving."

"The tunnel leads to the Tiber," Desi said, "do you see any sign of Feli yet?"

"No, my dear girl, I'm afraid she's dead."

"Tell me, deacon," a little boy asked, "aren't the lions going to chase us?"

"No, Cyril, I closed the door of their cage and secured

260

the latch again."

"Now she tells us!" Desi thought, "and how about Feli, then!?"

"I don't know what happened out there," the same man as before remarked, "but it looks to me like a miracle from God!"

"You can say that again, Cephas! We're all here... we've escaped: this is a miracle if I ever saw one."

Desi, who now accepted that Feli was dead, and that it was not Plautilla's fault, still felt a sudden and unexpected burst of anger.

"Miracle, my foot!" she exclaimed, "Feli and I *planned* all this very carefully, you know."

"Oh, but don't you understand? God has been fulfilling his own plans through you and poor Feli. Obviously you two were God's instruments, perhaps without even realizing it."

"Praise the Lord!" some of the others answered, "let his will be accomplished."

"Well, all I can say is that you have to be careful with this kind of reasoning, Plautilla. If *you* always get to decide what is God's will and what isn't, then in the end no one will ever be allowed to contradict you."

"Oh? Ah... maybe you have a point. I'll keep that in mind... in the future."

They walked on in silence through the tunnel, getting closer to the end of it. In a few hundred yards they would emerge by the sluices near the riverbank, Desi knew. They would be able to hide until nightfall in the copses and bushes along the shore. Later they might follow the river upstream to the north, round the city, outside the walls, towards the east, and reach the cemeteries along the *Via Tiburtina* unseen. Desi knew there were some abandoned catacombs there, underground burial sites, where they could hide and lie low for a while, until things turned back to normal...

The deacon stroked her shoulder. "Are you holding out, there? You're awfully quiet. Are we still good, you and I?"

"Yes... but it's just, now that Feli is dead, I feel as if my heart has been torn out of my chest... and I can't even weep! From now on I am dead to the world."

As they kept walking towards the light, Plautilla put her arm around Desi's shoulders, and she said quietly, "You know, we Christians are also dead to the world. That is how we live."

THE END

A brief note on the History

Nero had the bad luck of being the last emperor of his dynasty, the Julio-Claudians. After his death, the historians of the next regime were immediately put to work to give him a bad name, and did so with great gusto. Eventually his reputation was further ruined by the resentful Christians, when *they* finally took over.

An example of this is when Tacitus tells us that Nero "did not return to Rome until the fire approached his house", implying he didn't care much until he was personally affect-ted. How can Tacitus possibly know what was going on inside Nero's head? Writing fifty years after the facts, it is not likely he found any documents in the state archives that al-lowed him to make this claim about the emperor's innermost state of mind.

As for the Christians, think about it: in AD 64, when the great fire took place, there could never have been that many Christians in Rome, only 32 years or so after Christ's cruci-fixion. Don't forget that this new faith was completely alien to the Roman mentality. Yet Tacitus reports nasty and exten-sive persecutions! Possibly a tall story based on the very first juicy rumours that emerged about the hated sect, just when he himself was writing the 'Annals' around AD 115.

Then nine months after the fire, in AD 65, Piso's Conju-ration came to light and failed miserably. The plotters were either exiled or 'invited' to commit suicide, which was astoni-shingly effective. If a Roman had to choose between death and dishonour, he'd choose death anytime. As the great fire occurred so close to this Piso business, I decided to blame it on the plotters in my novel, although there is no historical evidence to support this. There is nothing to *disprove* my crazy theory either.

So a Roman emperor could be untypically lenient for the members of his own class who tried to get rid of him. This was all part of the game. Maybe that is what happens when such military geniuses as the Romans conquer the world, plunder the riches of the conquered, and take away as many slaves as they want. They end up in their mighty city with too much leisure on their hands. And there's nothing like power and boredom for breeding mayhem.

In AD 68, three years after Piso's Conjuration was slapped down, Nero was finally done in by the 'Revolt of Vindex and Galba'. This time it was Nero himself, aged 30, who was invited to commit suicide, which he did reluctantly, with a little help from a friendly slave. Or is that yet more bad-mouthing, this time from Suetonius? At any rate 'The Year of the Four Emperors' then followed, four contenders slugging it out on the battlefield until Vespasian was finally able to prevail. Talk about mayhem!

But all this could become the subject of another novel... or two.

Acknowledgements

Dear reader, thank you ever so much for reading this story through to the end. I hope you liked it. Support your indie writer, don't forget to sprinkle some stars on Amazon and GoodReads, or actually post a review. Just a few words to help other readers would be great.

I would like to thank Hanna, as usual, for the subtle hints that helped me a lot in editing the first drafts. Also many thanks to Pablo Stam, whose help with my Latin was invaluable. He came to the rescue although he didn't have much time at his disposal.

Author's homepage: www.nickaaronauthor.com

Milton Keynes UK
Ingram Content Group UK Ltd.
UKHW010636040324
438885UK00001B/74